RANCH AND RING

Books by
FLORENCE CRANNELL MEANS

PENNY FOR LUCK
A BOWLFUL OF STARS
A CANDLE IN THE MIST
RANCH AND RING
DUSKY DAY
TANGLED WATERS
THE SINGING WOOD

'YOU LET GO OF ME' (*page* 58)

Ranch and Ring

A Story of the Pioneer West

BY

FLORENCE CRANNELL MEANS

WITH ILLUSTRATIONS BY

HENRY J. PECK

Boston and New York
HOUGHTON MIFFLIN COMPANY
The Riverside Press Cambridge

The Riverside Press
CAMBRIDGE · MASSACHUSETTS
PRINTED IN THE U.S.A.

LOVINGLY DEDICATED

TO THE TWO MOST CRITICAL OF KIN

AND KINDEST OF CRITICS

MY HUSBAND AND MY FATHER

CONTENTS

ILLUSTRATIONS

Ranch and Ring

.·.

CHAPTER I

JANEY'S ROAD TURNS

JANEY GRANT could name the exact day when her quiet road twisted itself about and turned toward Colorado Territory.

It happened without the least warning. That morning — April 17, 1874 — she could see nothing ahead but the sunshiny commonplaces of Normal School with Emily Lewis and Susan Sloane. That afternoon, she found herself pushed irresistibly toward Colorado's wild frontier, dazzling with golden adventure and threatening with Indian war-whoops and the bark of six-shooters.

It was the last day of the Normal School term. Just as usual, Janey had plunged up the stairs of their boarding-house, three at a time. Just as usual, she had caught herself and gone on mincingly when one of the teachers opened a warning door on the floor below.

'She almost caught me that time,' Janey told her room-mates breathlessly. '"One step at a time, young ladies!"' she mimicked, thrusting her circle comb through her fly-ing curls, and tying an apron around her waist with a jerk.

'"Place your right foot on the step, and bring your left foot to a position beside it, and so with the next,"' Emily continued.

'"Young ladies will under no circumstances exhibit either haste or discomposure,"' Janey chanted, pirouetting so fast that her generous ankle-length flounces stood out around her like a crinoline.

'However can you jig around so?' Susan asked with in-dulgent wonder. 'You've had as many tests as I have this morning, and I feel as if I'd been drawn through a knot-hole. That examination in philosophy! Honest, I got so mixed up I didn't know but Sir Isaac Newton invented the solar system.'

Janey stopped, flushed and panting in her tight-boned bodice, and surveyed Susan. Janey, with her tilted nose and wide-set hazel eyes, and the brown ringlets flying about her round forehead again, looked a gay little girl rather than the proper Normal School young lady. Nor was Emily much more sedate. It was Susan who had lost her childish-ness this year: the dark hair piled on her head in an intricate twining of plaits looked too heavy for her thin flushed face, and her lustrous gray eyes held an anxious look. Yet all winter through, the childish Janey and Emily had mothered the motherless Susan like two worried chicks nursing a troublesome hen.

Susan coughed and drew her three-cornered plaid shawl tighter around her shoulders, and they both studied her sharply.

'If you've caught more cold —!' Janey scolded. 'We ought to have managed to spread our firewood a little thinner. It's been frosty, these last few days, even if it is April. I guess it's good we're going home if you can't keep from catching cold, Susan Sloane.'

They looked regretfully around the room where they had spent so many happy hours. For Janey it had been the goal of childhood dreams. Years ago, when she was eleven or twelve, Normal School had been the pot of gold at the end of her rainbow. To go to Normal School and be a teacher, a very good teacher; and all the while to be writing stories and poems, like Harriet Beecher Stowe and Felicia Hemans! Emily Lewis had shared those childhood dreams, clinging to them even after Janey and their new friend Susan had moved away from the Wisconsin neighborhood to the Minnesota frontier.

Except for the chill, their room was a pleasant one, the whole attic story of a rooming house for students. The beds were gay with patched quilts and starched pillow shams, and the floor was covered with rag carpeting stretched over straw. A marble-topped bureau filled the space between the high dormer windows; on its top shelf, fenced in with a gingerbready black walnut railing, sat a black-haired china doll sprucely dressed in scarlet merino and white muslin. Angelica was a doll with a history, and she had come to Normal the autumn before as Janey's mascot and guardian of her few bits of jewelry, which she carried on wrists and neck when Janey was not wearing them. Beside the study table with its fringed brown cover stood the pot-bellied little stove, coldly black, and flanked by an empty scuttle.

Susan shivered again.

'Yes, sir, I'll feel safer to get you home. And yet — oh, dear! our precious year at Normal!' Janey said sorrowfully.

'Oh, well, it isn't as if there wasn't another one coming,' Emily consoled herself.

'I — hope so,' Janey said slowly.

'*Hope* so? When we all have our board and tuition put away safe and sound?' protested Emily.

'I'm not so sure about mine,' Susan answered, interrupting herself with a gasping cough. '— Pop's been awful queer about money. You know the panic last year. Well, sometimes I think Pop must have lost a lot more than he let on.'

'I — haven't got my hundred and fifty put away, either,' Janey confessed hesitantly. 'Something — happened. There's just fifty dollars left.'

'Why, Janey Grant!' Emily's voice was tremulous with pained surprise. 'But you can manage somehow!'

'Oh, yes. You can manage anything when you want to so hard.'

They were halted by a sound between a yelp and a bellow, issuing uncannily from the wall beside the south dormer. 'Outlandish contraption!' Susan snorted.

'That you, Peetohlemy?' Janey called into a tin can that protruded from the window-frame.

She pushed her hair behind her ear and pressed the ear to the can to listen.

'Well, all right. I'll be down in half a minute,' she answered, putting her mouth to the opening again.

'Peetohlemy's got the mail, and there's a letter for me,' she explained to the girls, jerking off her apron as she turned away from the 'outlandish contraption.'

'Remember, young lady, one step at a time!' Emily warned mechanically as Janey darted to the stairs. Janey always needed that warning, for her usual descent was a light gallop: brumpity-*dump*, brumpity-*dump*, brumpity-*dump*.

In the sitting-room she found Ptolemy Jones, their land-lady's only son, stamping impatiently up and down, arms Napoleonically folded and chin sunk on chest.

Though his name was spelled Ptolemy, everyone but teachers and minister called him Pee-toh-lemy: why a *P* at all if it were not to be pronounced?

Ptolemy let his hair grow rather long, and one lock grati-fied him by falling heavily over the large bulge of his brow. The backward fling of that lock was a gesture that consoled him for the too abrupt taper of his chin beneath his beaklike nose. He had hectored his mother into making him white shirts that he left unbuttoned at the throat, to roll back with Byronic negligence.

The girls were of two minds about Ptolemy.

'When all's said and done,' Susan would argue, 'he's smart; terrible smart.'

'A footless kind of smartness,' Emily would object. 'Smart about everything that doesn't matter, and not knowing half the time whether he's afoot or horseback.'

'But this audiphone he's rigged up,' Janey usually pro-tested; 'and the one he's working on that he claims will carry your voice a mile! I can't even get the straight of it when he explains it to me: membranes and magnets and electro-magnets! And all he's had to go by is reading what those men in the East are doing — Mr. Bell and Mr. Gray and those. And then — good gracious! — that horseless buggy of his, with the steam engine ——'

'Hm!' Emily countered scornfully. 'Lots of use in horse-less buggies, isn't there? Especially when they blow up first time you try 'em. And he's so play-acty. Just as if he's coming on the platform to speak a piece, every time he moves.'

'The thing that bothers me,' Janey had criticized, 'is his

treating his mother so. All those silly white shirts to do up!
And her toiling and moiling till all hours, while Peetohlemy
lies on the sofa and reads dime novels.'

Now, in the sitting-room, Ptolemy thrust out a bulky
letter to Janey. 'From your dude friend in the East,' he
accused her.

'You mean my brother Haakon?' she parried placidly.

'Brother!' Ptolemy snorted. 'How comes it his name's
Haakonsson then?'

'Well, foster-brother, if you're so fussy,' Janey amended,
tearing the envelope open with such vigor that its contents
went tumbling to the floor. '— He did! He sent me a
picture of the Dartmouth boat crew!' She retrieved letter
and picture, while Ptolemy watched, scowling. 'See! there's
Haakon!' She tapped one of the jerseyed figures triumphantly, and held the photograph out to the girls, who had
followed her down the stairs.

'Why, I'd never have known him!' cried Emily. 'Well —
except for his cowlick. And the scar on his chin. But, goodness, Janey, he looks like a grown-up man.'

'You'd look like a grown man yourself if you were going to
be twenty your next birthday,' Janey said abstractedly,
studying the pictured face, with its deep scar like a one-
sided cleft in the chin, and its familiar lock of blond hair
waving defiance at the crown of the head. That one unruly
lock was much more noticeable, now that he was old enough
to keep the rest brushed shining-smooth as a helmet.

'A bunch of Eastern sissies, that's all I've got to say,'
Ptolemy dismissed the whole crew.

'Sissies!' Janey laughed tolerantly. 'Goodness, Peetohlemy, you ought to see Haakon once. And maybe you forgot that he lived with the Indians until he ran away and
came to our house. Indians don't raise sissies.'

'With the Injuns? Him? In a horn he did!' Ptolemy exclaimed incredulously.

'Well, Peetohlemy, I must say! Certainly he did.' And then, as Ptolemy listened, scornfully envious, Janey gave him the high points of Haakon's story.

Somewhere about 1856 his father and mother had come to Minneapolis from Norway with their baby son. A few years later, while traveling on business through the State, Mr. Haakonsson had been taken ill, and his wife had hastened to join him in the town where he was detained, taking with her the small Haakon, her maidservant, Ingrid, and a manservant to drive the carriage.

This was in 1862, at the time when the long-smouldering resentment of the Sioux Indians flared up against the whites in a consuming flame. And into the path of that raging fire rode Mrs. Haakonsson, not suspecting her danger until too late.

Janey and Thad had always shivered with terror at Haakon's story of the moment when the painted savages whooped about the horses' heads and tomahawked the hapless driver before the child's eyes. His mother had gone limp and white — mercifully dead of the shock before a dripping blade could touch her. Ingrid's very queerness turned to mental unbalance by terror, saved her from their superstitious hands. And the boy Haakon had been adopted by the chief and his wife.

After thirty-eight of the ringleaders of the Sioux had been sentenced by the Great White Father and had died on the gallows, the rest had been sent permanently from the State of Minnesota. For five or six years after that, the child Haakon had wandered with them, growing and prospering in the tipi of the chief, and half-content with his lot.

All that while, Ingrid was restless and unhappy, and

again and again she attempted escape, only to be followed
and brought back by her captors. At length, when Haakon
was twelve, he had followed her in one such flight, tracking
her alone by her footprints in the fresh snow. He had over-
taken her near a little Wisconsin village, and there, almost
overcome by exhaustion and cold, the two had been sheltered
by the Grants.

And there they had remained, the Sioux, evidently baffled
by the swirling storm that covered their trail, never finding
them. With the Grants, Ingrid, indeed, had stayed to that
day; though Haakon, caught in a sad web of circumstances,
had returned for a time to his Indian companions when he
was sixteen. It was after his white foster-family had also
left the old Wisconsin home and settled at Lucerne, on the
Minnesota frontier, that he had found them again.

When Janey had started away to Normal School that
fall, Haakon, too, had realized a long-time dream. During
his winters with the Sioux he had trapped and hunted busily, and the sale of his furs had brought him a substantial
nest-egg. With this money he had gone East to Dartmouth
College. There he had succeeded in scraping through the
entrance examinations; and there he had spent a year as
fresh and exciting as any in his life.

'Hmph. Injun trash.' Ptolemy curled an unconvincingly
scornful lip when the story had been told.

'Trash, my eye!' Susan gasped indignantly on the tail
end of a cough. 'Why, he's an earl or something, according
to what the lawyers have been writing him. Like in a novel.'

That was another chapter of Haakon's varied history, a
chapter only lately revealed. His father, it seemed, had
been of a noble Norwegian family, but with other heirs between him and the estate. And now these other heirs had
been wiped out, and Haakon himself was next in succession.

'All he's got to do is to prove he is who he is!' persisted Susan, wrathful at Ptolemy's unbelief.

'That may not be so easy!' sneered Ptolemy.

'I'd like to know why not! Look at the old family ring he gave Janey when they were children.' Susan lifted Janey's hand, but it was bare of ornament. 'Well, anyhow, you've seen it times enough, the one with the Haakonsson crest and all those green-and-white stones.'

Janey stuffed letter and photograph back into the envelope.

'Let's go out into the sunshine, girls. It's pleasanter out than in,' she said pointedly, 'and we've time for a little walk before we pack up.' They sailed past the frowning Ptolemy and out at the door.

'We can go over by the Sioux gibbet and see what Haakon has to say,' Janey suggested, when they were out of hearing. 'That Peetohlemy makes me tired. He'd only sneer at everything.'

They sauntered across the road to a parklike clearing within sight of the house. On a day twelve years earlier, the place had been thronged with spectators, morbid, curious, vengeful. For it was here that the thirty-eight Indians condemned to die for the great Sioux massacre mounted the platform and wailed the death chant hand in hand before the planks fell from beneath their feet.

The square gallows still stood, but grass had crept in on the trodden earth, and spring violets were blooming. Quiet houses enclosed the little park, their trees and lilac bushes leafing out delicately under the tender April sky. It was hard to believe that hatred and fear and violent death had ever beaten in upon this gentle stillness.

Emily and Susan drew their ruffles and pleats smooth, and seated themselves tidily; but Janey plumped down re-

gardless of skirts, absorbed in running through the letter.
While the other girls nibbled the sweet white ends of grass
blades, she shared bits of news with them.

'It seems that man at the end of the picture is terribly
rich,' she said, 'but — well, I'll read what Haakon says.
"Rich as dirt, but common as an old shoe. Has rooms that
cost him a hundred a year, I have heard, with gas light and
a built-in bathtub with running water. Eats at the most
elegant place in town, where they charge four dollars a week
just for meals. But with all that, he is not a bit snobbish.
There are several other fellows on the crew I certainly do
hate to say good-bye to, now that I know I am not coming
back." — Not coming back?' Janey echoed blankly, her
eyes scrambling ahead. 'Girls, listen to this!

'"Janey, I am going to teach next year! Guess where!
Greeley's Union Colony, in Colorado Territory. And guess
what it is I am going to do on the side! Start a cattle ranch.

'"You know that is what I have always hankered after —
a grand big stock farm. It looks to me as if this Colorado
Territory was a young man's chance. At present, of course,
I cannot take up government land, but I shall be of age before long. And I am so lucky (at least I hope it proves to be
luck) as to have hooked up with a fellow who has almost all
the money there is: Ralph Farnum. He wants to go into the
ranching business with me: wants to furnish the funds until
I get returns on the Haakonsson estate.

'"You know how I feel about borrowing, Janey. Your pa
drilled that into me. But, anyway, Ralph Farnum wouldn't
give me a minute's peace until I consented.

'"Union Colony seems to be first-rate. I was only ten or
eleven the last time I was through that country with the
Sioux, and so I have only a vague sort of memory of it; but
the East has gone wild over it.

'"They say there's no richer soil in the world, once you get water onto it: potatoes grow big as your head. Of course there is open range for cattle, and the grass winter-cures so that they fatten on it all year. Besides all that, a man could earn a living panning gold out of the streams, if there was no other way.

'"And such a climate! Folks recover even from lung complaint and without dosing themselves with nostrums."' Janey's reading grew slower, and she and Emily both glanced toward Susan. '"Other ailments, too. It made me wonder whether it might not help Grandmother Grant's rheumatism.

'"Ralph and I want to bring blooded cattle onto the range. There is nothing much there now except the long-horns from down in Texas and Mexico: lean, rangy critters that are no good for milk and very little for meat; and I guess there are some of the common roans and reds such as they have in Minnesota. To be brief, Ralph has not only sent in the money for membership in the Colony, but he's contracted for five hundred cows — long-horns, to be driven up from Texas — and ten short-horn bulls, fine stock, so that we can gradually grade up a herd.

'"As for myself, I have been so fortunate as to secure a teaching position in their fine new school in the town of Greeley. The building cost thirty thousand dollars, imagine that! I understand they need more well-trained teachers. Why don't you girls apply? Salaries are high: sixty dollars a month is about the average for lady teachers. And you would have a chance to see new country. You may think Lucerne, Minnesota, is new enough, Janey, but wait until you see Colorado Territory, with Indians still plenty, and buffalo pounding across the plains, and mountains like nothing you can dream of.

'"The only thing worrying me is this borrowing business. I hate it. The estate is not going to bring me an awful lot of ready money when I do get it, but it looks big to a fellow who was not expecting anything at all. You see, it was my father's brother that had the title and the estate, and he had a son who was heir to it. But it seems that he and his wife and son all died of some sort of plague. I should not be surprised if it was the same thing that came so near taking me, a little over a year ago. I understand it swept the world.

'"I am talking as if I were cocksure about it all; but to tell the truth, there is an awfully uneasy feeling in the back of my mind, and a kind of sinking in the pit of my stomach. As Grandmother Grant says, 'There's many a slip 'twixt the cup and the lip.' Sometimes I wake up in the night, cold all over. What if I should not be able to prove my identity to their satisfaction? I have heard of stranger things. After I've tied myself up with a debt for thousands! Gosh, Janey, I do wonder if I have bitten off more than I can chew.

'"And while of course Ralph is a good enough fellow, he's not the one I'd have chosen to hook up with, either. I would do a picture of him if I had your turn for drawing, Janey. That surely was a pippin you made of your friend Ptolemy. I am returning it with care, knowing how deeply you must treasure it."'

Janey peered into the envelope. 'I guess he forgot to put it in.'

'Unless you didn't pick it up when you dropped that letter,' worried Susan. 'It wasn't the awful one with his arms folded, Janey?'

'Yes, it was. If anyone was to find it — ! I felt mean about it as soon as I'd sent it. Probably Haakon just forgot to stick it in: I'm always doing that. But we'll look, as soon as we get back.'

They scrambled to their feet, smoothing their flounces.

'Of course he was joking about us going to Union Colony,' Susan said wistfully. 'I wonder if it's really as healthy as they say.'

'You'll be all right, Susan, if you'll only take the cod-liver oil and drink milk and cream the way Dr. Taylor said,' Janey encouraged her soberly.

Susan made a wry face. 'Cod-liver oil! It does go against me dreadfully. I wish you hadn't made me go to him, Janey.'

Janey had not only made Susan go, but had escorted her there and conferred with the doctor afterward, because Susan was so fatalistically afraid of the disease that had carried her mother away. That conference had left Janey more troubled than ever, and she had dared report only a part of it to Susan.

'Honestly, Susan,' she said now, with sudden energy, 'I don't know whether it's such a joke: about our going to Union Colony, I mean. The doctor said it would — would just make you over if you could spend a year in Arizona or Nevada. And Colorado's just as good. Why couldn't we all go next year — supposing we could get places to teach?'

'But — Janey!' Emily bit her lip and stopped.

'Well, why not?' crowed Janey. 'Susan could keep house for you and me and be well again in no time at all. And there are trappers and cattle-men and Indians. And we might find us a gold mine,' she rattled on excitedly. 'It would be a real adventure; and think how much I'd have to write stories about!'

'Couldn't we — put it off till we're through this next year of Normal?' Emily quavered. 'There's no use my thinking of going now. My father and mother wouldn't listen to my quitting before I've finished.'

She and Janey looked long into each other's eyes, past the unconscious Susan, whose cheeks blazed with eager color. Janey mournfully shook her head. For they both knew that Susan should not wait another year. And to Janey it had come with the suddenness of a blow that Susan's health was her problem, and this perhaps her opportunity. Poor Pop Sloane — as Grandmother said — 'he was like a man with his head in a poke' as far as anything was concerned except farming; and, crippled as he was by the panic of '73, he could not move on again for what would seem to him a doubtful experiment.

The road seemed opening at Janey's very feet.

Silently the three walked on, tangled in their separate skeins of thought. Silently they entered the house.

'You were going to see if you dropped that picture in the sitting-room,' Emily reminded Janey, her voice thick.

The room was unused at that time of day. The paper shades were carefully lowered, shutting out the sunlight which would have been so grateful in the spring chill. The girls stepped inside and looked around: there was no scrap of paper to be seen. Janey dropped to her knees, impatiently yanking up her cashmere flounces. She looked under the sagging springs of the haircloth sofa; pressed her cheek against the musty-smelling blue Brussels roses, and peered under the parlor organ.

'Haakon forgot to put it in,' she concluded.

They climbed the two flights of stairs, so sedately that the most precise of teachers could not have reproved them, and set about their packing.

'Janey!' Susan's voice shook with dismay. 'Would you look at this?'

She was standing before the bureau, staring up at the doll Angelica.

Behind the walnut curlicues gleamed a slip of paper, pinned to Angelica's muslin apron.

'Oh, forevermore!' breathed Janey.

There was her drawing of Ptolemy, done in a dozen deft strokes. His poetic forelock fell more heavily than in life over a brow more bulging; a nose more beaklike dominated a chin that retreated more rapidly.

Beneath it, Haakon had written: 'A perfect portrait of Ma Grant's leghorn rooster.' And beneath that, in a scrawl which Janey recognized as Ptolemy's, were penciled the words: 'Ptolemy Jones may be a laughing-stalk, but he has a human heart, and it is one that will never forget friend nor forgive foe. Remember that, Miss Jane E. Grant.'

CHAPTER II

THE RING DISAPPEARS

PACKING was a difficult task for Janey, that afternoon, little though she had to take home. Distress over her own heartless cartoon added itself to excitement about Colorado and the pain of losing Emily again.

So her hands trembled and her eyes blurred, and she walked to and fro mechanically, picking things up and laying them down again. She folded the doll Angelica carefully in her best plum-colored taffeta bodice, and stuffed the bundle firmly into the bottom of the satchel. She wrapped her dusty shoes as carefully in the plum-colored taffeta skirt, ruthlessly crushing pleated ruffles and puffs, until Susan, chancing to look around, took it from her hands and folded it properly on the bed. She packed her brush and comb securely under everything else, and sent everything else flying when she needed to tidy her tumbled curls.

At the last moment she missed Emily. Following a stifled sniff, she pushed into a dark store-closet under the eaves, and found a crumpled figure huddled on a box in the farthest corner. It was there in the cobwebby dimness, smelling faintly of mice and dust and mothballs, that they said good-bye, clinging together with sobbing, salty kisses.

A half-hour later, Janey paused with one foot on the car steps, and stared at her hand and then up at Susan.

'My ring!' she faltered.

'Hurry, Janey!' urged Susan. 'You must have left it on the doll-baby's wrist, as usual.'

'I must have, but I don't remember — ' Janey followed reluctantly into the car. 'Susan, I feel like unpacking her before the train pulls out. I wouldn't for anything lose ——'

'Oh, Janey!' Susan coaxed. 'There are the boys waiting under the window now to bid you good-bye.'

Janey put aside her worry and dragged her drooping lips into a smile until the train had slid on its way and the group of fellow students had vanished from their sight. Then she pulled out the valise and started to open it.

'I'm not going to!' she declared, shoving it back again. 'It's so cram full I never could get things back in again. And I do despise the kind of folks that are always running back to see if they locked the door or shut up the chickens. Besides, what good would it do me now?'

Yet the ring hung uneasily in her mind during the whole of the ride, and dropped out of her thoughts only when the train puffed into the lighted home station that evening, and drew to a stop with a great jangle and bang that sent the two girls swaying where they waited in the aisle.

'There's Pa!' Janey cried eagerly.

Pa Grant was standing in the flickering shadows at the head of his team. Zuleika and Marie, the bay mares, quivered and shifted away from the noisy monster with its hot acrid breath: Pa would drive none but thoroughbred horses, and they were nervous creatures. Pa's bright eyes scanned one lighted coach after another. And standing near him, consciously manly, was Janey's fifteen-year-old brother Thad.

'Why, Thad Grant, if you aren't in long trousers!' Janey murmured in his ear as he ducked her teasing kiss. ' — And if there isn't Lucy!'

Six-year-old Lucy poised eagerly on the back seat of the spring wagon and sprang into her sister's embrace, curling arms and legs around her like a monkey. Janey kissed her elfin face soundly, and pulled her hood up from where it hung by its strings on her shoulders.

'Well, Daughtie!' Pa's blue eyes were bright upon her, his mouth bracketed in the smile lines she loved. 'Did you pass? — Good land, Susan! haven't they been feeding you at that school? Once Grandmother lays eyes on you, she'll not rest till she's cosseted you up and put some flesh on your bones. I told 'Lijah we'd swing around by your place, Susan.'

They drove through the main street, its stores, with their high false fronts, in darkness now, except for a few glaring corners from which Janey could imagine the sourish smell of beer. Past the stores, onto streets where log houses irregularly set were dimly lighted for evening; to a corner where a half-finished building glimmered in the moonlight.

'Whoa!' said Pa, and sat regarding the structure proudly.

'Why, Pa, what is it?'

'The new meeting-house. We've been working at it every minute the weather favored us. Hoped we'd have it farther along when you got home, Daughtie.'

'Won't it seem good to have a real church here!'

'I tell you, a town isn't a real town till church bells ring out on its Sabbath mornings.'

He clucked to the horses and they trotted on, out into the

open prairie and to the soddie that was Susan's home. When they had seen the door flung open and the girl clasped in Pop Sloane's awkward embrace, Pa slapped the reins gently against the bay backs, and the mares quickened their trot.

'Ma and Grandmother will be fair standing on their heads with hurry,' chuckled Pa. 'And Ingrid's been bobbing round all day like a hen with its head cut off.'

Thad snorted at the picture of gentle Ma and ramrod-straight Grandmother standing on their heads, and Janey giggled.

'The prairie's lovely, Pa,' she said. 'The night sky doesn't look like this when it's all broken up with roofs and chimneys. But Lucerne's grown a lot in a year. And now with a church!'

'Haakon says this Union Colony town — Greeley, they've named it — has several churches already; fine meeting-houses, too.'

'Oh, Pa!' Janey hesitated, clutched at her firm intention of awaiting a more auspicious time, and then plunged, helter-skelter. 'Pa, Susan and I —— Would you think we were crazy if we wanted to go out there and teach next year? Haakon says the average lady teacher gets sixty dollars a month.'

Pa slowly revolved his head to stare at her, while Thad, always slow of speech, opened and closed his mouth in helpless amazement.

'Out there?' Pa echoed. 'What on earth you talking about, Janey?'

'Out to Greeley,' Janey explained earnestly. 'You know Haakon's going.'

'You?' Pa muttered in a daze. 'Well, I'll be —— Why not Lucy, here?'

Janey laughed. 'But, Pa, I'll soon be seventeen. I've got sense enough to come in when it rains, and all that. And Susan's nineteen. Anyway, I thought maybe we could take Ingrid along, just to be proper. She isn't much help to Ma, and she could take up land, couldn't she?'

'But, Daughtie,' Pa remonstrated, 'you know what your grandmother would say: "A rolling stone gathers no moss." Looks like you ought anyway to finish at Normal. Why, after the way you set your whole heart on Normal, it looks —— '

Janey interrupted eagerly. 'Pa, I know it does; but here's how it is: —— '

And while Pa drew the horses down to a jog, and listened intently; while Thad leaned forward wide-eyed, and Lucy strangled Janey from behind, oblivious to grown-up talk; Janey told him about Susan's fever and her troublesome cough; told him what the doctor had said.

'Well, Janey,' said Pa, as they drew near the house, 'let's wait till tomorrow to spring it on 'em. Mind, Thad.'

The pioneer house stood on a 'sightly' rise of ground, slender saplings surrounding it and forming a narrow avenue from road to door. It was an uncompromisingly square little, plain little dwelling; yet it was a source of just pride, for it was the first 'frame house' in all that community of log cabins and soddies; it was the first to be painted glossily white and green; its shade trees were the first set in the county.

Three yellow rectangles shone out of the gloom, a woman's figure silhouetted at each. Marie and Zuleika's whinnies were answered by whinnies from the barn. Shep stood waiting at the gate. Janey was home.

She leaped out almost before Pa could cramp the wheel for her, dropped a hand on Shep's raised head, and met Ma halfway up the board walk. 'Janey, baby!' Why, she couldn't remember Ma's ever calling her that, except when they came home after their three days' imprisonment in the Great Blizzard. Grandmother waited inside the door and kissed Janey quietly on the forehead (oh, poor Grandmother! how stiffly and painfully she moved ahead of them into the living-room), while Ingrid fidgeted about them, and took Janey's hands in hers, laughing and crying and mumbling brokenly, 'Ai ban glad — Yaney, ai ban knit you new mitten —— !' Poor old fuzzy-witted Ingrid.

When she had looked at them all, and kissed them all, she swung open the back door and, putting her thumbs in her mouth with a peculiar twist Haakon had taught her long ago, she whistled. Again came the answering whinny, loud and eager.

'Mind if I run out with a lump of sugar?' she asked.

'But hurry back,' Ma assented. 'Supper's getting cold.'

Pa was unhitching the mares by lantern light in the dim, clean barn. 'There, girl. So now, Marie,' his kindly voice admonished them.

The ponies nickered at Janey's entrance, ears pricked forward, velvet muzzles outstretched, lustrous eyes catching the light. She let them reach into her pockets for the coveted sweets, and stroked their fine heads affectionately. Hiawatha and Minnehaha were special pets, Indian ponies belonging to Janey and Haakon.

'Goodness, Pa,' Janey quavered as they started toward the house to make ready for supper, 'if it's so wonderful to be home again after being away seven months and two hundred miles, what would it be if we went way off to Union Colony?'

'Huh, Janey? Huh?' demanded Lucy's small voice, as Lucy swung possessively on her big sister's arm.

'Nothing, you little pitcher. Nothing at all, till to-morrow.'

'And you wait and let me sort of bring the matter up, Daughtie,' Pa counseled as he followed her in.

As soon as supper was over, Janey turned to her luggage, eager to resolve her doubts. With Lucy squatting on the floor opposite her, gravely watching each move, she unclasped the bulging satchel, which opened with a relieved pop, and took out one article after another. There were a few trinkets to put into Lucy's unconsciously extended hands — a string of beads Emily had sent, a peach pit Ptolemy had carved into a basket, a row of paper dolls with clasped hands that Janey had learned to cut in her primary course. Janey had scarcely a glance for the child's eager delight. Her heart beating fast, she flung the taffeta skirt on the bed and carefully lifted out the other rumpled taffeta roll.

'Oh! 'Gelica!' cried Lucy, dropping her new treasures to reach for the coveted doll.

But Janey was staring blankly at Angelica's slender kid wrist, where she had been wont to slip the ring bracelet-fashion when she was not wearing it.

The ring was not there.

CHAPTER III

GRANDMOTHER TURNS ADVENTURER

THE whole family helped ransack Janey's belongings in the search for the ring. The satchels were emptied and their contents spread out on the bed, and they themselves brushed and shaken upside down. All the intricate puffings and pleatings of Janey's 'good' dresses were felt with meticulous finger-tips. Angelica was undressed and probed. Not until Janey, in her nightgown, had examined the clothing worn that day, could she believe that the ring had really disappeared.

'I can't sleep a wink till I've written Mrs. Jones to be on the lookout for it,' she worried; and she slipped into Ma's flannel wrapper and wrote the letter that night, her eyes swimming with sleep and the tears of the day.

Next day, the inquiry mailed and everything possible done, Janey's attention focused on Colorado Territory again. It was not until evening that Pa found the right moment to introduce the subject. He was sitting in the kitchen looking through the new county *Herald* while Ma patiently climbed round him and stepped over his extended foot and prepared supper. Janey set the table, sniffing with relish the delicately browned biscuits and the sizzling meat. Grandmother knitted swiftly, erect and unrocking in her rocking-chair just inside the sitting-room door.

'Quite a report here from Union Colony,' Pa observed, crackling the paper open with a twinkle for Janey. 'Frost out of the ground in February, last year: think of that! Got their crops in early, and everything's looking fine, except for grasshoppers. Sometimes I do wonder at myself that I didn't try to make it through to Colorado Territory when we pulled up stakes in Wisconsin, instead of stopping here in Minnesota.'

'Why, Pa' — Ma, quite unruffled, beat rich milk into the potatoes and added an unwonted spoonful of butter in honor of the returned child — 'how could we have bettered ourselves much by that? They had the hoppers there, same as here. And soon's we've weathered that pest, we'll be doing well.'

'Now, Ma,' Pa argued, 'there's other things than mere money to consider. Look at the kind of town Greeley is. Look at the good solid meeting-houses already built. Look at the rules against any trafficking whatsoever in spirituous liquors and all intoxicating drink. Look at the kind of men that are forming the community. Look at the men that founded it.'

Pa drew a deep breath and shook the curling red-brown hair back from his white forehead. His blue eyes glowed. Janey smiled tenderly: he was working himself up to a tremendous enthusiasm.

'Why,' he went on, 'Nathan Meeker is a scholar, a gentleman, and a philanthropist.'

'Some say that he's sort of impractical, though,' Ma observed, still beating that creamy swirl of potato.

'QUITE A REPORT HERE FROM UNION COLONY'

'Aren't there always some to "say"?' Pa demanded, hotly indignant at the unknown critics. 'Clods that call a man a dreamer if he has a vision! How could Nathan Meeker be agricultural editor of a paper like the *New York Tribune* if he was so impractical? It doesn't stand to reason. And he's been cogitating over such a colony scheme for years, and studying its problems. But when Horace Greeley joined hands with him on the project, it was the union of all the needful elements. Impractical? What is there impractical about the way they've gone to work?'

Punctuating the story with crackling jerks of the *Herald*, Pa reviewed the forming of the Colony.

It was in 1869 that Meeker began to advocate, through the columns of the *Tribune*, the founding of a farming colony in the West, and from the start Horace Greeley had been his ardent supporter in the idea. Followers had swarmed to their ranks, and when Mr. Meeker made a tour of the great new West and found at the foot of the Rockies a region which seemed to him the very Garden of Eden, Eastern enthusiasm flamed high.

'But, Pa,' Ma objected, 'I can't get the straight of it yet. In our geography books it's labeled the Great American Desert.'

'Irrigation, Ma, irrigation! They've been using canals in Egypt and India since way-way back. European countries, too. Why shouldn't we? Not that folks didn't get some wild ideas about the Territory,' he admitted, with the manner of one making a generous concession to his opponents. 'Man's got to earn his bread in the sweat of his brow as long as he's here in this vale of woe, I take it. And some of these Eastern men were put out when they found they had to callus their hands to make a living — not lie in the sun and let their wheat grow of itself in the Colony fields.'

But in general, he said, the colonists were sticking to it. Together, Greeley and Meeker had assembled a group of solid citizens. They had discouraged drifters by asking references as to character, and by requiring a substantial membership fee. Membership entitled the holder to a town lot and a tract of farming land — land which the founders had purchased from the railway that was pushing through the vast wild desert. Excess funds were used for construction of canals and other improvements.

The town of Greeley had been incorporated in May, 1871, carefully laid out, with thought for churches and schools, and provision against any sale of intoxicants within the colony limits. At first it had been a group of tents and shacks, but already, three years later, it was becoming substantial, and little by little the trees were beginning to grow along its wide streets.

Horace Greeley himself had been untiring in his urgency that trees be set. He had loved the Colony and the town that bore his name, and had expected to settle there. Death had ended that plan two years after the founding of the town, but his spirit seemed still to inspire it.

'And anything Horace Greeley set his seal of approval to,' Pa went on, 'is worthy of the highest consideration. It's a source of pride to me that he was my personal friend. I count that the man truly died a martyr to his country's progress; I count that he perished of a broken heart after his bitter presidential defeat two years ago.' Pa's voice and his enthusiasm mounted steadily, and the paper swished and crackled in his clenched hand. 'I don't know but it's the bounden duty of his friends and admirers to show their admiration of the man and their respect for his judgment by helping build up the project which was the darling of his heart — the Union Colony of Colorado!'

Pa took breath and wiped his brow with a flourish of clean bandanna. Ma flicked him an indulgent smile and went on beating the potatoes.

'But what could you do about it, Pa? We're not exactly footloose.'

'And what of that?' Pa demanded oratorically. 'Why not cast in our lot, even at some personal sacrifice, with this little band of God-fearing, high-principled men who hope to build a Paradise on earth? Shall we let ourselves be root-bound by the property we've acquired in this community? By the few dollars we should lose if we sold out and went on?'

'Yes; till after we've picked up from the grasshoppers and can get a fair price for our property,' Ma responded with her soft imperturbability; 'yes; I think we *should* let ourselves be bound.'

'But, Ma, consider!' Pa launched into a glowing description of twelve-inch turnips, forty-pound cabbages, and other marvels of irrigation. He paused in full tilt to listen: went to the door and peered into the night.

Nearer it came, a thin high voice in song:

> Helloo, helloo, my little dog Koomy!
> It's mide-amide well in the roo,
> In the row-atum-scow, in the eastable waggy.

'Come in, come in, Inch-Along!' Pa held open the door and hailed the small bent figure pausing at the gate. 'You're just in time for supper. — Set another place, Daughtie. — Our Janey's come home from school.'

Inch-Along limped up the walk and shifted his pack to the floor, blinking and beaming in the lamplight.

'I kinda calc'lated the little lass might be home. Kinda figgered it that way,' he chuckled. 'Well — well — well.'

The subject of Union Colony was shelved until Inch-Along had washed tidily at the bench with Grandmother's famous cake soap, and they were all crowded together at the table, the light picking out the farther faces but dimly. Inch-Along was always hailed with pleasure; he was a 'pack-peddler' who had made his rounds ever since Janey and Thad could remember, heralded by the mysterious song, and bearing treasure of needles and pins, gingerbread and spices, lace and combs, and now and then a precious volume of verse or story.

'And where is the lad Haakon?' he asked, peering from end to end of the table.

'Haakon has spent the year at Dartmouth College, in the East,' Pa told him, 'but he is going to start up for himself in the Union Colony, Colorado Territory. You have any personal knowledge of Colorado Territory, Inch-Along?'

The old man chuckled again. 'Have I?' he ruminated. 'Friend Grant, if I had a dollar for every time I've tramped through Coloraydo Territory —— ! Not a pack-peddler then, for I was still strong and quick on my feet. It was in Coloraydo Territory, to be sure, that I came by the mishap that's made me inch along the balance of my days. But I don't hold it no grudge for that.'

'Aw, Inch-Along! you never told us that one.' Thad's voice, always deliberate and strangely deep of pitch, had added to itself a shrill falsetto break which came at the least expected moments, plunging him into crimson embarrassment.

Inch-Along ignored it. 'It's little enough there is to tell, lad. We were prospecting, and I was fool enough to try to see why the dynamite didn't go off as it should. But before those days I panned gold in the streams, and went after it with my miners' pick; and I'd take some furs on the side now and then; but mostly not, because my good friends the Injuns might not have been such good friends if I'd poached too much on their preserves. Gold don't concern 'em; but furs —— !'

'I've heard tell it was wonderful country,' Pa encouraged him.

'Fine country it is. Up here the mountins' — Inch-Along drew a diagram on the tablecloth with his fork — 'and here the plains where the Utes hold the fort. And the Sioux and the Arapahoes and others aren't supposed to come past Cherry Creek here. But every year they venture up into the mountins after bear and lion and other game; and every year the Utes venture out onto the plain after buffalo. And — glory! what battles they do put up!'

'Haakon says he was there with Two-Toes and Weenonah,' Thad broke in.

Inch-Along paused and nodded thoughtfully. 'And I remember the laddie myself: no bigger than a jack-rabbit; no bigger than Lucy, here, or not much; and just beginning to tan brown so his white hair put you in mind of milkweed silk.... So Haakon's going to try his fortune in Coloraydo? Well — well — well. Good for the lad, say I: it's bonny country. Grand even for the farmer, 'tis said, once they get the water onto it. Though it's little faith I have in growing crops with rain from below.'

'I'd like to try my luck there myself,' said Pa.

'Pa, how can you talk so,' Ma protested, 'when we're just getting on our feet here? With a new cow for the old one lost in the blizzard, poor creature; and the note paid, and a new barn —— '

Grandmother spoke for the first time. Seeing her firm lips unclose, Janey squirmed uneasily. Grandmother was always wise; always unwilling to embark on wild schemes. And in her heart Janey knew this scheme had its wild features. But to her surprise, Grandmother's voice was halting, wistful.

'They say the climate is — is very salubrious?' she asked. 'I've heard it does wonders for folks with all sorts of ailments.'

'And right you are, ma'am,' Inch-Along assented heartily. 'Almost as soon as white men broke into the region at all, they discovered the queer effects of the mountin air. I can't rightly say what it is, ma'am, but it's like drinking in the good God's own medicine. I've seen men carried in on stretchers, and going out in a few years on their own two feet, fit as a fiddle.'

Grandmother sighed. Poor Grandmother! her own two feet were becoming less and less obedient to her will.

'I'd like to end my days there myself,' Inch-Along went on.

'And I,' Pa seconded him.

'Now, Pa!' Ma chided, her voice shading into anxiety.

Pa seized the moment. 'Well, Ma, if you're plumb set against it, how about letting Janey go and spy out the land for us, so we could move out in a year or two when we got a good price on our holdings here?'

Ma's cup hung in mid-air. Grandmother leaned tremulously forward. The whole table turned astonished eyes on the speaker. All, that is, except Janey, who was self-consciously crumbing her bread into bits and holding her breath.

The whole table voiced its question: '*Janey?*'

So Pa explained it. First he told them about Susan. Nothing that should not clear up in a year, the doctor said, in that life-giving climate, but, going on as she was — Pa shook his head.

'The poor girl!' Ma murmured. 'The poor motherless girl. Think if it was our Janey.'

'Garsh, Pa!' Thad broke in, spots of red on his tanned cheeks. 'Mountains — and wild horses — and Injuns. Injuns, Pa! Oh, Pa, wouldn't they need a boy along? Ingrid wouldn't be any 'count.'

Ingrid, refilling the platter of crisp-fried sidemeat, set the dish down with a crash and backed away into the wall, her face white and her pale hair unwinding from its loose coil.

'Inyins?' she pleaded. 'Ai not going. Please, Ai not going!'

Grandmother spoke up with decision, decision that held underlayers of hope and fear. 'If you are really considering such an adventure,' she said, 'why shouldn't I be the one to go with the girls? I — find it hard to face the possibility of being a — a burden helpless in my chair.'

It was their turn to stare at Grandmother. *Grandmother* to go into pioneer country? Why, grandmothers were supposed to ——

'Doubtless you're thinking my place is in the chimney-corner.' Grandmother spoke with vigor. 'I'm not so old. I'm just sixty. I could hold my own with any woman of forty if once I was rid of this rheumatism.'

'You'd be the one to take up a homestead, Mother,' Pa nodded slowly; 'you could prove up in no time at all, on account of Father's service in the War. They subtract the years of service, you know, from the homesteading time, for a veteran or his widow either.'

With the impetus given by Inch-Along, who had been there, and by Grandmother, who so amazingly wished to go, talk of the Colony shuttled back and forth across the supper table, weaving a web of romance, adventure, health.

The Seth Thomas in the sitting-room struck the hour. Involuntarily the company paused to count. Ten o'clock.

Ma rose from the foot of the table. 'We'd best leave the talk for tonight,' she said, 'and get these dishes cleared away. Anyhow, who knows that Janey and Susan can get teaching to do? First thing, it seems to me, is to send their applications in and see what comes of it.'

Janey's glance of triumph met Pa's. With Ma on her side, the wild adventure began to swing into the realm of the possible.

CHAPTER IV
WESTWARD HO!

EXCITED conferences with Susan Sloane. Long discussions between Pa and Ma and Pop Sloane. Careful penning of applications with Mankato Normal as reference. Restless waiting for replies.

Mrs. Jones's answer came with gratifying promptness; but that was the only pleasant thing about it. 'I do hope you have found the ring by this time, Miss Janey. I have hunted everything over as careful as anybody could, and Ptolemy hunted, too, before he left, but we never found hide or hair of it. I am going to get at the spring cleaning next month, and I will watch all the sweepings when the carpets are took up, though I would be almost willing to swear it is not here.'

It was late May before they received the answers to their applications.

The few farmers waiting for their mail that morning were all talking at once. 'It ban mos' too much,' Mr. Sanson whined, his voice squeaky with emotion. 'Ai tank Ai pool oop an' try agan someveres else.' — 'They ain't like last year's hoppers,' protested another. 'These here are sech leetle fellers. And it beats all where they come from. One minute they wa'n't there, and the next they was. Ground jest swarmin' with 'em, and all eatin' like shoats.' — 'Well, nacherly the ground's swarmin' with 'em. They hatched out of those eggs the pests left last summer.'

Lucerne and its county were gloomy, despairing, fighting mad, or grimly determined, under this new invasion of locusts. Last year's siege had come near ruining the whole countryside. What would this year mean?

The day seemed so somber that Janey did not expect any good from it, when at length the postmistress, who had been shuffling the mail deliberately and portioning it to its pigeonholes, came to the grated window and opened the slide. Janey's heart lurched at sight of a long envelope with the Greeley postmark. She waited till Susan received one, too, and they retreated together to a far corner of the store, where they teetered precariously on a cracker barrel and slit the envelopes solemnly with one of Susan's hairpins.

The communications were drowned in formal wording, and Janey dived hurriedly for the meat of hers.

'Susan!'

Susan looked up from her patient perusal, her gray eyes still unenlightened.

'Susan!' Janey could say nothing more till a series of chuckles had welled up and burst in her throat. 'They have! Honestly they have! I mean I am! They're going to! Oh —— ' She shoved the letter under Susan's nose and pointed to the middle of it:

'We have the honor to inform you that your Normal School grades, as forwarded to us by the president of that institution, were sufficiently high to permit us to engage you for next year's teaching without the customary examination by the county superintendent. Such an examination

will be necessary, however, before you can be granted a
second year's contract. Your previous teaching experience
in the Lucerne school, and your training in primary work,
combine to influence our decision. We have the honor to
offer you a salary of seventy dollars per month, for a nine
months' school year.'

'Oh, Susan, Susan, Susan!'

Susan smiled at her maternally. 'I never for a minute
doubted they'd grab onto you, Janey. But me — I haven't
got the straight of this letter yet, the handwriting's so
fancy.'

Janey craned to see, and in an instant her hovering finger
pounced. It trailed along a line, slowed, stopped, went
back. Susan, following it, swallowed hard.

'But, Susan, that's all right!' Janey assured her hurriedly. 'If you'd taught a year, they'd have taken you sight
unseen, too. The examinations 'll be easy.'

Susan winked rapidly. 'Well, I'm going,' she announced
defiantly. 'I — honest, Janey, I can't hardly wait to get
there.'

And now, indeed, the days were crowded with plans and
preparations, peppered with Thad's explosive pleadings,
and sparkling with Lucy's funniness, as she darted into
everybody's way and stuck her little finger into every possible pie.

Inch-Along came in on the plans. Ma had made him a
comfortable bed in the hayloft, since the small house would
stretch no further, and he helped with odd jobs during
the days of waiting. Each day had increased his determination to go with them if they went, taking up a homestead where he could spend his last days on 'soil that's my
own.'

'And I'll feel safer for the little lass if I'm some'rs near by,' he said soberly to Pa and Ma as he helped with the milk on an early June evening.

'You've taken quite a fancy to our Janey,' Pa commented, glancing curiously at the old man's face, browned and reddened with wind and sun, and all its wrinkles curving upward.

'I always fancied her,' Inch-Along nodded, pouring the foamy fragrant whiteness through a strainer into a shining pan. 'Well do I mind the first time ever I hobbled over your stile on the old Wisconsin place. She wasn't but a yearling, Janey wasn't, and me a pretty tough-looking old customer. Setting on a quilt on the grass she was, and she held up her bits of bare dimpled arms and gurgled like an angel. But that ain't all,' he added thoughtfully, 'nor even the friendliness of her all the years sence, up to now, when some book-learned young ladies would turn up their pretty noses at a lame old pack-peddler. No.'

He set the pail down and reached a clean, gnarled old hand into an inside pocket; drew out, slowly, a case like a small embossed black book, and with a lingering look inside, passed it over to Ma.

It was a daguerreotype, beginning to show the iridescence of age around the edges. From the center, eternally young, looked a girl, her hair folded in quaint braided loops over her ears and escaping in curling tendrils, her brow childlike and round, her eyes wide-set and singularly direct, her chin unexpectedly squared under a curving mouth.

'Why, it *does* favor our Janey!' Pa exclaimed. 'Barring the queer old hair-do, and the dress. Mother, do you mind when you wore a dress like that, with the wide sleeves filled in with lace? Janey, would you look?'

Janey came in shyly, because she had been there longer than they supposed, and had heard what was said. She took the daguerreotype respectfully. 'Oh, but she's much pret-tier than I am,' she protested.

'Not anything but the nose,' Inch-Along assured her seriously, and Janey laid a protective palm over the nonde-script little feature.

'But — who was she, Inch-Along?' she asked timidly.

Inch-Along cradled the case tenderly in his hand before closing it and returning it to his inner pocket.

'You mind the frill of lace — Spanish silk lace it was — I gave you when you were a bit of a lass, Janey?'

'Of course. I have it put away in my treasure-box.' Janey flushed, remembering the old man's words: 'For a frill beneath your pretty chin. On your wedding day, be-like.'

Inch-Along's eyes dreamed through the twilight. 'She was going to trim her wedding dress with a bit of that same lace, lassie, my Lisbeth was. And the dress half-made, and me with my broadcloth at the tailor's, when she — when she went from us. — So it's like as if — like as if you were our grandbaby, Janey, and you favoring her so.'

Pa gripped Inch-Along's hand in a hearty clasp. 'Some-times I've feared it was a wild thing I was letting the child do. But not with you by, Inch-Along.'

It had been decided that Inch-Along should set out with the two ponies, enough ahead of the women-folk, who were going by train, to reach there only a little later than they. He could pack what he needed on one animal and ride the other, changing about to rest them. In that way he would save not only his own railway fare, but the cost of shipping Hiawatha and Minnehaha.

'Susan says her father would give her a good pony, if it didn't cost so much to get it there,' Janey mused aloud.

At that Thad waxed eloquent. 'Oh, Pa! why couldn't I

ride one of 'em and go with Inch-Along? Oh, Pa — Ma!
Please can't I?'

Again Grandmother proved an ally.

'Son, Thad would be a wonderful help with the work
we'd have to do proving my claim. He's small yet, but he's
handy.'

Thad stretched to his slim five-feet-two and implored his
father with pleading hazel eyes.

'I don't see how I can spare him myself,' Pa countered.

'But hired help is dreadfully dear at the Colony, I've
read. And my notion would be this' — Grandmother hesitated — 'if Thad helped me prove up, I'd deed the land over
to him as soon as it was proved on; then he'd have his start.'

'Garsh, Gramma!' Thad said solemnly.

'And he'd get enough sight better schooling in the Greeley
school than he's getting here, with that Sanson niece for
teacher.'

So Inch-Along and Thad set out two weeks ahead of the
train travelers, riding Hiawatha and Minnehaha, and leading Susan's wiry Gitchee Gummee, renamed to match its
companions.

Those two weeks were busy ones. There were wardrobes
to be considered. Fortunately, Janey hadn't been hard on
her clothes that year at school, and she had had an unprecedented number: a best dress, a second best, and an
everyday! Best would still be best — the plum color with
the robin's-egg blue facings, that was; and second best
would be fine for school — a blue and cream woolen, spun
and woven at home. Pa brought home a pattern of king's-
blue henrietta for another dress, and they all set about making it up. For summer, two ruffled muslins were devised, a
straw-colored and a blue. Pa took her to Beaver Rapids,
where there was a milliner, and got her a smart little hat

that tilted fetchingly over her eyes, leaving all her curls to
show behind; and at the general store, a pair of cloth-top
shoes laced on the side, the first Janey had ever possessed.
For winter she had her beautiful gray squirrel cape and
muff: Haakon had saved her the finest pelts for two years.

Grandmother's clothes were little worn and always in
perfect order, so they took no time at all.

Betweentimes, everyone helped fight grasshoppers. The
voracious infants devoured every green thing that appeared, and grew and grew, and developed to the winged
stage, and flew onward. The roads and sidewalks were foul
with them, and neighbors came a half-mile to draw water
from the Grants' covered well, for the open ones were
sickening with drowned locusts.

'There's still time for the gardens to come on again,' Pa
rejoiced, 'and the crops haven't been quite so bad hurt this
year. If only this is the end of the vermin!'

Altogether, the two weeks hurtled by. Once more, Zuleika and Marie stood twitching outside the little station.
Pa had already brought down Grandmother's cowhide
trunk and Janey's box and the bulging carpet-bag. Now the
spring wagon unloaded Grandmother, stiff and slow, and
Janey, quick and eager, their two brown leather satchels,
Ma, Lucy, and Ingrid. The Sloane wagon was as crowded,
and a half-hour before train time, the stuffy waiting-room
was thronged with most of Lucerne and the surrounding
country, come to bid the three adventurers farewell.

'Goodness! isn't saying good-bye the *hardest!*' breathed
Janey, when they had at last chugged out of town and were
sliding smoothly into the open country. She dabbed at her
eyes and nose with a moist handkerchief. 'Much as I hated
to leave Pa and Ma and that blessed baby, it got so I just
longed to hear the train whistle. That lump in your throat

swells and swells, and the tears sting in your nose, and you have to keep on standing on one foot and then on the other and saying the same thing over and over.'

'Seems to me we listened to quite a variety of speeches,' Grandmother said dryly.

'"Janey, you clean forgot to write in my album,"' mimicked Janey, blinking back the tears. '"Be sure you send me an invitation to your wedding." — "Don't forget your old friends." — "Don't get run off with by an Injun chief." — "Watch out for rattlesnakes." — But the funniest were the ones that took us by the hand in a farewell-forever kind of way, and you knew they didn't expect you to come back alive.'

The trip was to take two days and three nights. For economy's sake they were riding in the day coach till the final night. Pa felt that Grandmother should not try her strength further, and that she might need the girls near her in the Pullman.

Darkness came upon them soon after their start, and though comfort was impossible on the stiff plush benches, Janey found it fascinating to doze and drowse and sleep, and wake to watch the countryside slip by: small sleeping towns and lighted stations; and silver-flashing ponds and streams; and inky black trees.

Babies woke and cried, and tired mother-voices soothed them, or stockinged feet padded lurchingly up and down the aisle as fathers tried to quiet the restless ones. The air was heavy with boxed lunches and orange peel and coal smoke, and the bump of a flat wheel wove the whirr of sound into a regular refrain. Janey started a poem about it:

> We glide, glide, glide, over the sounding steel,
> To the rhythmical song of the wheel,
> With its chug — chug — chug, like a galloping horse at night;
> Like a monster horse, with iron might.

The first part of the day was interesting, too, with its
continual change of scene. And when Grandmother spread
out their breakfast-lunch on little fringed napkins, it tasted
delicious.

'What's the matter with the napkin, Susan?' Janey
asked in surprise.

Susan was scrutinizing it closely. 'Janey, it is!' she said
solemnly, 'and I do believe it's a good sign.'

'Is what? What's a good sign?' Janey demanded in impatient amusement.

'Do you remember when we first began to be friends —
way off in Wisconsin in the little schoolhouse, three whole
years ago?'

'Well, of course.'

Indeed, Janey remembered it somewhat uneasily — her
first contempt of Susan, the newcomer, with her lank dark
hair cut bowl-shaped, and her queer gray eyes, and her outlandish dresses. Susan's 'looks' no longer mattered to her,
for they were the looks of the truest friend a girl could have.
But when first the teacher made them seat-mates, Janey's
tilted nose had tilted higher, and at lunch-time Janey had
eaten with eyes straight ahead, until ——

'I asked you if your lunch was always so pretty,' Susan
reminded her. 'And, Janey, it was this very same fringed
napkin.'

'What makes you think so?' Janey doubted.

'I know so. It had a teentsy hole right in this red plaid,
and it was darned as dainty as if it had been embroidered,
with a little red-and-white thread. And see!' Triumphantly
she showed the darn to Grandmother and Janey. 'It does
make me feel like — well, that was the start of an awful nice
friendship for me; and maybe this is the start of something
just as good.'

As the day wore on, the sun beat mercilessly on the speeding train, and the air grew sticky, the odor of lunches staler, and the babies more fretful. Janey amused a few of the older ones with finger plays and stories; but life seemed to wilt out of the day coach and everyone in it. At noon all the sandwiches tasted of fried chicken, and the fried chicken tasted of cake, and the cake tasted of cheese. None of the three did more than nibble at their dinner. By night they voted unanimously for a cup of hot tea and nothing else, and the girls carried one rather sloppily from the station lunch-room to Grandmother. Grandmother's face was drawn and gray. 'Rheumatism full as bad as usual,' she responded briefly to the girls' questioning.

Susan was coughing, and her cheeks were hotly flushed. Janey watched them both, worriedly, as she rolled up her coat and tried to fit herself to the obtrusive angles of the seat. She was too tired and sickish-feeling to sleep. And the next she knew, she woke to find the lamps out and the thin gray light of early morning filtering into the car. She was lying on the seat, almost full length, with her own coat under her head and Susan's under her shoulders.

'The idea!' she scolded. 'Did you do that, Susan Sloane? And me the healthiest one of the lot.'

'Well,' Susan said reasonably, 'you're the only one small enough to come any way near stretching out on that sofa, so why not?'

They were all relieved to change into the 'elegant Pull-man palace car' that day.

'Babies are fine, but on a train —! And there aren't half so many on this car. And the smells aren't so smelly.'

Besides that, there was a porter who gave some attention to ventilation, and flapped around the window-sills to scatter the cinders.

'I suppose that hired man calls it dusting,' Grandmother observed caustically.

Late in the day this porter pointed out to the girls the stacks of bleached bones piled up on each side of the track. Buffalo skeletons, they were; the hunters had brought the carcasses to the railway, skinned them there, and shipped the hides to market. Already the great herds had dwindled to almost nothing, though once that evening the porter came hurriedly to show the girls a cluster of dark specks on the horizon: 'sho' 'nough live buffalo, yes, ma'am.'

But it was at dusk that Janey surveyed her new domain with awe. The porter lighted the lamps that hung from the ceiling ('swinging silver lamps,' Janey wrote Ma), moving soundlessly on the thick soft carpet, and then began to make up the beds.

Pullman sleeping-cars had been invented only a few years earlier, and this was the first either Grandmother or the girls had ever seen. It was like watching a magic act to see the hidden shelves spring into being, and the flying skill of the porter's dark fingers as he placed the double mattresses and spread the fresh sheets and good blankets.

'It seems almost against nature,' said Grandmother, 'for a man-body to be so able at making beds.'

'But how ever are you going to manage, Grandmother? To get settled? When it's so hard for you to get into bed at home, where you have a whole room.'

'You tend to your own managing and leave me to mine,' Grandmother advised them, her voice a trifle tart with pain. 'How the two of you are going to climb up on that closet shelf and undress there is more than I can figure.'

It really was an acrobatic stunt, especially with double rows of hooks and eyes on their tight bodices, and Janey's proud new shoes that laced on the sides. They twisted and turned on their narrow perch, and laughed till they were out of breath and Susan went into a coughing spell.

'And for land sakes, where are we to put them when we've got them off?' inquired Susan.

''Spose we can pin them up to these lovely curtains?' wondered Janey.

She was kneeling on her shelf busily pinning up the waists and skirts when a sudden lurch of the train sent her sprawling forward. 'Oh!' she squeaked wildly, and Susan gripped her firmly by the petticoats and saved her from pitching into the aisle.

At length they were abed on their 'closet shelf,' the lights of the hanging lamps were lowered to mere taper flames, and a new and delicious coolness seeped into the car. The girls, and even Grandmother, slept soundly.

With her usual foresight, Grandmother was up before dawn, and — as perfectly tidy as if she were at home — wakened the girls before the drowsy porter had quenched the lamps. They dressed with stifled laughter, and made their way to the washroom before anyone else was stirring, so that they were able to comb their hair and wash without waiting. The train was to stop at Cheyenne for breakfast. There they would change to the Denver line; and after that it was only a few hours to Greeley. 'We ought to last that long,' said Janey — 'clean, I mean'; and she pinned a fresh white collar into her straw-colored muslin dress and tilted her best hat smartly over her fresh curls.

They were both 'neat as new pins' when they drew into the Cheyenne station. And fortunate it was; for scarcely had they clambered down from the train before Haakon came striding toward them, both hands outstretched in greeting.

'And this is my friend and partner, Ralph Farnum,' he introduced the young man at his side.

Ralph Farnum swept off his huge felt hat and held it grandly against his heart. Janey kept her giggles sternly in control and greeted him demurely, while Susan's mouth stayed ajar in frank bewilderment. The young Easterner had spent the previous afternoon purchasing the most violently Western togs he could find in the Cheyenne shops. He was highly decorative in a silk shirt and vivid silk neckerchief, gun-belt, buckskin breeches, and boots with glistening spurs. It may have cost him some pain to discover that all his art and dollars could not change the bulbous commonplace of his features; but probably he never discovered it.

'We could do some of our buying here as well as in Denver,' Haakon explained, 'and we thought it would be good fun to surprise you. — Great guns, Janey, but you've grown!'

'More beautiful!' bowed Ralph Farnum.

A muscle twitched in Haakon's jaw, and he cleared his throat. 'We'd better be thinking about breakfast. Where's Grandmother Grant? And your satchels?'

'The colored man offered to take our things to the other train; and Grandmother's waiting for us.'

When Haakon returned, helping the stiffly erect Grandmother, Ralph was offering his arm, elegantly akimbo, to Janey. Startled, she glanced back, and saw Haakon, his eyes dancing, offer his free arm, elegantly akimbo, to Susan. So she accepted the challenge, and they went into the station lunchroom, where they ate an appetizing breakfast.

'No hurry,' a trainman told them, as they looked anxiously at the clock. 'There's a hot box. Have to hold up a bit for repairs.'

There was still a margin of time when they had finished eating, and so they settled Grandmother in her seat in the

Denver train and walked out into the town. Not much of a town, 'Cheyanne,' as it was called by the Westerners: an untidy huddle of small buildings, adobe and log and lumber, the stores with false fronts facing each other superciliously across a dusty expanse of street.

'But what a funny house!' cried Janey, stopping beside an adobe whose one side window showed a sill two feet deep. She scurried on and peered cautiously at the window on the other side. 'Why, this wall isn't any thicker than a regular soddie!' she exclaimed.

She had not lowered her voice, and a woman came to the door and flashed her a good-humored Irish grin.

'An' did yez want to know fer why?'

Janey nodded, blushing.

The woman flipped a thumb at the building next them on the thick side, and Janey noticed for the first time that it was a saloon. 'Shure, an' the firrst year we was here, me man an' me, 'twas more nor wan bullet come bustin' through from that saloon into our kitchen. So Mike, he up an' sticks another layer of 'dobe bricks on that side, to save us from sudden death. But things has changed; Cheyanne ain't the place it wanst was.'

It was raw enough and wild enough still, Janey thought, with every other building a saloon, the click of dice insistent, and hard-eyed men swaggering on the corners, and ——

'Oh, do look!' she said softly.

Down the street sauntered a picturesque figure, yellow ringlets showing under a hat like Ralph's, buckskin breeches, and a fringed shirt brightened by a crimson sash.

'Doesn't he look like a dime novel?'

'That's his aim.' Haakon dismissed him contemptuously, even while Ralph's eyes were devouring him. 'They come here mild as dishwater, and rig themselves out like that, and grow some curls if they can, and tack on a name like Apache Mike or Pawnee Jack; only most of them are Bill.'

'But surely Buffalo Bill and Wild Bill Hickock — they aren't as mild as dishwater?' Janey asked disappointedly.

'No, they're the originals, and these are the copies. And there's always more copies than originals. There's another of the copies, if I'm not mistaken.'

They had turned to look when the train clanged and buckled. 'Allll aboarrd!' challenged the brakeman. The boys strode toward the train, the girls scurrying beside them. As she ran, Janey glanced over her shoulder at the slight youth with his fringes and his pistol belt. He seemed to be returning her stare from under the jaunty brim of his hat.

'My goodness, Susan!' she gasped, as Haakon boosted her onto the car step. 'If I didn't know it couldn't be, I'd say that was Peetohlemy Jones.'

CHAPTER V

GREELEY

'Let's ride on the steps of the last car and see more of the country,' Haakon suggested. 'If you don't mind our leaving you, Grandmother Grant?'

It was something the girls had longed to do, but without quite daring. 'It's all right?' Janey asked the conductor timidly when they had established themselves.

'So long as you're careful,' he nodded. 'I guess these young men can look after you.'

Janey soon found it necessary to tie Haakon's big handkerchief over her hat and wildly blowing curls, but the fresh air was pleasant, in spite of fluttering finery. The hours to Greeley fled past in a race of new and amusing prairie-dog towns, cactus, gardens of wild flowers — red, blue, violet, yellow — and shining steel rails. And, hung against the western sky, the Rocky Mountains, shimmering blue and unreal in the morning sunshine, and dominated by gleaming white peaks.

As they approached the town, the steady song of the steel was broken, and the train jerked almost to a standstill, the wheels spinning madly.

'More grasshoppers!' Haakon ejaculated.

Grasshoppers it was, the rails slippery with them, and the fields on each side as ragged as finger-nails bitten to the quick.

Haakon smoothed his brow determinedly. 'Our land lies in another direction. Likely as not they haven't touched it.'

'I thought you'd best go straight to your boarding-house, Grandmother Grant,' he said, when he helped her from the train. 'You'll have time to snatch forty winks before dinner.'

When they had looked after the baggage, they stepped out into the Greeley streets for the first time.

The little town baked in the mid-morning sun. Store buildings straggled around the 'park,' a square of parched earth broken with sickly young trees. Saddle ponies and teams were tied to the hitching-rails that bounded the road, switching and stamping at the flies that pestered them. Small dwelling-houses straggled out from the business section, with here and there a determined spot of greenery.

'Anyway,' Janey murmured, 'it's nice not to have the saloons and gamblers.'

'Land sakes!' protested Susan, 'I'd just as lieve have gamblers as Injuns — Injuns like those.'

The quintet turned to follow her gaze. Against the wall of a 'dry goods emporium' sat a gayly decked group. Janey's eyes slipped over the squaws, sitting with their children in their arms; over a young boy who crouched a little apart, a fuzzy black pup clasped to his breast; and fixed themselves with unwilling fascination on the massive figure at the center of the company.

A bottle-green shirt strained across his corpulent chest, and the brilliant blue blanket that swathed him from waist to knees increased his monstrous bulk. The greasy copper of his face was adorned with a rainbow of color: crimson streaks on his forehead, a yellow band across his eyes, and bands of red, yellow, and blue down his cheeks. The rainbow was surmounted by a tall plug hat of shiny beaver. tilted over one eye.

Janey could find no amusement in the comic contrast. The face was too gross and evil, too assured in its wickedness, and the small eyes followed them too intently.

'Those aren't Sioux?' she asked breathlessly.

'No, Utes.'

'I suppose the fat one isn't really so bad as he looks.'

'Colorow? Say, folks are frightened to death of him,' Ralph informed them with evident relish, 'the length and breadth of this fair Territory.'

'Well,' Haakon amended, 'I've always had a sneaking notion that the old fellow was more bark than bite. Yet he's bad enough at that — one chief I've never heard a good word for. — But he's not often around Greeley,' he reassured them. 'Once in a while he camps up here a way, but not often.'

The boarding-house was only a few steps farther, and Janey was visioning a cool and quiet sitting-room, and bedrooms where they could drop into a deep, sweet sleep after the hard journey. The dusty town danced dizzily before her, and her ears rang. Susan had grown pale and hollow-eyed, and Grandmother's straight mouth pinched straighter.

Haakon noticed it. 'You'd all best keep quiet awhile,' he cautioned them as he twisted the doorbell. 'This altitude

gets you going, at first. — Mrs. Pertle, this is the lady I engaged a room for — Mrs. Grant; and the young ladies, Miss
Grant and Miss Sloane.'

Mrs. Pertle wiped moist hands on her apron and held
open the door. 'Shoo!' she hissed venomously, and flapped
her apron almost in their faces. 'Them flies!' she explained
in the same vindictive tone. 'Not that it does a speck of
good to fight 'em; they're one too many for me. Come in.
Not that I've got much to offer you. What with the hard
times, and that triflin' Indiana skursely worth the salt to
pickle her.' She was ushering them into the 'best room,' and
she talked steadily on, and flapped the damp apron with
utter disregard of consequences. ('We'll be back for dinner,'
Haakon told Janey, and he and Ralph disappeared.) 'Like
enough you rather go up to your room and clean up a mite
and rest before dinner-time. Not that it's much of a room,
but them as comes to Greeley expecting much is going to
wish they was back where they come from.'

She led the way up the steep narrow stairs, her voice lost
as she talked ahead of her and dabbed at flies. Janey helped
Grandmother make the difficult climb. Mrs. Pertle held
open the door for them, closed it after them, descended, still
mournfully vocal.

Left alone, the three surveyed their longed-for bedroom
with blank disappointment.

Grandmother broke the silence. 'Well,' she said with
businesslike decision, 'we may's well lay down and take our
rest.' After a scrutiny of the sheeted cot, she dropped
stiffly upon it and closed her eyes.

'She's certainly beat out,' murmured Janey, as she un-
hooked her clothes and wriggled out of them; 'did you take
notice she lay down in her dress?'

The two girls, on their lumpy cots, gazed about them at

the canvas partitions, black with flies; at the soapbox wash-
stand, with its chipped white washbowl and cracked blue
pitcher and discolored pink soapdish; at the salmon-colored
building-paper ceiling; at the one small-paned window
propped a trifle open with a chunk of stovewood.

The heat, high under the peaked roof, was sickening.
Janey's courage oozed out at every sick pore. What a ninny
— oh, what a ninny she had been to urge this venture! How
could they live through a year of it? What wouldn't she
give to be back on the edge of Lucerne, a paradise after this
desolation? Susan blew her nose; and Janey shut her eyes,
for she knew just how Susan was feeling. Janey shut her
eyes, and felt the tears sting her hot cheeks as they trickled
through her lashes...

They were wakened by the clangor of a dinner-bell, deaf-
ening through the thin floor boards.

'I don't know's I ever had an hour's nap that did me less
good,' Grandmother conceded, as the three of them staggered to their feet and hastily tidied themselves for the
meal.

Haakon met them at the foot of the stairs and escorted
them into the dining-room. 'Feel pretty wretched right
now, don't you?' he sympathized. 'But you wait!'

Somehow they sat through the meal, a most uninviting
agglomeration of food spread on an oilcloth-covered table.
Janey had a confused impression of numberless men, in
checked trousers, in fringed buckskins, in ordinary dark
suits and 'boiled shirts'; men who exchanged few words
except to ask their neighbors to 'kindly reach me the pie,'
and who speared the bread with their forks; of Mrs. Pertle's
steady monotone, entirely lost only when she disappeared
into the kitchen; of the triflin' Indiana, shuffling round
the table in carpet slippers, pale eyes fixedly on the girls;

of flies, flies, flies, in buzzing swarms, invading every dish.

Somehow, too, they lasted through the afternoon, trying the stifling bedroom again till they could stand it no longer; sitting in the scarcely less stifling best room, as gracious as the interior of a packing-box.

It was late in the afternoon when the turn came. Grandmother sat stiffly in the squeaky wooden rocker, staring ahead of her. Susan stifled her yawns as she leafed through the blue plush album that had graced the center table. Janey was drowsily reading a story in the current *Peterson's*. No one had said a word for an hour. Suddenly Janey's well-known chuckle welled up and exploded behind her compressed lips. Grandmother's grim face relaxed. Susan looked up questioningly from the family photographs.

'We're so funny!' Janey gasped. 'Just as if we were waiting to be hung or something.'

'That's about the way I feel,' Susan assented.

'Honestly, I don't believe it's going to be so bad.' Janey stood up and stretched herself. 'I do feel better. I've stopped riding in the train the way I'd been doing ever since we got here. And my ears don't ring near so much as they did.' She shook herself inquiringly. 'Why, I'm feeling almost good!'

The others agreed that they didn't feel so bad themselves. As a matter of fact, it was not only their feelings that had changed, but the atmosphere. The air had freshened, and a sweet coolness flowed through the open window, so that the supper odors were not unbearable, as the dinner odors had been, but surprisingly welcome after their partial fast.

'Why do you suppose Haakon and Ralph Farnum don't get back?' Janey thought aloud, when the supper-bell dinned in the entry.

As if summoned by the words, a young man towered in the doorway, stooping to avoid the lintel. It was neither Haakon nor Ralph, but a cattle-man whom Janey dimly remembered seeing at the dinner-table, a tall chap in checked shirt and bandanna, with blue eyes that squinted from the sun. He jerked his hat awkwardly from a mop of flaming hair, and ducked a bow.

'I'm Sandy McPhee,' he mumbled, 'your servant, ma'am. Haakon, he ask' me to see to you ladies till him and his pardner could git here,' he explained. 'They had to look after some critters.'

'Anything wrong?' Janey asked in quick alarm.

'Wal, it could mebbe be righter. But he said you wasn't to worry none, Miss.'

He herded them into the dining-room, stooping through each door, his face congested with the effort his attentions cost him. Janey, though pitying his misery, only increased it by motioning him to the chair between her and Susan, where he sat unable to eat.

'Buffalo meat, ma'am?' he muttered, passing the platter.

'Honestly, Mr. Sandy?' Janey sampled it eagerly.

The flies still clustered thick about the table. Indiana still left the imprint of her thumb on the butter. Mrs. Pertle still carried on her unbroken discourse. Nevertheless, the girls, and even Grandmother, ate with appetite, and saw through altered eyes — 'Like after dusty windows have been washed,' Janey commented to Susan.

'You young ladies should walk out in the cool of the evening,' observed the young gentleman directly opposite. Mr. Bancroft, they were calling him. Bancroft? Bancroft? Why, how stupid of her: he was her new principal! He was young and curly-haired and scarcely larger than Janey, and he spoke rather pompously, as if to give himself the weight he lacked otherwise, and looked rather anxious, as if his responsibilities rested heavily on his slim shoulders. Janey remembered her first days of teaching, and sympathized.

Susan and Janey did 'walk out,' leaving the schoolmaster conversing politely with Grandmother in the best room.

'He did so want to come with us, poor dear!' Janey murmured, when they were out of hearing. 'But he was much too polite to leave Grandmother.'

'Poor dear? The *principal?*' asked Susan, unshakable reverence in her voice.

'Well, and our friend Sandy, too. But he was much too bashful. — Oh, Susan!' — she had glanced back over her shoulder — 'there he actually is — Sandy, I mean — a block behind us.'

'I do feel for him,' Susan said soberly, 'being bashful myself and always scared I'll put my foot in it. I'd give anything if I could act natural, the way you do, Janey.'

Janey gave a little skipping run of good spirits. 'Susan,' she cried, 'oh, Sukey Sloane! I do believe this is going to be a wonderful year!'

The cool evening air was bitter-sweet with silvery sage and prairie clover. The prairie rolled away to the majesty of the mountains, and a splendid sunset blazed above them, such brilliant color as the girls had never seen.

They had changed to heavier shoes, and now they gathered up their flounces and ventured onto the unbroken ground — 'Ouch, so many prickers!' — watching the changing sky with fascinated eyes.

'He's still walking with us, about two hundred yards behind!' Janey whispered gleefully.

'We — I s'pose there wouldn't be any proper way to let on that we didn't mind?' Susan asked anxiously; and Janey laughed unsympathetically.

They were beyond the scattering village now. The cloud flames had smouldered out, and a clear green glowed above the peaks. When the girls turned back, a great red moon hung low above the plain. Janey would never forget that evening: the magic lift of spirits after the weary day, the new wild tang in the air, the green sky and the red moon and the bigness of everything.

'Janey, aren't those the Injun camps Haakon spoke of?' Susan interrupted her delight. Sharply they veered from the cluster of tipis among the cottonwoods that fringed the Cache La Poudre River, hoping they had not been seen.

'Let's hurry home!' Janey shivered, and Susan needed no urging, though she coughed breathlessly. But fast as they could hurry — 'Oh, Janey!' she gasped, 'there's that awful fat Injun!'

It might have looked comic to an uninterested unlooker. There were the two of them, looping their muslins as high as propriety permitted, and walking so fast that the walk sometimes broke into a run. There was the blessed ungainly figure of Sandy McPhee, who had dropped back, but now was swinging into a long lope to retrieve the distance. There was Colorow, a monstrous animate Buddha in green and blue, striding with inexorable swiftness, and followed by the scurrying figure of a young lad, who was followed in turn by an occasionally glimpsed ball of black fur. It was painfully evident that the paths of Colorow and the girls would converge before Sandy's could reach the juncture, and that at a point well outside the friendly town.

Comic!

But there was not a whisper of laughter in Janey and Susan: their feet simply followed one another jerkily, like the feet of puppets, and they seemed to cover no more space than as if they were walking in a nightmare.

Then Colorow met them, stopped them, laid a cushiony
brown hand on Janey's wrist. He spoke rapidly, repeating
one word again and again. The young lad was pulling at
him from behind, but Colorow paid no attention to his apparent remonstrances other than a backward kick.

'You let go of me!' Janey chattered stoutly, wondering
wildly what she should do next. And then Sandy came loping up, took Janey's other arm, and smiled — smiled with a
cold and level eye — at Colorow, while he pulled something
from his pocket.

Colorow dropped Janey's arm and extended his hand,
scowling. Janey's bewildered eyes dropped to see that
Sandy had not drawn out the wicked-looking pistol she expected to see, but a large stick of peppermint candy.

With slow and simple majesty, the Ute turned toward
his tents, gripping the candy in one hand and cuffing the
little lad with the other. Janey, secure on Sandy's arm,
stared after him blankly. The ball of black fur bounced in
Colorow's way and he kicked it. There was a shrill cre-
scendo of yelps and the poor puppy picked itself up and
limped in distracted circles. Janey, catching an appealing
backward roll of black eyes from the boy, gathered the hurt
animal into her arms.

'He's broke its leg, like enough,' guessed Sandy, 'the big
brute.'

'Was it all just a joke?' marveled Janey. 'Wasn't there
any danger at all?'

'Wal, that Colorow — yes, he's a dang bad joke. Like
enough he was jest begging for sugar or a biscuit. "Beeskit,"
and "wheesky"; that's their tune.'

'And it didn't take anything but a stick of candy to make
him quit!'

'Candy *with* a six-shooter behind it.' Sandy tapped his

bulging holster. 'That's Colorow all over. Myself, I think he's a big bully, and you can 'most always call his bluff. But not every time.'

The ragged village, flung down on the vast brooding lap of the plains, looked safe and reassuring as they sauntered back toward it. On the outskirts they met a fourth stroller, walking sedately with eyes on the horizon, but breathing rather more rapidly than the slowness of his pace seemed to warrant. Mr. Bancroft lifted his hat and turned to join them. Presently Janey was explaining the puppy and their recent fright, while Sandy and Susan walked on ahead.

'You'll be careful?' Mr. Bancroft urged. 'I didn't think of your walking so far. I suspect, though, that Mr. McPhee is not wholly in error in his estimate of this Ute Colorow. — It frightened your friend Miss Sloane?'

Susan was laughing and coughing at once, and he watched her with a troubled face.

'She is — not in the best of health? Miss Janey, would it be a serious disappointment to Miss Sloane if we could not engage her for the coming term? Perhaps after Christmas — You know the medical men do not think it safe for children to bring them in contact with coughs like hers.'

They talked in lowered voices till the boarding-house was reached. 'Grandmother and I can manage it,' Janey agreed quietly. 'It won't be necessary to explain to Susan.'

It was dark, and the two oil lamps guttered dispiritedly in the best room, when galloping horses clattered to a stop before Mrs. Pertle's door, and Haakon entered, Ralph glowering behind him. Haakon's face was calm and cool, so calm and cool that Janey knew banked fires burned behind it: there was something afoot when Haakon looked like that.

'Anything wrong with your stock?' asked Grandmother.

'Oh, no!' Ralph snarled, 'everything's fine and dandy. To hear Haakon talk, this was a Utopia where nothing could possibly go wrong. As if it wasn't enough to go out there this morning in that darn' blistering sun and find a new army of locusts eating our wheat down to the ground. No, that wasn't enough —— ' Ralph's rage frothed and sputtered and put out his words. Grandmother looked to Haakon.

'It was our own fault,' Haakon said. 'We didn't salt the cattle, and it seems they got hold of some old bones — buffalo bones, Sneeth, the cattle-man, says — and chewed them up for salt. A dozen cows, maybe, and —— '

'Maybe you wouldn't take it so coolly if it was your own money had bought 'em,' foamed Ralph. 'A dozen cows and one of our blooded bulls. Cost a flat five hundred, that bull did.'

'*Bones?* What do bones do?'

'Do you mean you found them sick, Haakon?' Grandmother asked.

Haakon grinned mirthlessly. 'Yes, ma'am, we *found* 'em sick. Awfully sick, past saving. We found them sick, and we left them dead.'

CHAPTER VI

ENTRANCE AND EXIT

MRS. PERTLE's boarders had scarcely risen from the breakfast-table next morning before Grandmother asked, 'Haakon, how soon can we set things in motion? We ought to be settling down.'

'I thought you'd ask that, Grandmother Grant. We picked out a likely-looking quarter-section, subject to your approval. Would you mind riding out in a common ordinary lumber wagon? It's all we have.'

'I take notice it's the regulation carriage hereabouts,' Grandmother approved, 'and good sense, too.'

'Your coach will be at the door within half an hour, ladies,' Ralph promised them, bowing himself out.

It was not the boys' own horses and wagon that he drove up to the door at the appointed time, however. Instead, the equipage was a high, spidery carriage, with fringes swinging gayly from the canopy, and it was drawn by two spidery horses who seemed to have had little to do with each other or the vehicle. Haakon regarded rig and driver with amazement.

'Where did you find that outfit?' he demanded.

Ralph smirked down at them. 'The only vehicle in Union Colony fit to be graced by so much worth and beauty!' he declaimed; and to Haakon, 'At the livery stable; where did you suppose?'

Haakon silently handed Grandmother and the girls into the back seat, the telltale muscle twitching in his jaw. When he had taken his place beside Ralph, he fished a small account book from his pocket, put a low-voiced question, added a numeral to a column of them in the book.

'You don't have the first notion how to treat the ladies,' Ralph grumbled in answer to his silence. 'Lumber wagon, I must say!'

Already the girls were gripping their hats and the sides of the carriage, for this team had none of the habits of carriage horses. Speed seemed their one desire, and their irregular canter soon broke into a gallop which sent the light carriage careening from side to side. Ralph grew red and then white.

'Ain't they running away?' gasped Susan.

'Looks a lot like it.'

Without a word, Haakon crowded Ralph over in the seat and wrenched the reins from his frozen clutch. 'Whoo-oa there! Steady!'

Janey relaxed. 'Now they won't run away. Haakon can handle anything,' she sighed her relief; and Ralph's ears reddened again.

'Want us to show you our place first?' Haakon asked over his shoulder when the ponies had raced a mile along the country road and dropped into a subdued jog.

'We'd be pleased,' Grandmother assented.

It was not far from the town, a piece of railroad land the boys had purchased at a comparatively low price. They had

had it fenced in and sown in spring wheat before they came. Sandy had looked after it for them, and had put up a temporary shack and a shelter for horses and equipment.

'The wheatfield was as pretty a sight as you'd wish to see' — Haakon pointed it out with the butt of his whip. 'But a new swarm of the pesky hoppers hit it, day before yesterday, Sandy says.'

'When you were meeting us in Cheyanne?' cried Janey, remorsefully.

'Better say, while we were buying our trousseau in Cheyanne,' Haakon corrected caustically. '"A gentleman must have clothes,"' he added, evidently quoting. 'But it isn't likely we could have done a thing if we'd been here, Janey. The hoppers are certainly bad. I notice one of our merchants has posted a notice offering a bounty for a million hoppers. Good public-spirited citizen, Obadiah is, but he loves a practical joke.'

'And here's our herd!' he broke off proudly.

'Gummy!' breathed Susan.

'I didn't suppose five hundred cows would be such a lot!' Janey cried.

'They're not all in sight, either.'

'Nor I didn't dream long-horns had — well, such monstrously long horns!'

'And these are all cows. You ought to see a long-horn steer,' Haakon told her. 'Nine feet, their horns sometimes measure.'

Rusty red the herd stretched on and on, the horns, gracefully spiral and as much as six feet in spread, glinting in the sun. The short-horn bulls which the boys pointed out were enormously stocky in contrast to their wiry leanness.

'Nine of 'em, where we had ten yesterday,' Ralph growled.

'Fortunes of war!' Haakon said incisively.

'What does the brand stand for?' Grandmother asked.

'Stands for FH — Farnum-Haakonsson. I heard a cow-hand call it the Lazy Stool, because of the way it lies on its side,' Haakon explained. — 'And here's our palatial abode.'

The girls looked curiously at the shack.

'Who redds it up?' asked Susan.

'We do. We take turns sweeping her out and making the beds. And now our month's up at Mrs. Pertle's, we're going to cook our own grub, too.' Haakon thrust out his chin and looked sidewise at his glumly silent partner.

'Ever do any cooking?' Grandmother inquired.

'I certainly haven't,' Ralph answered stiffly.

'Nor I; but we can't learn any younger,' Haakon said good-humoredly. 'And I don't see but we have as much sense as other chaps that are baching it around here.'

Grandmother was thoughtfully silent, as they drove past the boys' place and on to the adjacent prairie land. Presently Haakon drew up and awaited her comment.

'This it? It lies well,' she conceded.

'Yes, doesn't it? And take notice how the prairie grasses and weeds grow greener and thicker hereabouts. Good soil and good drainage. The Cache La Poudre runs through a corner of it, and it's under ditch, too.'

'Under ditch?'

'Irrigation ditch. All this land has to be irrigated, you know, and it costs a lot to put the ditches through so's to water it all. Without the ditches — well, it's like this' — he waved his hand at the untouched prairie — 'but with ditches,' he declaimed with humorous oratory, 'it blossoms like the rose.'

'Like our wheatfield back there, you understand,' Ralph grunted.

'Like our wheatfield day before yesterday,' Haakon rejoined dauntlessly. 'Grasshoppers are liable to happen anywhere. Can't blame them on the soil; or on the government; or even on me!'

'This looks — first-rate.' Grandmother delivered the ultimatum slowly. 'How comes it such a sightly piece wasn't taken up, Haakon?'

'It was.' Haakon helped her out of the carriage and led her over to a rectangle of darkened ground that had been hidden from them by the waving grasses. 'Smart Eastern fellow it was that filed here, and they say he had a good house put up on it. But he didn't have a lick of sense.

'You see those cottonwoods down the river a piece? Well, some Utes had used them for a burial place, years ago. You know: wrapped the bodies in bark-cloth and skins and lashed them high in the branches. Well, what did this Easterner do but yank one of 'em down to see what it was like — nothing but a skeleton, probably, with some jewelry on it.

'He thought there wasn't an Indian in a hundred miles, and maybe there wasn't. But lo and behold! not a month passed before he was waked out of a sound sleep to find his house on fire over his head and a dozen painted Utes dancing around it.'

Janey drew a deep breath. 'Did he — did he get killed?' she whispered awesomely.

'No, he sneaked out and hid in the well till dawn, and then they scattered, and he made tracks for town and took the next train back to Boston.'

'This country ought to run down every one of the red rascals and put a bullet through him,' Ralph said irascibly. 'It's the only answer to the Indian question.'

Grandmother surveyed him coolly over her steel-rimmed

spectacles. 'I suppose you'd be pleased to have somebody dig up your grandfather's grave and take his seal ring, young man?'

'Is there any land right close that Inch-Along could file on?' Janey asked hastily.

'This is a quarter-section?' asked Grandmother. 'Why not let Inch-Along have a piece of it? Seeing it's such choice land.'

'Good Lord!' Ralph exploded, drawing another severe glance over the spectacles. 'I thought this Inch-Along or Crawl-Along or whatever's his crazy name was a mere pack-peddler? Then what's he to you? What call have you to split your good land with him? Let such riffraff fend for themselves.'

'So if you'll help us go through the law part,' Grandmother went on, addressing Haakon as if Ralph were a mosquito, 'we can be getting ready to settle down. How soon do you think we can get onto the ground?'

'If you could use our shack for a while' — Haakon glanced at the flattened Ralph — 'we could easily make shift with that tent of ours, couldn't we, Ralph?'

'No,' Grandmother declined decisively. 'The tent will do us till we can build a cabin. I was thinking,' she added slowly, 'that Mr. Farnum maybe has the right of it. About your baching it. I never did hold with men-folks fiddling round the housework when there's women-folks to do it.'

'But, Grandmother Grant, it's a matter of expense.'

'Oh, hang the expense, Haakonsson!' said Ralph. 'Don't be such a pinchpenny. Didn't I tell you I'd stand good for things till your estate was settled?'

'It wouldn't be any more costly,' Grandmother went on. 'We women-folks would cook for the whole outfit, and you boys could lend a hand with our heavy work.'

'But, Grandmother Grant!' Haakon looked down at her with admiration and reproof combined. 'Until you get over this rheumatism it's a chore for you to get around, even. You'd better not take on any extras. You know Janey and Susan'll be pretty well tied down to their teaching.'

'I was coming to that.' Grandmother tied the strings of her bonnet tighter as a sage-laden breeze tilted it over one eye. 'I think it would be full as well if one of the girls was to stay home with me this fall. Suppose Susan was to do the teaching and Janey was to be my help in the house.'

Janey flashed an admiring glance at Grandmother. How well she played the game!

'But, Mrs. Grant,' Susan protested, 'Janey's already signed her contract.'

'Mercy-*to*-us!' Grandmother exclaimed composedly.

'Would — would I do?' Susan proposed timidly. She had never conquered her awe of Grandmother Grant. 'Could you put up with me around the house, Mis' Grant?'

'I don't know why not,' Grandmother reflected. 'Fact is, I'm never sure when Janey'll leave the flatiron in the middle of a petticoat she's doing up, and run to write a poem.'

Janey bit her lip. Grandmother's eye glinted with sardonic humor and Janey managed to laugh. Clever of Grandmother to make a joke of it.

'I reckon there ain't a living thing Janey can't beat me at,' Susan declared loyally. 'But this way would suit me right down to the ground. The longer I can put off teaching, the better pleased I'll be. I never did hanker after it. And those examinations! Why, I've dreamt of them ever' single night. Education don't take on me the way it does on Janey.'

'Then that's settled. If you boys will set up that tent and maybe fix us a shelter for our stove…'

The remainder of the day whirled with activity. The claim had to be filed on, Grandmother's little leather trunk and the satchels brought out, and the ticks she had brought from home filled with clean yellow straw. The boys put up a shelter for the stove, knocked together a table for present use, and then ransacked the town for wooden boxes which could serve as cupboards and chairs.

The girls shopped for food supplies, and came home shocked at the prices.

'Imagine butter at forty-five cents a pound!' Janey said solemnly; 'and eggs thirty-five cents a dozen!'

'We'll have a hen and a cow and a churn on the job in-stanter: I see it in Grandmother's eyes,' said Haakon, handing bundles out of the wagon. 'Grandmother Grant, here's a dozen lemons. They say lemon juice is great for rheumatism.'

'Potatoes two cents a pound, Mis' Grant.'

'By the *pound?*'

'Yes'm, that's the way they sell 'em: by the pound. This sack — I hate to say how much it was. And this flour was five dollars.'

'But meat isn't so dear, Grandmother. Here's ham for four cents a pound.'

'Ham? What kind of ham?'

'Buffalo! And they've got antelope and wild duck and wild geese. And bear.'

'Well, I see where we've got to get a garden in, even this late,' said Grandmother. 'Susan, if you'll kindle a fire and get the tea-kettle over, and put a couple of slices of buffalo in the spider, I'll peel the potatoes and we'll have supper in two jerks. I don't know when I've been so sharp-set.'

Grandmother sat serenely on a soapbox under the prairie sky, peeling potatoes and directing the activities of the others. The 'store stove' had not yet been purchased, so the tea-kettle boiled on the open fire and the meat sizzled and the potatoes bubbled merrily and the muslin tablecloth billowed in the evening breeze.

'We'll dish up, Susan,' Grandmother directed.

'You think the potatoes are done?' Susan asked dubiously.

'They've boiled hard for a good twenty minutes,' Grandmother nodded.

Susan dished them out on the plates and cut up the meat, while Janey measured the tea into the new black teapot.

'The festive board!' Ralph declaimed, when they had sat down. 'Strange how the plainest food gains aroma at the fair hands of cooks like these!' He savored a morsel of buffalo meat with gusto.

Janey fidgeted, but Grandmother merely sat.

'I once heard a story,' she observed, 'of a young man sitting down as a guest at a family table and beginning to eat. And the father of the family bowed his head and returned thanks like this: "For what we are about to receive, and for what this young man has already received, may the Lord make us truly thankful." Haakon, please ask the blessing.'

'The meat is awfully good,' Janey said with enthusiasm when they had begun. She cast a placating glance at Ralph. Goodness! he'd been hammered enough for one day. Ralph didn't respond to her overtures. He was jabbing his potato viciously.

'A new variety?' he inquired coldly. 'A fossil form, maybe?'

They all tried their potatoes. Fine and large and white,

the famous Greeley tubers had promised good eating. That promise they were far from fulfilling.

'Hard as rocks!' agreed Grandmother. 'What on earth ails 'em?'

Yet the keen outdoor air made any food edible, and there was not one of the company who did not eat heartily of the meat and solid potatoes, the store bread and butter and tea.

'We'll put a mess of beans to soak before we go to bed,' Grandmother said, 'and you tell your man Sandy he can come eat with us any time now.'

The next twenty-four hours brought their new boarder and unexpected happenings besides. First of all was a night of rest such as none of the newcomers had known for some time. Scarcely had the last glory of sunset faded when Grandmother observed that she didn't know how the rest of them felt, but for her part she was ready for bed. Ralph had already sulked himself off; now Haakon gathered up the Indian puppy, which had lain in a box of soft grass all day, following them with suffering brown eyes.

'I'll take this little feller home with me, Janey. He's sure to keep Grandmother awake if he's here; and I think I can get that splint fixed more comfortably, too.'

'Your partner will appreciate being kept awake,' Janey warned him.

'I hope we haven't made things harder for you, Haakon; with him, I mean. I don't know's I ought to have raked him over the coals that last time,' Grandmother grudged.

'Ralph's pretty touchy.'

'It's not often folks rub me the wrong way like that Farnum young one,' Grandmother went on when Haakon had gone.

'He looks like common, everyday folks, under that circus

rig of his,' Susan commented thoughtfully; 'and every so often his genteel ways slip up and show that he *is* common — common as dirt. And land sakes, what a temper!'

'I'm afraid Haakon's let himself in for something, getting tied up with the likes of Ralph.'

That night of rest! They fastened back their tent flap and let the fragrant air flow over them like cool water. So cool, indeed, after the hot day, that they pulled the quilts up to their chins.

They had scarcely cleared away the breakfast things next morning when Grandmother sighted riders on the horizon. 'One — two — three horses!' she counted, peering under her slatted sunbonnet. 'Janey! Susan!'

Janey dropped her writing-board — she was perched on a soapbox writing home — and sprang to her feet. 'I do believe it is! Oh, glory, won't it be good to see Thad, and know he's all right!'

They came nearer, two riders and a led horse. Nearer; and Janey's keen eyes could distinguish the black ponies and Susan's red one. She thrust her thumbs into her mouth and gave the old, shrill whistle. A faint whinny answered her. Haakon also answered, riding up pellmell. His anxious face cleared as he saw her scanning the distance.

'I thought — I didn't know if anybody'd warned you about rattlers,' he panted.

Tired and hot and stiff, the riders presently dropped from their horses, submitted to handclasps and sisterly hugs, and stretched themselves in the grateful shade of the tent.

'Garsh!' Thad fanned his burned face with his hat. 'I never did know just how much that Bible verse meant: the one that goes, "the shadow of a rock in a thirsty land."'

'This is a sightly resting-place,' Inch-Along mused, his eyes feasting on the tall grasses and the rich mingling of wild flowers, and on the gleam of the river between the cottonwoods.

'But no Injuns,' Thad objected, ''s far's I see.'

Janey laughed at his disappointment. 'We've had enough for a starter.' And she told them about their encounter with Colorow, and about the puppy, hobbling comically with his splinted leg, who had already found Thad's coaxing hand. 'We've named him Bute, because he's a beauty of a Ute puppy. Or a beaut of a Utey.'

'All this talk isn't getting our dinner.' Grandmother roused herself suddenly from her listening and knitting. 'And these folks must have made an early start, instead of oversleeping like us. We better get those beans cooking again, and my cake in.'

'Beans! Cake!' Thad exulted.

The tired old man and boy lay on their backs in the shade of the tent and slept. The tired horses grazed on the succulent grass. Grandmother whipped up a cake, and Janey and Susan kindled the fire and put over the beans, which had been set to boil with the breakfast. Presently, when the sun had climbed to the top of the sky, Ralph came riding his fine gray horse, and Sandy jogged in on his skinny calico mare.

Susan pulled the cake out of the Dutch oven Grandmother had improvised out of an iron kettle and two pans, and bent above it uncertainly.

'Done, Susan? You can test it with a grass stem.'

'Well, yes'm, it's done. But Mis' Grant, it looks awful odd.'

Grandmother adjusted her spectacles and looked.

'Mercy-*to*-us!'

'Why, Grandmother, it's the first time I ever knew one of your cakes to fall.'

'Three times they have, all the years I've used this receet, girl and woman,' Grandmother said accurately.

This one was fallen indeed; and thin; and crisped round the rim; and pale in the middle.

Inch-Along, wakened by the discussion, pulled himself creakingly to his feet, blinked at the cake, and started to speak.

'Land sakes, Mis' Grant,' Susan exclaimed, 'here's the meat done to a turn, and these beans still hard as bullets. Shall I cook some potatoes real quick?'

'Quit it, Janey!' yawned Thad, jerking the teasing grass-blade from his sister's hand and jumping up. 'Seems like I can't hardly wait for some of Gramma's cooking.'

'Seems like you'll have to,' Grandmother observed grimly. 'Are things witched? — No, not potatoes, Susan. Don't you mind how poor they were?'

'Poor?' puzzled Inch-Along. 'Greeley spuds poor? How's that, ma'am?'

His face twisted into laughter at their explanation.

'Hadn't nobody took thought to warn you?' he asked. 'This altitude plays hob with the cooking. You'll have to allow about thirty-five minutes for your spuds to bile mealy. And beans have to cook all day, mighty nigh.'

'The cake — that doesn't boil,' Janey pondered.

'No, little lass. But I've heard that cake receets have to be changed a good bit for this altitude, too.'

'Now that don't stand to reason,' Grandmother protested, even while she stirred up a batch of sour-cream biscuits to help out the diminishing meal.

At last dinner was ready, the table lengthened, and the boxes set for eight. Inch-Along started to seat himself beside Janey, but Ralph shoved him carelessly aside.

'Permit me to sit by the young lady, my good man,' he said in his best society manner.

Janey stared incredulously.

'Who're you calling your good man?' she demanded. Maybe he had meant it as a joke.

Ralph lifted surprised brows.

'He's not your good man!' Janey flared. 'He's not anybody's good man! And I much prefer to have him sit beside me, where we can talk.'

She had done it again. After all their resolutions not to offend Ralph, she had done it again.

'I'm sorry I spoke so rudely,' she hurried. 'We hadn't made it clear, I guess, but Inch-Along is our old friend; and our very good and respected one.'

Ralph sat down grumpily and ate in silence.

'You came through Denver?' Grandmother asked. 'Sightly city, Thad?'

'Biggest I — ever saw, anyway,' Thad mumbled the words around a whole biscuit, apparently. 'Twenty thousand, they claim, but I don't believe it. Lots of big brick store buildings; but, garsh! the streets are an inch deep in dust. There's little ditches of nice clear water running alongside the roads, and out where the houses are, folks have got trees started.'

Grandmother nodded approval.

'But say, what you suppose? The street cars had stopped running, the day we come through, because all the horses had took sick. Eight miles of street car they've got, yes, sir! Something catching, the horses had. What was the name of it, Inch-Along?'

'Epizoötic,' the old man answered, and relapsed into the abstraction that had held him since the unlucky beginning of the meal. Janey patted his knee and he smiled at her.

'You don't suppose that could be what's ailing our

horses?' Haakon asked worriedly. 'Two of them were acting droopy this morning, and off their feed. Your Comet,
Ralph, and Nigger.'

'Is it serious?' Ralph asked sharply, glancing up at Inch-
Along from the food he was scorning with his fork. 'Dangerous? I noticed Comet acted lazy. And that horse cost
me ——'

'Most of 'em gets over it,' Inch-Along answered.

Ralph shoved back from the table and went over to his
horse, picketed not far away. There was no doubt of it: the
beautiful gray stood with all four feet bunched and head
drooping. Even from that distance they could see that his
eyes were wet and dull.

Ralph strode back to the table, jamming his hat on his
head and shaking a violent fist under Haakon's nose.

'If Comet dies,' he shouted, 'I've got a good mind to take
the price of him out of your skin, you fine-talking crook,
you!'

Haakon rose leisurely and stared down his nose at the
clamorous youth.

'There's a saying out here' — he spoke with scornful
slow incisiveness — '"If you call me a name, *smile!*" Nobody calls me a crook in sober earnest, Farnum.'

'I'm not smiling any,' Ralph snarled.

Without haste or effort, Haakon lifted his partner by the
silk-handkerchiefed neck, held him dangling a moment,
gave him a single resounding spank with his large hard
palm, and set him down, speechlessly goggling.

Grandmother took another sip of tea, and eyed them
calmly.

'I'll — I'll sue you!' Ralph chattered with rage when he
could find any voice. 'You g-got me out here under false
pretenses, y-you big whiteheaded Swede, you!'

Haakon smashed Ralph's hat down over his eyes with a tolerant slap. 'Ai ban Norsk, you loony!' he drawled.

Ralph tore off the hat and threw it on the ground. 'Inveigled me into putting up ten thousand dollars, and got me into a hole like this! I thought you were a gentleman, but here you expect me to hobnob with peddlers and other riffraff ——'

Haakon's smile froze.

'You aren't funny any longer, little man,' he gritted, and seizing Ralph by the shoulders, he shook him vigorously and thumped him down on one of the soapboxes. All these seats had been vacated except Inch-Along's and Grandmother's. She, having finished her tea, had taken her knitting out of the bag at her belt, and was toeing off a sock.

'You want to sell out your share in the partnership?' Haakon asked, his face a glare of white and his eyes a blaze of blue. 'Either you get out or I do.'

Janey shivered. She could remember just one other time when she had seen him in a rage. It was when some of the big boys in the Wisconsin neighborhood had followed and tormented poor witless Ingrid.

'You want to sell out to me?' Haakon repeated.

'You haven't got any money.'

'Want to take my note for it, payable in ninety days?'

Ralph nodded, his face venomous.

CHAPTER VII
CROOKED STICK

'It's a whole lot nicer,' Thad exulted next day at supper, 'with that old bag of wind out of the way.'

'Isn't it, though?' agreed Janey. 'He sort of stiffened everything up, and now we're all so easy and comfortable, just us together.'

'Easy as an old shoe,' Inch-Along nodded. 'That lad was like ——'

'A chestnut bur under the saddle,' offered Sandy, absently pouring his tea into his saucer and hastily pouring it back.

'But it's awful for you to have such a debt, Haakon — ten thousand dollars,' Janey fretted. 'Just think how we felt when Pa owed four thousand: it was as if we were being crushed to death.'

'That why you're so awful quiet, Hawk? Worried, huh?' Thad demanded.

'No, not awfully worried, Thad. There'll be at least that much from the estate. And it seems as if the estate was bound to come in time. It belongs to Haakonsson; and I'm Haakonsson.'

'There's many a slip,' warned Grandmother.

'I oughtn't to have got into it in the first place. I can see that now,' Haakon acknowledged. 'But since I have — what quotation fits me now?'

'"But being in"' — Janey was quoting Shakespeare from the almanac again — '"bear't that the opposed may beware of thee."'

'"As well be hung for a sheep as a lamb,"' Grandmother added. 'Haakon, is your note for ninety days? Foolish thing to offer.'

'Yes'm, I know it. But Ralph was decent enough to say he'd extend it as much as I might need. The money's really nothing to him.'

'Put it in writing?'

'No — o,' Haakon grudged, 'but I'm not worried about that.'

'More fool you,' Grandmother commented succinctly.

'You're fretted about something or other,' Thad persisted, and then, waving an emphatic knife at him, 'I bet another of your horses is sick.'

'I didn't see any use mentioning it, but you've hit the nail on the head, youngster. Comet's coming out all right, and I promised to ship him back to Ralph as soon as he's in shape. But Nigger's not going to pull through. — Well, it's the fortunes of war. Don't let's spoil this good supper with it.'

It was a good supper. Grandmother had analyzed the fallen cake of the day before and tried again without waste of time, increasing the flour and decreasing the sugar.

'Not up to standard yet,' she pronounced critically when it came out. But it tasted delicious to appetites sharpened by the fresh pure air. Sour-cream biscuits, heaping plates of warmed-up potatoes, golden-brown and savory, hot tea, cake. Over them the unbroken prairie sky, its deep blue paling with evening and clouds like flakes of gold floating above the misty blue mountains. Around them the undulant prairie, its green bitten by the grasshoppers and browned by the scorching July sun, but fragrant with keen prairie odors and embroidered with color; lavender pentstemon, white and pink and rose and red gilia, yellow squaw weed, magenta loco, golden pulsatilla, vermilion paintbrush. Janey and Susan had already begun to gather specimens of them all and press them, so that they might look up their names in the botany keys at school.

'It reminds me a little bit of eating outside the shack in Lucerne that first summer,' Janey commented, 'only there are more flowers here ——'

'And the air is different,' Susan added.

Grandmother looked silently toward the beauty of the peaks.

'Yes, and there's those funny prairie dogs,' Thad said. 'I think they're the cutest, sitting up that way like little trick dogs. They look like — I know what! Just exactly like Mrs. Jonas at Lucerne when she sings a hymn, sort of fat and important with her hands folded across her stomach. And the way they dive into their holes when you scare 'em!'

'Speaking of shacks,' Grandmother said, 'how about starting ours?'

'Hadn't we men better turn to and knock up a couple of cabins before we get at ploughing for the winter wheat?'

'I'd like a piece of ground broken for garden, too.'

'Late as this, Grandmother? And with the grasshoppers? Did I tell you Sandy found his best suit fairly riddled by the pests?'

'Garsh! do they eat clo'es, too?'

'They're death on wool.'

'Well, perhaps the hoppers are about done for this year. And turnips ought to grow. And maybe lettuce and radishes.'

They broke the prairie sod for Grandmother's garden that very afternoon, and Haakon finished it by hand in the cool of the evening. 'We can easily ditch it and bring the water between the rows,' he showed her.

Inch-Along, who had been helping, tossed Thad an Indian arrowhead he had turned up, and leaned on his spade. 'I never did get the straight of this irrigating,' he mused aloud. 'It always looked to me like the daftest body could see the Lord meant rain to come *down* on growing things. I don't know how you can look to have the crops prosper when you try to satisfy them with rain from below. Well — well — well.'

Sandy had hitched up, that afternoon, and brought the lumber from the experimental sawmill above the town, and next morning they set to work, Grandmother, stiff and straight, appointing the place for the dwelling.

'No manner of use putting up two separate shacks, if that suits Inch-Along,' she decreed. 'We can build on the line between our claims, with a room for him on his side of it.'

'That will save lumber,' Haakon assented. 'Fuel, too, in winter.'

Inch-Along puckered his lips to a rollicking whistle and hobbled zestfully about, lining up the building-to-be with sticks and strings. In no time at all, the air was cheerfully noisy with the shrill song of saws and the drumbeat of hammers, while the clean smell of new wood mingled with the other outdoor odors.

The yellow shavings that curled out under the plane gave

Janey a homesick pang. Lucy had decked her flaxen head with such ringlets when the Lucerne house was building. Janey captured the rolypoly black Bute, tumbling underfoot, clumsy but content in his stiff splint, and hung him with a row of the glistening spirals, twining them into his fur so that he had to roll and wriggle to rid himself of them.

It was a brief task, the erection of the shack: a long, one-story affair, with a sloping roof and no foundation. Grandmother insisted on double walls and floor. 'No saving to heat the whole outdoors, come winter.' So they used a good layer of building-paper, and sheathed the outside with weather-boarding: 'snug as a bug in a rug,' Inch-Along commended.

'Three pairs of strong young arms, they make light work,' he said wistfully, 'while the old man just hobbles around. But never you mind! Inch-Along's got a surprise for you.'

'If it wasn't for Inch-Along,' Janey smiled at him, 'I guess this shack would not be so near done as it is.'

'Nor so true-built; nor with such a good pitch of the roof to shed the rain.'

'Jack of all trades and master of none,' the old man deprecated, though his eyes sparkled with pleasure at their praise.

As a matter of fact, he was skillful along a dozen lines. He could match Grandmother's knowledge of medicinal herbs, and carried a packet always with him, together with a cup of quassia wood, that turned its draft of water to a bitter tonic. Among other things, he knew the technique of constructing cord bedsteads in the corners of the rooms, and had soon made four, strong and springy.

The shack had a large living-dining-cooking-room for its

center, Inch-Along's sleeping apartment on one side, with a
bed for Thad, and Grandmother's on the other. Inch-Along
had suggested that Janey and Susan's room, built beyond
Grandmother's, be made with canvas sides; and he showed
them how it should be sided up part-way, to protect them
from the severer cold, and how the canvas could be but-
toned back to admit more air in warm weather. And finally
it was Inch-Along who came home from town with a bucket
of paint, and spread it on with the smooth flow of a profes-
sional, so that the little shack bloomed shiningly white and
belied its humble name. That last was Inch-Along's surprise.

'Let's call it the White House!' Janey proposed.

'Come spring we'll set some willow and cottonwood,'
mused Grandmother, 'and start a vine or two. Nothing like
greenery to make a place homey.'

'Horace Greeley agreed with you in that,' Haakon told
her. 'I don't know how many thousand trees he had set
out, or else the seed sown for them. Most of them winter-
killed, or died out one way or another.'

Sandy made no comment, but he disappeared before supper that night, asking for a few sandwiches to carry with
him. He returned at mid-morning, his pinto laden with
sprays of evergreen and masses of trailing hop vines, and
two small spruces.

'If these here trees don't ketch aholt and grow,' he explained, shifting from one foot to the other and loosening
the bandanna round his throat, where his Adam's apple was
working painfully, 'they'll anyways keep nice and green till
spring. And if you want to nail up the other green stuff inside, it might look kinda good and make a nice smell.'

Exclaiming with delight, the girls dragged in the rude
ladder, and climbed on it to nail the spruce boughs against

the two-by-fours in a feathery green frieze, with trailing festoons of hop between.

'Sandy, it makes all the difference!' Janey cried.

'It was awful clever of you,' Susan added diffidently.

Sandy flushed, twisted his hat in his hands, and went away beaming.

'That lad seems pecooliarly pleased to do for our lassies,' Inch-Along observed indulgently.

'Ever'body likes to do for Janey!' Susan tilted her head to observe the smaller girl with a devotion almost motherly. 'Now ain't she a picture?'

'Freckling the way I do?' Janey protested.

'I like you freckled.'

'And my hair's not nearly so curly out here.'

'I like it the way it is, and I reckon Sandy does, too.'

Haakon's eyes were indulgently admiring, also, as he looked at the golden freckle-splashes on the well-tanned face, the softly waving brown hair curling into loose ringlets on her shoulders. But he chuckled when Susan mentioned Sandy.

'So you thought the spruce and hops were all for Janey's sake, Susan? Let me tell you something. Sandy confided to me that he thought Susan Sloane was the neatest-looking girl he'd set eyes on in a coon's age: which in Sandy's lexicon means the prettiest.'

'Who? Me?' Susan was frankly incredulous.

Janey, too, stared her wonder. 'Why, Susan!' her voice sagged with amazement. 'Why, Susan, you really are! Handsome, I mean!'

Grandmother laughed her dry laugh. 'First time you noticed it, Janey?'

It was. 'Plain as a fencepost' had been her first precise description of Susan, and she hadn't really looked at her

since. Now, as the other girl shrank, blushing, from their
sudden scrutiny, Janey saw a new Susan, tall and trim and
slim, with dark braids forming a glossy crown above a face
grown clear and bright of skin. The funny high peak of her
forehead was concealed by dark bangs; and the steady eyes
that had been so queerly pale in her tanned face sparkled
brilliantly, like brook water over gray stone and moss. 'I
didn't remember your eyelashes were so thick and black,'
Janey marveled, 'and your eyebrows such thin straight
lines. I don't wonder Sandy thinks you're pretty.'

Susan pressed an unconscious hand to her hot cheek. 'I
always did like *his* looks,' she murmured.

'His *looks?*' shouted Thad, dropping a queer contrivance
he was working on (a trap, he said evasively). '*Sandy's*
looks?'

'I wouldn't call him handsome,' Janey demurred.

'Well — maybe not. I never did fancy a handsome man
or boy: they do think so well of theirselfs.'

'Not always they don't!' Janey cast an indignant glance
at Haakon's silver-gold head and gray-blue eyes, as he tus-
sled with an unwieldy length of stovepipe.

'But most generally they do,' he drawled, quite unconscious of her thought. 'I side with Susan. And Sandy's certainly a chap you can count on, looks or no looks.'

'Admiration party over?' asked Grandmother. 'Suppose
we make a list of what we need from town.'

Presently they set out in the lumber wagon drawn by
Minnehaha and Hiawatha, the two girls and Thad and
Haakon and Inch-Along, with Bute curled in Thad's lap.
They discussed their purchases as they went, though Susan's contributions were vague and disconnected. Susan
still wore an expression of profound bewilderment: the expression of the ugly duckling when first it has been told it is
a swan.

'There, now!' Janey spoke her exasperation. 'We never asked her about a table and chairs.'

'No need to buy those,' Inch-Along advised. 'We can knock together a table easy enough. Paint it yellow if She wants.' Inch-Along always referred to Grandmother by the simple pronoun, as if she were a Superior Being. 'And a long bench for each side will be no trick at all, and do us plenty good at present. But I see a splint-bottomed rocker in a store down here. That would finish things out nice and look more respectful-like to Her, even if She doesn't ever lean back nor rock.'

'We didn't ask her about rugs, either.'

'She said we'd paint the floor a nice clean yellow; and She'd begin braiding rag rugs, soon's we begun to wear out any clothes.'

Haakon had drawn up before the general store and was tying the team to the hitching-rail.

'Keep quiet, Bute,' Thad commanded. 'What you so worked up over?'

The puppy was wriggling excitedly in Thad's arms, and whimpering, small, eager whimpers. Janey looked at the edge of the wooden walk and saw a slender figure crouched there.

'Oh, it's Colorow's boy!' she exclaimed, smiling at him as he shrank timidly away, his big dark eyes on the puppy. 'The puppy was his, Thad.'

Thad jumped from the wagon and approached shyly, holding out the puppy, which squirmed delightedly and kissed the dark face with a lavish pink tongue. The Indian boy held the warm bundle against his breast, touched the bandaged leg appreciatively, glanced apprehensively over his shoulder, handed the puppy back, while Thad smiled and nodded steadily, like a toy mandarin.

'Me — Thad,' he said loudly, tapping his breast. 'Who you?' and he tapped the other boy inquiringly.

The Indian answered hesitantly.

'That's funny,' Haakon commented. 'That's a Sioux word. Means Crooked Stick. Well, you look more Sioux than Ute, even if you are sort of undersized and crooked in the back, little fellow.'

They went into the store, leaving Crooked Stick huddled against the hitching-rail watching them.

The needed lengths of unbleached 'factory' and thinner white muslin purchased, for shades and curtains, and the rocker loaded into the wagon with the cook-stove, and food bought, Janey inquired at the post-office for their mail. She came back to the wagon inspecting their 'catch.'

'One for you, Sukey, from 'Lijah. And from Pa, for Grandmother. And an awfully long solemn one for you, Haakon. What are you looking at?'

'At a real show,' murmured Haakon.

Janey turned and followed the direction of his eyes. Two men had come out of the hotel across the street, one a dashing personage in most sophisticated hunting garb; the other much like the men they had noticed in Cheyenne, as far as externals went: broad-brimmed hat, fair curls, beaded buckskins, bristling weapons, scarlet sash.

'Probably another of the copies,' said Haakon. 'Sandy tells me of a new one that's been shooting around up in Cheyenne this summer. Paiute Pete, he calls himself, or Pete the Kid, take your choice. They say he's got half a dozen notches on his six-shooter.'

'Notches?'

'Each notch is supposed to mean a man he's killed. — Whew!' he whistled as the men turned and started toward them, 'I take it all back, Colonel Cody!' He doffed his hat respectfully. 'That's no copy, folks: it's the real Buffalo Bill.'

'Who do you suppose it is with him?' gasped Janey, studying Cody's finely cut high-held head.

'Him? Say, but ain't he the howling swell?' muttered Thad admiringly.

'Well, rather!' chuckled Haakon. 'Buffalo Bill's conducting a buffalo hunt for the Grand Duke Alexis, according to the *Tribune*. I'll wager this is ——'

'*The Grand Duke?*'

'No two ways about it,' said Inch-Along. 'But Grand Dukes don't butter no parsnips. Better climb in, little lass, or She'll be worried.'

'Grand Dukes and Buffalo Bills and Injun boys,' sighed Susan. 'What a lot to tell Mis' Grant — and Sandy.'

'Garsh, I like that Crooked Stick.'

'He's real folksy,' agreed Inch-Along. 'Lots more like a Sioux than a Ute. Not that there aren't good Utes. Ouray now, one of their chiefs: say, you'd be put to it to pick a whiter man than Ouray, or his squaw Chipeta, either. He's as fur removed from Colorow as white from black. — I took note that this Crooked Stick has got one beauty in common with Haakon here.'

'One beauty?'

'His cowlick!' Janey said triumphantly.

'Yes, ma'am, his cowlick. 'Course, his hair didn't hardly look's if it had ever met up with a comb; but he had a lock that stuck up like a squirrel's tail, as like Haakon's as two peas, barring the color.'

Haakon, tearing his letter open with his teeth as he drove, paused and looked interested.

'You can poke all the fun you please at my cowlick,' he growled, his eyes laughing, 'but it's worth more to me than all the rest of my lint-white locks together.'

'Why, Haakon, however do you mean?'

'Just so. Yes, for a fact.'

'Well — keep on teasing, why don't you? Only tell us when you get good and ready.'

'That's what I mean to do, Spitfire. When we get home, maybe. — Oh, well, you might run up a fever if you had to wait so long. It's a long, sad story. I shouldn't laugh at it, though, for it held sorrow enough.

'Weenonah has often told me how they came bringing Ingrid and me into camp. They hadn't hurt me — yet; but the fact is they were of no notion to keep me: the tribe had plenty of young ones just then. Weenonah and Two-Toes had opposed the massacre, and she stood at her tipi door looking out, sickened at the sights and sounds, because that's the kind of Indian she is. And here she heard them sort of joking over what they'd do with me — no, Janey, I won't go into that — and she glanced at me, just a frightened little fellow, and looking ugly as the dickens, my face all swollen with crying for my mother, but mad, too, she said, and sticking my lips out and scowling. And she was just about to turn and go back into the tipi when a brave yanked off my cap.'

'Yanked off your cap? Oh, hurry *up*, Hawk!'

'Yanked off my cap. To scalp me, maybe. But if he'd left my cap on one minute longer ——

'Because there was my comical hair sticking straight up. as Inch-Along says, like a squirrel's tail. Only it didn't look comical to Weenonah. Because only a year before, when they had come up into the mountains — somewhere here in the Rockies they always did come — her year-old baby boy had been stolen from her by another tribe: the Utes, they always thought.'

He drove on, leaning forward with his elbows on his

knees, a slow smile curving his lips. Janey jiggled in her little-girl way.

'What under the sun did her lost baby have to do with your cowlick?'

'Haven't you guessed that? And you a schoolmarm. Well, well. — Why, her lost child had a cowlick, too, and as mothers do, she loved it — it sort of made all cowlicks precious. So when she saw mine, though I was even more of a towhead than I am now, why, it was all up with her. She "owned" me for her son, then and there, and saved me from the savage sport they'd planned.'

'Excuse me if I look at my letter?'

He slipped the folded sheet out of its envelope and read, while Janey waited eagerly to hear what it was about. Without telling her, he thrust it into his pocket. 'Giddap, girl! Giddap, boy!' he called dryly to the horses, and slapped the reins across their shining backs.

'Haakon!' Janey questioned sharply. 'Is it something bad?'

'Well, not so bad. And not so good, either.'

'From your lawyers?'

'Umhum.'

'Oh, you old close-mouth!' Janey jiggled again, shaking her curls and gritting her teeth. 'What did they say, Haakon?'

'They — aren't exactly satisfied with my proof. Well, they say I haven't offered any real proof.'

'Well, what do they want? Haakon, whatever do they want?'

'Oh, they suggest that I offer something tangible.' Haakon's tone was carefully indifferent. 'Never you mind, Janey. I *am* Haakon Haakonsson, and there's sure to be a way to convince them of it. I don't see how it can mean anything worse than a delay.'

'A delay — but won't Ralph get ugly and make trouble?'

'Oh, well; that's the fortunes of war. — Gosh, Janey, look at the way the grasshoppers have stripped these fields since morning.'

Janey stared somberly ahead. 'Haakon' — she turned to him suddenly — 'I'll bet they said you'd have to produce that ring? Didn't they? Wasn't the ring in it, Haakon?'

'Don't you worry yourself about that, Janey. They don't claim the ring would be proof enough.'

'What *did* they say about it?'

'Well, they did suggest that it looked sort of fishy, my claiming to have the Haakonsson ring, and then writing that it had disappeared just when it was needed.'

CHAPTER VIII

THAD'S GRASSHOPPERS

'Oh, Haakon!' Janey wailed, her eyes darkening with tears. 'It's all my fault! D-ding bust the old ring, any-way!'

''S good Pa didn't hear you swear like that, Janey Grant!' Thad ejaculated.

'I don't care! And what about you, Thad Grant? You put a "garsh" in every other sentence,' Janey sniffed an-grily, dabbing at her eyes with the back of her hand. 'Oh, Haakon!'

'Aw, Janey-girl, don't you get all worked up! Just a ring can't make so much difference. There'll be a way to prove who I am,' Haakon reiterated.

'If only we could offer a good big reward,' she thought aloud. 'Two or three times what it's worth, even, so any-body that picked it up just couldn't keep from returning it. Fifty dollars, maybe' — Haakon's lips twitched in a small smile. 'Isn't it just the luck that we haven't any of us got any ready money?'

'*She'd* say "the destruction of the poor is their poverty,"' Inch-Along agreed.

'Yes; if we had any money,' Thad grumbled, 'I know where I could get me a horse for twenty-five dollars. And, garsh, but I want a horse.'

'What kind of old crow-bait could you get for twenty-five dollars?' Haakon demanded, glad to turn the tide of talk.

'A stage horse, and she's been treated bad.'

'Yes, but old stage horses have been selling lively for a hundred.'

'Well, this man that's got her, he did pay a hundred; but now he needs his money, and besides he thinks he's got cheated; he thinks the mare's bad off.'

'Then what would you want her for?'

'Well, garsh, the man hasn't got a lick of sense. He oughtn't to tried to work this Fidgets till he'd rested her up. He thinks the mare's done for, but I know better,' Thad said with conviction. 'Garsh, if only I could earn some money. I bet I'm going to earn me a suit of store clo'es. But I got a suit of clo'es already. I wish it was money.'

'You lotting on ketching that million grasshoppers, Thaddie? That what your traps were for?' asked Inch-Along.

Thad nodded sturdily. 'I bet I got most a million now.'

'And you're not hankering for the suit of clothes?'

'Well, I got to begin to grow sometime, I hope. I hope I can't wear *this* size of clo'es much longer.'

'Didn't Mr. Obadiah say "Any suit of clothes in the store"?'

Thad nodded, inquiring eyes on the old man, who sat ruminating.

'Seems 's if I heard Sandy sayin' 't he had money laid by for a Sunday suit, didn't I, Haakon?'

'That's right. Sandy's taken to sprucing up lately' —
Haakon glanced past Janey in time to catch Susan's blush.
'And now the hoppers have ruined his "other clothes," he's
in a bad fix, poor fellow.'

'I was thinking, laddie, you might get Sandy to hold off a
bit, and buy his suit from you, s'posin' you really ketch a
million hoppers.'

'Say!' Thad ejaculated. 'Say! — There's Sandy riding
over to our place now. I'm going to ask him if he won't.'

The wagon and Sandy's pinto met before the White
House.

'What's he lugging in front of him?' wondered Thad,
scrambling out.

'Want to bring up a norphan, young un?' asked Sandy.
'Seems to be a left-behind June lamb, and about tuckered
out.'

Thad gathered the leggy creature into his arms, 'Sure. I
can fix him up a bottle easy. We've done that lots of times,
haven't we, Janey? I'm going to call him Oliver Twist.'

'It's a wonder you don't name your grasshoppers,'
Janey teased. 'You're just off your head about animals.'

'Say, Sandy' — Thad looked up from the gangling lamb
— 'would you buy a suit of clo'es off of me? Haakon says
you're sprucin' up lately.'

Sandy's freckles stood out pale against his brick-red
blush. 'Sure,' he gulped, looking reproachfully at Haakon.
'Let's see the clo'es.'

'I haven't got 'em yet. Not till I take my million hoppers
down to Mr. Obadiah's store.'

That evening, after he had fed his new pet, patiently
holding a twist of rag soaked in milk for it to suck, he bor-
rowed Hiawatha and disappeared, to return presently with
a bran sack, almost full. Janey poked it with an inquiring

finger, and sniffed. 'Ugh! what under the sun have you got there, Thad Grant?'

'My grasshoppers. They're getting kind of stale. But I figure I'll have my million by tomorrow night, if only they keep up like they have been.'

'Reckon Thad's the only person in Union Colony that's hoping the hoppers'll keep up,' chuckled Inch-Along.

'No one else trying to catch a million?' asked Grand-mother, looking up from her sewing. She and the girls were hemming the muslin curtains, and the 'factory' for shades.

'I don't reckon there is, Mis' Grant. 'Most everybody took it for a joke.'

'Well, he's got it printed out plain, right in front of his store,' Thad insisted.

'But, Thad, you can't count a million,' Janey protested. 'It'll take from now to doomsday.'

'I weigh 'em.' Thad thrust the hook of the scales through the knotted sack and squinted at the figure.

'But Mr. Obadiah said a million.'

'Well,' Thad explained proudly, 'I figured out a way to manage that. I counted enough to make an ounce, and then I figured from that how many pounds it would take to make a million. Gee, but they don't weigh hardly anything at all.'

'Why, that wasn't such a bad idea, for a boy,' Janey praised with sisterly moderation, 'if you did your sums right.'

'I thought maybe you'd kind of go over them for me,' he suggested hopefully.

For the next half-hour the household figured, Janey, Susan, Grandmother, Inch-Along, taking their turns with scraps of paper and pencil in the yellow circle of the lamp-light. Thad sat on the floor with Bute curled contentedly in his lap and Twist cuddled against him, and watched them anxiously. Finally Grandmother nodded, and handed him the paper.

'Gr-racious! It's closer'n I thought. Say, Gramma, couldn't I put in tomorrow afternoon just ketchin' the rest? They're kind of spoilin' on me.'

'There's the ploughing for our little piece of winter wheat,' she reminded him.

'I an' Hawk kin do his share, ma'am,' offered Sandy.

So Thad spent the hot August day pushing tar-smeared traps through infested places, and visiting some special contraptions of his own, set in likely fields. It was not until evening that he came laboring in, sweat-streaked and dusty and fagged, with grasshoppers enough to reach the required weight.

'Take your sack well off from the house before you try to weigh it,' Grandmother had ordered. 'And then wash up good for supper.'

'Obadiah keeps open evenings,' Inch-Along answered Thad's unspoken protest. 'I'll go along with you, laddie.'

After supper the two departed, riding Hiawatha and Gitchee.

An hour or so later they returned.

Silently Thad picketed his horse and came in, after dropping the sack outside with a thump. Janey looked up from her sewing.

'Didn't he play fair?' she demanded.

'Not the way I look at it, the old skinflint,' mumbled Thad.

They waited in sympathetic silence.

'Said he—meant live hoppers. And mine was awful dead.'

'Mercy-to-us!'

'Well, gummy, he didn't say anything about their being alive, did he?' Susan snapped indignantly.

'He took us out and pointed to the notice, and said "grasshoppers" meant live ones, in the nature of things; if he'd meant dead ones, he'd have so specified, and writ in "grasshopper corpses," or, "alive or dead." And then all the men that was loafin' round haw-hawed fit to make you sick,' Thad said in deep disgust.

'Thad, I'm awfully sorry!' Janey condoled, throwing an arm across his shoulder.

He wriggled away ungratefully. 'Don't bother to cry over me!' he advised her. 'I ain't beat yet.'

'What are you going to do?'

'Well, if Gramma'll just let me off a coupla days, I'll ketch another million and keep 'em alive, and see if the old joker can get around that.'

He was so tired next night that he walked in his sleep and came prowling to the girls' door, muttering and groaning until they were frightened almost out of their senses. Nor had his catch been very great. 'But I found another awful big batch in a man's tomato patch,' he yawned at breakfast. 'Now if only a new lot will settle down!'

When he dragged home, late for supper, the whole family helped him empty into his murmurous sack the hoppers that he had been keeping in a screen-covered barrel, and then waited expectant while he lifted them on the scale. He waited for the pointer to come to rest, his arm quivering with strain, and his eyes narrowed. Then his pursed lips parted in a broad grin.

'Garsh! I got 'em!'

Supper and dishes were hurried through, and they all piled into the wagon to accompany him.

'I hope there's a nice crowd this time,' Janey said vindictively, 'to see Mr. Obadiah get his comeuppance.'

'He's likely got something else up his sleeve, lassie,'

'I'VE BROUGHT YOU A MILLION HOPPERS'

Inch-Along warned her. 'He won't let go a good suit of clothes so easy. He's a good fellow, Obadiah, but he'd got this up as a joke and he naturally won't want it to turn out a joke on him.'

The store was well lined with townsmen, sitting on the broad wooden counters, when Thad stumped in, the sack over his shoulder and the rest of the family behind him. Dimly lighted with oil lamps and festooned with lengths of calico and woolen and silk draped on lines above the counters, it made an interesting setting for a comedy. Janey stifled a laugh at sight of Mr. Obadiah's face. For an instant his mouth dropped; then it tightened into an assured smile.

'And what can I do for young Mr. Grant tonight?' he asked. 'Or for the other ladies and gentlemen?'

Thad swung his sack to the floor.

'I've brought you a million hoppers.'

'They have to be alive,' the merchant reminded him gently.

'They are,' Thad assured him.

Mr. Obadiah prodded the sack with a gingerly forefinger. It pulsated convincingly.

'But how do I know there are a million?'

Thad reached into his pocket and drew out a sheet of paper, which he held out for Mr. Obadiah's inspection, while the loafers slipped down from the counters and came to peer over his shoulder.

'It's all worked out there,' Thad explained. 'It takes this many to make an ounce' — he pointed out the figures with a square boy finger-tip — 'and here's what the whole caboodle weighs up. — Sandy, kin I have the scales, for Mr. Obadiah to weigh them himself?'

But Mr. Obadiah waved away scales and sack and paper.

'You're a real enterprisin' little cuss,' he said pityingly. 'I'll hand it to you for that. But I didn't say a thing about weights and measures. I specified in black and white a million — a MILLION grasshoppers by actual count. — No, no, wait a minute! You see, young feller, it's this way: the ounce you counted may have run all runt hoppers, or infants, even. And this sack of yours' — he prodded it with his toe — 'it like enough has the grampas and the Goliaths. Anyway, I don't know if it has or hasn't. It was a real smart idea of yours; and I can see by your good honest face that you didn't mean to put anything over on a poor storekeeper; but that's the way it is, and I'll have to stand on my rights.'

The crowd guffawed, stamping with delight, and slapping their knees.

'Shan't I biff the old geezer one?' Sandy muttered. 'Just an easy one?'

Haakon thrust down the clenched fist and shook his head. 'Wait a bit,' he whispered, 'I'm betting on Grandmother.'

Thad stood belligerent and uncertain.

'Well, bub,' drawled the merchant, 'I'm a fair man. You certainly done a good work, getting shut of two sackfuls of hoppers. Take this and get yourself and the family a sody.' He extracted a fifty-cent shin-plaster from his bulging wallet and held it out to the boy.

'One minute, Mr. Obadiah.' Grandmother spoke out of the dimness. 'Thaddeus couldn't take fifty cents he hadn't earned. But I believe he can satisfy you. — Shut the door, Haakon. Open your sack, Thaddeus. We'll count 'em.'

Mr. Obadiah gulped. An old man opened his mouth in a silent laugh that showed all his toothless gums. Thad hesitated for an instant, and then, at Grandmother's decisive nod, snorted and bent to untie the knot.

'Boy! Stop! Quit it, for land sakes!' bellowed the merchant.

Thaddeus went on slowly untying the knot.

'Quit it, I say! You let those pesky vermin loose and I won't have a whole piece of goods in the place.'

Thaddeus raised inquiring eyebrows and went on fumbling with the knot.

'Quit it, I say!' Mr. Obadiah threw his hands wide in a gesture of surrender. 'Great guns, have it your own way! And I must say you're pretty cute!'

He waved so violently toward a rack of boys' suits that he sent two convulsed listeners crashing backward over the counter, pulling down a bolt of calico draped above them and swathing themselves in its indigo lengths. 'Anyway, you're a little feller and won't take a big size.'

Thad stood solidly and stared at him. 'You said any suit in the store.'

Mr. Obadiah groaned and waved helpless hands. 'Sure, I said it and I stick by it. I'm a man of my word, I am.'

'Any suit in the store, bar none?'

'I said it.'

Without a smile, Thad grasped the six-foot Sandy by the checked flannel elbow and pulled him forward.

'All right, sir,' he said. 'I want a blue broadcloth for Sandy McPhee.'

CHAPTER IX

FIDGETS

HAAKON and Sandy stopped at the White House, that night, for a jubilee over Thad's victory. Susan lighted both lamps in celebration, while Janey lowered the new shades to make the room cozier.

They were proud of those shades. Grandmother had made them of 'factory,' unbleached muslin, stiffened with potato starch; and to fasten them when they were rolled up, she had twisted fancy cords of green string, with tassels at the ends. 'I never see the beat of your grandmom!' said Susan.

Grandmother sat in the rocker and braided rags for a rug which grew slowly because of lack of material. 'I'm scared to go to bed before Gramma does,' Thad declared solemnly, 'for fear she'll take my clo'es for rags.' Inch-Along, perched on a bench, was knitting himself a woolen sock. The rest of the family occupied the shiny yellow floor with Bute and Twist, and Sandy pulled a harmonica from his pocket, wiped it lovingly, and launched into 'Oh, Susanna!' with Haakon singing bass, Susan alto, Janey soprano, and the rest un-identified parts.

'I do wish Pa and Ma could see how cozy and homey we are here,' Janey said. 'It doesn't seem a bit as if we were way off in the Great American Desert.'

It was just then that Bute wriggled from Thad's clasp, to squirm through the partly opened door. When he pattered back, long minutes later, Thad opened the door and looked out, curiously.

'Seemed just as if I heard someone out here,' he said.

There was no one in sight, but the moonlight showed an object lying on the doorstep.

'Whatever is it, Thad?'

'I don't know. Some kind of an Injun bag,' he said, hold-ing it close to the lamp. 'Garsh, but it's pretty nice stuff.'

'One of the pouches they use so many of,' Haakon pro-nounced it. 'A fine piece of quill embroidery.'

'What's the pattern there in the middle?' asked Thad.

'A boy — a white boy, I should think, because he's wearing trousers. And shoes.' He turned it over. 'And on the other side, you see, the design's different. It might be forked lightning. No, not that, or it wouldn't be worked in brown quills.'

'Why — Crooked Stick!' exclaimed Janey, peering at it more closely. 'Don't you suppose it means it's for Thad, from Crooked Stick?'

'Bute smelled his old master, the smart puppy!' Thad cried, rumpling him affectionately with his toe. 'Bute! what ails you?'

This time the pup was growling, and sniffing at the door, which Thad had closed after him. Suddenly he pricked up his ears and dashed at the opposite wall. With two swift strides, Haakon blew out the lamps.

Pale gray, but fairly distinct against the white window-shade, as if it were pressed close to the glass, loomed a bulky shadow, its top cylindrical. Scarcely had it appeared before it dropped out of sight.

'We'll give him a minute to *get!*' murmured Haakon; and as soon as the minute had passed, he and Sandy threw open the kitchen door with a bang, Janey and Thad peering around the edge of it, and Susan huddled shivering in the corner. There was nothing to be seen.

'Trust Mr. Lo to melt into the shadows,' Haakon said cheerfully. 'I thought that plaguey Colorow was breaking camp to go up into Middle Park, where he usually spends the winter. Sooner he gets going, better it suits me.'

'D'you suppose Crooked Stick was saying good-bye?' asked Thad.

'Likely enough. And then his father either followed him, or else was curious about our lights and wanted to know what we were about and where we kept things. Nothing can beat Lo for curiosity, either, unless it's an antelope or a wild turkey.'

'Think there's any danger?' Grandmother inquired calmly over her braiding.

'No, I don't. If you and the girls were alone, and he thought you didn't have any firearms —— But even then, all he'd be likely to do would be to scare you into giving him anything in the house that took his fancy.'

'Why, I wouldn't do it!' Janey bristled.

'I don't want you should be alone, long as that old bully's anywhere round. The Great American Desert isn't quite as safe as Ma Grant's parlor yet, Janey. But if he should ever find you alone, don't show you're scared. Only don't make him mad, either,' Haakon told her soberly.

'And that's right, lassie,' nodded Inch-Along.

'He isn't likely to come pottering around again tonight,' Grandmother observed, folding away her work and laying it tidily in a box Inch-Along had painted white for her. 'May as well wind the watch, Thaddeus.'

Haakon chuckled, 'Which is to say, "Good night!" Sandy.'

'Yes, ma'am, if you'll just wait a minute.' Pulling a wallet from his pocket, Sandy wadded a roll of bills into Thad's hand.

'Lookit!' crowed Thad, waving the bills over his head. 'Here's my mare Fidgets, and now Janey won't be the only one to have a horse of her own. Only' — his brow furrowed, and he ran the bills uneasily through his fingers — 'I'll let you have it to offer a reward for that old ring, if you want, Hawk,' he sighed.

'Couldn't think of it, old chap,' Haakon laughed at his reluctant generosity. 'Wouldn't take it if you threw me down and tied me.'

'Honest, wouldn't you?' Thad struggled visibly with his own relief. 'Hawk, I *will* give it to you; honest I will.'

'No, you'll not, old man!' Haakon had always seemed far more than four years older than Thad; now his amusement was that of an indulgent senior. 'Might as well quit trying to force it on me, for I won't take it, and that's final.'

Thad sighed once more. 'Well, then,' he said dolefully, 'I'll have to go after Fidgets. Guess I'll go first thing to-morrow morning.'

Indeed, he rode Hiawatha up to the front door and hallooed to them next morning before they knew that he was awake. He was leading a sorry-looking yellowish chestnut, which stood with drooping head.

'Meet Fidgets!' Thad introduced her proudly.

Susan surveyed the new animal dubiously from the doorway, and Janey was frank in her questioning.

'Why, but, Thad! she looks as if she had one foot in the grave. Her eyes are so dull and sunken. And look how thin she is.'

'Her eyes are sunk because she had the epizoötic. She ain't so old.'

'"If the old mare can turn over, she's worth a hundred dollars,"' Grandmother quoted laconically.

'And I seen her turn over all right,' Thad triumphed. 'But lookit, folks! She's got awful good lines. Look how long her neck is, and how it's sort of cut out neat at the throat. And did you ever see a pair of ears stand up so straight and little?' Janey smothered a laugh, and he glared at her. 'You just wait till she's grazed on this grama grass all winter, and I've curried her regular. Hawk!' he appealed to the boys, riding up for breakfast, 'Janey's making fun of Fidgets.'

Haakon leaped from his saddle and came over to inspect the new mare gravely. He went over her again, this time with more consideration.

'Breakfast!' called Grandmother.

Thad waited restlessly until the meal had begun.

'Honest, don't you think the mare's a good buy?' he appealed to Haakon.

'Good-bye to your twenty-five dollars?' Janey asked.

'Aw, Janey, nobody asked you!'

'"Honest," I think the mare may prove a good purchase,' Haakon answered him seriously. 'Of course there's always a risk. But a few months of good grazing and rest do marvels for some of these broken-down stage horses that look to be done for. And I must say this Fidgets of yours has all the marks of a high-class piece of horse-flesh. I always cotton to a mare that has those wide flat bones in the leg, and that high carriage.'

'I dickered with the man till he threw in the bridle,' Thad told them, flooding his cakes with molasses. 'He hadn't got up yet, and he said he'd give the bridle to be rid of me.'

'I see you wore your new pouch,' Janey observed.

'Say, that reminds me. I saw the whole Ute bunch going off toward the hills with their ponies and travoises and dogs. They were almost out of sight already.'

'Land sakes, but I'm glad of that,' murmured Susan.

That day brought Susan one of Pop Sloane's infrequent letters. It held a post-office money-order, and she sat looking at it bewilderedly before she read the accompanying message.

'Well, Janey!' she ejaculated then, leveling a straight glance at Janey, who was scratching away in her old notebook with little heed for anyone else, looking out from time to time at the rolling plains, golden with early fall flowers and purple with snakeroot and wild asters. 'Well, Janey!'

Janey looked vaguely at Susan.

'Well, *Janey!*' Susan repeated for the third time, her tone mingling amazement and admiration and reproach.

'Why, Sukey, whatever's the matter?' But innocent though her tone, Janey colored at sight of the official-looking slip.

'I see you know. I'll read you what Pop says, and if you couldn't have knocked me over with a feather, Janey Grant! He says, "Our crops weren't hurt as much as some by the hoppers, and prices are good, so I've been able to squeeze out twenty-five dollars to help on your expenses, and thirty-five on the loan from Janey."'

Susan lifted large eyes to Janey as she read the words.

'"*The loan from Janey!* I s'pose she's told you by this time: how I lost all my ready cash last summer when the banks went under in the panic; and we asked Janey how to break it to you that you couldn't go to Normal, like you'd set your heart on. So Janey, she just insists on splitting even what she's got for Normal, and not letting on to you. And once Janey's sot, she's sot."

'Janey, is it true?' Susan gulped back her tears and regarded her friend shiningly as she held out the money-order. 'Was that why you didn't have but fifty dollars left, this spring? And now — what good will the thirty-five dollars do you now?'

'Susan! I can send and offer that reward!'

'But Haakon wouldn't hear to taking Thad's money.'

'It wasn't Thad that lost the ring. Anyway, I guess I don't have to ask Haakon's leave.'

Sweeping her curls back from her face with a thrust of the comb, she ran into the house and sat down to the table to pen the letter.

'"Dear Mrs. Jones,"' she read it aloud to Grandmother and Susan. '"We are well and happy, here in Colorado Territory, and hope you are the same. I am writing to ask if you will be so kind as to put up one of these signs in your dining-room, and have the others put up in the school and the post-office. Respectfully yours, Jane Eleanor Grant." And then I'll write out the notices — let's see, how'd this sound? "A reward of Thirty-Five Dollars for the return of a gold ring with green sets" — Are they emeralds, Grandmother? Or maybe I'd better just say green stones — "green stones, and small white ones, and engraving inside band, 'Semper Fidelis. H.H. to R.C.' Please communicate with Jane Eleanor Grant, Greeley, Colorado Territory."'

The copies were made in Janey's fine even Spencerian, and

the girls mounted their horses and galloped across the plains
to the post-office.

'Can't you imagine how Mis' Jones will turn the house
inside out again?' asked Susan, as they returned.

'One thing's sure,' Janey said happily: 'nobody's going
to keep a ring when they can get *thirty-five dollars* reward
for it, not even supposing they were dishonest. We're sure
to get it now, unless it's been dropped outdoors. And I
can't see how that could be. It does seem as if I can't wait
to hear.'

CHAPTER X

AND MIGNONETTE!

It was well for the impatient Janey that the next weeks were crowded with other interests. For they brought no letter from Mrs. Jones.

Janey's heart skipped a beat every time the boys came loping over the prairie on their way from town and reined up before the White House, to reach into their pockets and pull out the mail. It pounded so hard as to suffocate her whenever she rode into town herself and tied Hiawatha at the post-office hitching-rail. Every time she took a bundle of new letters into her hands, she pictured Haakon's surprise and delight when she should hand him the notification that The Ring was being forwarded by the next mail. But every time she fingered them through, the picture faded to nothing.

There were letters in Pa's angular hand: things were picking up, in spite of the hoppers, so that he had great hope of selling without loss, in a year or so; and the church was plastered, and pretty neat; and he was doing the preaching till they could get a minister; and teaching class meeting, and going back in the afternoons to conduct a service specially for boys and girls — something pretty new.

There were letters in Ma's delicate tiny writing, slender and rounded and firm like herself; she and Ingrid were canning garden sauce and putting up a deal of jam.

There were postscripts from little Lucy; school was soon to begin, and the Sanson niece who had taken Janey's place as teacher would be there again this year; and she was 'verry horid; she dident youse enny finger plays or let them sow; and she never plaid with them at resecc like you.'

But from Mankato came no mail at all from Mrs. Jones or from a finder of the ring; only an occasional one of Emily's faithful letters.

School was soon to open in Greeley, also.

'How'd it be if we were to take just one trip into the mountains before vacation's over?' Haakon suggested on a dreamy warm day in early September.

'I'll stay behind and look after the stock, what they need,' Inch-Along offered.

They set out early one morning, bedding and provisions in the wagon, and drove across the plains to the hills, to a road that followed the stream up, and up, a long canyon. Inch-Along had told them where they would find a group of lumbermen's cabins which would probably be empty, and they steered for these, stopping only long enough to eat the lunch the girls had put up.

It was a long, slow drive up the rough road, but so filled with novelty and charm that the hours passed quickly. Thad was continually shouting aloud at the flicker of wings and the scurry of feet: at every turn in the road a chipmunk, elfin-tiny, flashed across their path, or a whistling marmot broke the stillness with its shrill cry, or a crested jay sailed on great spread wings from tree to ground.

'I keep hoping you'll hear one of our Rocky Mountain canaries,' said Haakon, with a glance at Sandy; and Janey kept watching for yellow wings and a fluted song.

To Janey, fascinating though she found the birds and beasts, the first sight of a mountain canyon held more of witchery in its beauty of scene.

'But I don't know whether it makes me gladder or sadder,' she murmured to Haakon. 'I want to keep it — make a picture of it somehow, with words or colors; and I know I can't.'

'Try!' encouraged Haakon, himself gazing wordlessly ahead.

The ravines seemed brimmed with sun, for their twinkling-leafed aspens were beginning to turn to gold and their sumach to red. The hillsides were purple with asters and smoky with the fluffy seed of wild clematis. The stream babbled and shouted over its granite bed. The pine and spruce were cool and deep and dark.

'The aspens dance on silver stems beneath a dreaming sky' — Janey tapped off the measure with her foot — 'All golden in the setting sun, the little clouds drift by.'

For the sun was setting when at length they reached their destination, the road branching off suddenly and leading them to the two log cabins perched high above the stream.

Stillness, save for the cheerful clamor of the water; and darkness, falling upon them suddenly, after the little drifting clouds had lost their gold. The boys had scarcely time to find wood and look after the team, and Grandmother and the girls to locate their provisions and get supper started, before night lay deep and dark around them.

'I never saw such darkness, and I never heard such stillness,' Janey murmured sleepily to Susan from her spruce-bough bed in the bunk opposite one of the windows.

Later she wakened to the sound of scurrying feet and gnawing teeth and strange little bumps and rattles. But she sat bolt upright in her bed the next instant, for a long shriek sounded through the forest — a wild scream that chilled her scalp and sent an icy trickle down her spine. The silence that followed was deeper than ever. Janey was sure Susan was sitting up, too, and Grandmother; but she could not bring herself to break that dreadful silence by speaking to them. At length Grandmother spoke.

'If there's a woman out in this wilderness alone, we've got to do something,' she said decisively, and Janey could hear her swinging stiffly to the floor and fumbling for a match.

Then came the glimmer of a lantern through the door-cracks, and Haakon's voice instead of the strange one they were dreading.

'It's just me. Go back to sleep, all of you. That was a panther, up a way on the hill.'

Next morning dawned mellowly fair, a typical September day in the Rockies.

'We men-folks'll try our luck with the trout,' Haakon proposed, 'and I suppose you women will want to pick cherries and such. We won't any of us get out of sight of that cluster of spruces by the cabins. So call if you need us.'

The chokecherry bushes were tasseled with purple-black, and Grandmother devoted herself to them, hanging her tin pail on a branch to save stooping. Susan was ranging here and there looking for the tiny, scarlet pin-cherries that made such delicious jelly. Janey gathered the bunches of Oregon grapes that grew close to the ground, richly blue, with crimson pulp. Now and then they could hear a shout from Thad, above the song of the stream; otherwise they might have been miles away from human life.

A chipmunk darted past Janey, sat up for a quick survey of something ahead, and skittered back the way it had come.

'They're like fairy animals —— ' Janey called.

'Hush!' hissed Grandmother.

Startled, Janey peered through the bushes. Down the slope, just below Grandmother's bush, a large black bear stood gazing from Grandmother to Susan, who stood with hands upraised, as if she were playing their childhood game of 'Statuary.' Janey crouched where she was, ready to run for the boys and their guns.

Grandmother went on picking.

Presently, with a little grunt, the bear padded away. And — Grandmother went on picking.

'What were you going to do if it started after you,' Janey asked through chattering teeth, when it was out of sight.

'Throw the bucket and yell. But I wasn't going to waste all those cherries before it was needful.'

The boys brought in a dozen great iridescent trout, which came to the table crisply golden, and fell apart in flakes of luscious whiteness under their hungry forks.

'I made out two kinds of chipmunks,' Thad told them, 'and I found where one of those marmots lived, and I found the funniest big nest like a ball of moss, right where the spray from the stream hits it; and I think I'm on the track of a skunk.'

'Mercy-*to*-us!' objected Grandmother.

'I'll tell you, Thad,' Haakon advised. 'You find the skunk's hole, if you can, and you and I might watch it to-night and see something interesting.'

'Oh, Haakon, can't I go too?' begged Janey.

'If it's all right with Grandmother.'

That midnight vigil was another of the experiences that Janey was to write large in her book of memories. She lay down and slept rather uneasily in her clothes until Haakon whistled softly outside the window, and then she slipped into her sacque, wide awake on the instant, and joined the two boys, waiting at the door with a lantern.

Thad had verified the trail of the skunk and followed it to a curious M-shaped bit of masonry, where he found a crevice that was rich with the characteristic odor. To this the three made their way, the lantern lighting their path a few steps at a time.

'This is a kind of blind the Indians make for shooting deer,' Haakon explained the M. He held the lantern ahead of them and examined the stones until he could make out the dark opening. 'Now we'll sit on the ground on one side of the hole, and set the lantern on the other. It's around two o'clock, so we oughtn't to have long to wait. But mind you keep still.'

The stars shone down piercingly bright between the pines. A breeze stirred far up in the tops like a sigh. Little night creatures scampered through the underbrush. Janey's legs cramped and went to sleep, but she didn't stir. At last, just as she shut her eyes to rest them, Thad nudged her sharply. She pulled her eyes open and focused them with difficulty.

Emerging from the deep darkness into the circle of dim light stepped a black animal showily striped with white, its plumy tail held high. It stopped and sniffed at the lantern, turned and sniffed at Haakon's boots, and disappeared into the hole.

After it — Janey could scarcely repress a gurgle at the

sight — stepped five miniatures of their mother, like her, sniffed at the lantern and the boots, and, like her, disappeared.

'She's been teaching them to hunt,' Haakon explained as they stumbled sleepily back to the cabins.

'Hunt what?' demanded Janey. 'Those little kitteny things?'

'Mostly grubs and insects of different kinds,' Haakon answered. 'Around the roots of weeds and bushes. Little lizards, too, and snakes, I guess.'

'Take me again tomorrow night, Hawk?' Thad yawned.

Next day, since the girls and Grandmother had filled every receptacle they could find ('Though I was certain I brought another pail,' Grandmother puzzled), they turned from berries to herbs: gentian and hops — heavy with their fluffy pale-green fruits — and other 'simples.'

Haakon came in triumphantly with a fine buck, which he skinned and cut up before nightfall.

Next morning they were up early and early on the way home. It was not until after they had started that Janey remembered to ask about the previous night's experience.

'Yes, we went,' Thad said, 'me and Hawk. Garsh! we waited till I'd pretty near gone to sleep —— '

'So near that I had to shake him till his teeth chattered before he could get his eyes open.'

'Aw, Hawk! — Well, not a single skunk put in an appearance! So finally Hawk, he scooped out some stones till he could look in the hole, and still no mother skunk. So he puts in his hand and feels around, and finds the young ones, all curled up inside. And we wait a while longer till the sky's beginning to get grayish, and then we pretty near know the mother's been trapped or killed or something.'

'The poor young ones!' said Grandmother.

'Garsh, Gramma, I should say so! And cuter'n any cat!' Thad said eagerly.

'It's a wonder you didn't ask to keep one,' Grandmother observed severely. 'I'm glad you can see there's limits.'

Thad fell abruptly silent, and Janey noticed that Haakon and Sandy were indulging in some private joke. 'Whatever are you boys laughing about?' she demanded.

Haakon shook his head at her, ever so slightly, 'Sandy, I insist!' he spoke rather huskily, his voice impeded with laughter. 'Show them how a panther goes!'

'Well, I'll have to do it kind of easy, or the team'll bolt on us. You get a good holt on the reins, Hawk.'

He cupped his hands to his mouth and shrieked so eerily that the girls jumped and the horses started up nervously.

'This fellow can do a coyote, too, and a Rocky Mountain canary, so natural their own brothers wouldn't know it wasn't the beasts themselves.'

'Beasts and birds,' corrected Janey. 'I didn't know Sandy could sing, or whistle either.'

Unaccountably, Sandy and Haakon roared at her comment. They had done their best for Thad, turning the attention completely away from him, but it proved not enough. Susan, with a bewildered stare for their unexplained mirth, turned to Thad again.

'Why, Thad!' she cried. 'Where did you get the cute kitten?'

Grandmother and Janey looked around from the wagon seat just in time to see Thad crowding a little nose back into his pocket with gentle haste.

'Kitten!' said Grandmother. 'Let's see the kitten, Thad.'

He dragged it forth, his eyes imploring. It was a beautiful little creature, scarcely so large as a squirrel. Its black

'MERCY-*TO*-US, WHAT DO YOU CALL THAT?'

fur was sleek and shining, and its white stripe clear and snowy.

'Mercy-*to*-us, Thad Grant, what will it be next?'

Before there was opportunity for further comment, they were interrupted by the violent shying of the horses. So strange an equipage was jolting along the rough road that attention was again drawn from Thad and the baby skunk.

First came a bunch of succulent grass, attached to a pole; next, craning her neck after the dainty, a small burro; beside her a burro colt; behind her a small two-wheeled cart, just large enough to carry a man even more mountainous than Colorow.

Haakon drew up his team and whistled. The burro also had stopped. Now it braced all four feet, lifted its head, and gave vent to a raucous 'Eehaw! Eeeeeehaw! Ehaw-ehaw-ehaw!' that sent the echoes ringing.

'Mercy-*to*-us, what do you call that?'

'We call it a Rocky Mountain canary!' Haakon informed her.

'Howdy, folks!' the fat man wheezed amiably, and then, to Thad, 'will you climb out and give Spuds the grass, Bub? I have to let her have it ever' so often, so's she won't git plumb discouraged. She's strong, and nice-tempered except around the heels; but she's even lazier'n the run of 'em.'

He sat and smiled at them while Thad complied. Then the boy gave his attention to the burro colt. It was a funny and appealing baby, with its innocent big head and soft furry body and long legs, and Thad, forgetting onlookers, threw his arms around it.

'What be ye got in yer pocket, Bub?' the man chuckled in his deep asthmatic voice. Bute was standing on his hind legs sniffing at the 'kitty' that peeped over the edge.

'Baby skunk,' Thad said. 'Garsh, but this donkey's a cute little tike, Mister.'

'They make nice, clean pets, skunks do,' the old man wheezed. 'Nice, clean pets, though most folks'll laugh at the idee. — Ye like to have a burro colt, would ye? Wal, I tell ye whut. After this here trip, I won't have no more use for Spuds, here, till spring comes round and I go back into the hills a-prospectin' agin, a-prospectin' agin. Mos' generly I jes' turns her loose; but this year, with a colt, and a hard winter promisin' — Wal, if you want to let her graze round your place till I need her — after this here trip — ye kin have the colt fer keeps, come spring.'

'Honest?' breathed Thad. 'Can I, Gramma? Thank you, Mister.'

'Wal, then, s'pose ye tie a fresh bunch of grass onto the pole' — He jerked a thumb toward the supply in the back of the cart — 'an' we'll jog along, me'n Spuds, we'll jog along. Where at kin I find ye, next month or two?'

They told him, and the comic equipage bumped along up the road, while they sat and watched it out of sight, after which Thad climbed into the wagon again, anxious eyes on Grandmother's profile.

'Our large friend was right, Grandmother Grant,' Haakon said persuasively as the wagon got under way, its pole brake squealing. 'Skunks have no — er — unpleasant attributes at all when taken early and treated kindly.'

'I never heard of such a thing.'

'Wouldn't Rose be a sweet name for it?' Janey suggested mock-seriously.

'Or Violet?' Susan seconded her.

'How about Petunia?' asked Haakon.

'Mignonette!' snapped Grandmother.

Thad sighed his relief and stroked the shy little head of the newly christened Mignonette.

Yet he had not entirely relaxed his uneasy tension when they reached the White House at sunset and began the process of unloading the wagon. He teetered anxiously from one foot to the other, and finally made a grab for an object hidden under wet canvas in a corner.

Grandmother leveled a dramatic forefinger.

'There's that pail!' she announced.

Thad lifted it nervously, slopping water from it in spite of his care. The canvas slipped off. Shiningly undulant in the half-filled pail swam a half-dozen rainbow trout.

'For dinner?' Grandmother asked dryly.

'Well — Well, but, Gramma! these are *pet* fish, I thought maybe I could make a kind of pool for them down beside the river.'

Inch-Along now came hobbling out, exclaiming over the abundance of wild fruits they had brought.

'Though I don't know what we're going to put 'em up in,' Grandmother soliloquized. 'Cans and glasses are too dear.'

'You get at makin' up your jam and jelly, come morning,' Inch-Along counseled, 'and I'll guarantee to figger out the cans, ma'am.'

So they put in a broiling morning over the stove, the flies buzzing stickily about the strong, sweet odors. And Inch-Along appeared at mid-morning, two bulging sacks across Gitchee's shoulders. He emptied them out with a clatter: old tin cans gathered from the dump that had already accumulated on the outskirts of town.

'I don't see ——' Janey surveyed the dingy pile doubtfully.

'You wait, lassie,' said Inch-Along.

He built a fire outdoors and hung a kettle over it. There he boiled the cans in soapy water, scoured them with ashes and boiled them again, after which he used the ends of a part of them for tops for another part, and put them on deftly with solder melted from the seams of the remainder, when Grandmother and the girls had them brimful of boiling jam and jelly.

While Inch-Along worked with the cans, Sandy put up a shelf for them, and Janey made a fancy shelf paper of folded newspaper cut to form lacy scallops. The bright double row of tins made a fine display there.

'Makes me feel a sight more folksy,' said Grandmother; 'and turnips to put away in our root cellar — when you boys dig us one.'

'Do we need a root cellar? They say there isn't any real winter here,' Janey objected. 'They say it's like Italy that way.'

'Don't you take any stock in such talk,' Inch-Along counseled. 'It ain't like winters East, to be sure. There's lots of open weather, so you don't get all wore out with solid stretches of cold. And with it so dry, the cold don't cut through like it does in other places. But sometimes I think winter kinda plays with the country out here, like a cat with a mouse. You think you've got clear of it, and then it grabs you again. Haakon, with all they do say about not needing shelter for the critters, I wish we could build us a sort of open shed for them. Can't run no risk with that shorthorn Liberty, and the other sires you give so much for.'

'I can't buy lumber,' Haakon frowned.

'None the less,' Inch-Along urged, pausing in his knitting, 'the way you say the moss is on the mountin trees, and the heavy crop of acorns and all, I look for a hard winter. Why can't we go after logs and make us a log shelter? Open to the south, it won't take so much.'

The young people had never known months so busy as these autumn ones. School opened, and Haakon and Janey started their teaching, while Thad entered a new class, both Thad and Janey awed and a trifle subdued by the brisk efficiency of the new building, grandly built of brick and equipped with all the convenience of large blackboards and 'boughten' seats and desks. Every morning the three cantered across to town on Hiawatha, Minnehaha, and Gitchee, and every afternoon they cantered back. After hours Haakon worked furiously at the digging of the root cellar, at the building of the cattle shed, at the fencing that must be kept in repair. On Friday afternoons he and Sandy drove up into the hills to bring down logs and firewood, or to Platteville, where they could buy coal directly from the mines for less than the six and seven dollars a ton it cost in town.

They would get home in the late hours of Saturday night, and the next morning church would be a misery. Haakon would bite his lips as they writhed in almost uncontrollable yawns, and Sandy, to whom church-going was a newly acquired habit, would nod and nod until wakened by a sharp jerk of his head, when he would glare steadfastly at the preacher as if daring him to suppose he had been dozing. Once, when Sandy's mouth had fallen open in complete abandonment to slumber, Thad pricked his knee with a pin. He never repeated the trick, for Sandy dreamed it was a fly, and drew the eyes of the whole congregation by slapping it resoundingly before he was fully awake.

As early fall slipped into late fall, Janey could not give up her belief in an Italian winter. The prairie herbage turned golden and russet and sent up puffs of aromatic dust underfoot, and the great round tumbleweeds broke loose from their stems and rolled idly here and there before the breeze. Nights and mornings were edged with chill, but midday was always balmy, with an ardent sun. Every possible moment the girls spent outdoors. Janey's face was powdered more lavishly with golden freckles, and Susan's acquired a deeper, warmer brown.

They laughed incredulously when they found Inch-Along, one particularly warm Saturday in November, stretching ropes behind the White House, and learned why he was doing it. There was a rope from the top of the back door to the small sod chicken-house; from the chicken-house to the shed that sheltered the four horses and Twist.

'Why, Inch-Along, whatever are you thinking of?'

'Never you mind, lassie! When a storm comes up in this open country — well, you'd ought to know what it can be like when you look back two years to the Great Blizzard in Minnesoty. And this kind of day, with the air so warm and still and the mountins looking that way — well, it's a weather-breeder, or I miss my guess.'

The first real storm of the season did break that very afternoon, and raged so blindingly that they were glad of the guiding ropes, which led them there and back again, when they went to feed and water the stock. Haakon had been to town, and he stopped only long enough to toss their mail in at the front door and gallop on to his own place to see that all was well with the short-horn bulls.

'My letter's come! From Mrs. Jones!' Janey cried joyously. She slit it open and stood close beside the darkened window to read it aloud.

My Dear Miss Grant: —

Yours rec'd, with notices enclosed, near two mo. ago, and I had them all put up acc'ding to your request, but sorry to say no result so far.

Everybody in this house has drove me near crazy hunting it, and the neighbor young ones have scratched up the yd.

till it looks like dogs have been fighting all over my garden.

I will drop you a line to let you know from time to time.

I suppose you heard about Ptolemy how he didn't pass his examinations last spring and I have not seen hide or hair of him since.

Hoping you are well, I remain,

Yrs resp'f'ly,

MRS. PHILURA JONES

CHAPTER XI

THANKSGIVING

'OH — gummy!' Susan mourned.

Janey turned the letter over and over, staring at it hopelessly. 'If anybody'd found it, they'd have brought it in double-quick, for fear I might take back the offer. Oh, dear! I thought it was going to be so grand if that letter said the ring was coming by next mail. Haakon's beginning to be — worried.'

They were interrupted by a halloo at the gateway. Janey ran to open the door, and Haakon leaned from his saddle and cupped his hand to call against the storm.

'Don't wait supper for us, Janey! We've got to head the cattle back from the hills.'

And he galloped away.

'Sandy says the cows have a way of making for the canyons in a storm, before they get used to the country,' Susan said, 'and it's sure death to a lot of 'em, because they get snowed up in those deep draws. I hope to goodness they haven't got far.'

Evening was already upon them, though it was not yet four o'clock. A lamp was lighted, and soon supper preparations were under way. One after another, Janey and Susan and Thad flattened their noses against the windows to peer into the swirling darkness. Thad fed and watered the stock, and cajoled Grandmother till she let him bring his lamb in with the rest of the family.

Supper was eaten, and Grandmother scooped out the boys' baked potatoes and seasoned them well and repacked them to keep warm and flavory in the oven with their portion of juicy bear steak.

'Keep the kettle boiling, Susan,' she adjured the girl. 'We'll dose them good with red pepper tea when they do come.'

Janey looked at Grandfather Grant's silver turnip of a watch, which hung from the lamp-shelf in lieu of a clock. 'Quarter after eight! Oh, dear, they'll be cold and hungry as anything.'

It was only a half-hour later when the adventurers rode past the window, put their horses under shelter in the shed, and came stumbling in at the door on a blast of biting air. Janey brushed off their snowy boots with the broom, and they unswathed themselves from their heavy whitened jackets and lappeted fur caps. Their faces, though cold-purpled, were happy enough.

'Lucky this time!' Haakon worked his fingers before the glowing fire, and pressed his ears with gingerly palms. 'A good share of the herd was making over toward the hills, a pretty good clip, too; but we found 'em in time to turn 'em, and I bet there aren't a dozen that aren't inside our fence tonight.'

'All the short-horns in safe?' asked Grandmother.

'Yes, ma'am, all nine.'

Haakon slipped onto a bench at the table and bowed his head briefly. 'Mmmm!' he said, as Janey placed his plate before him, steaming hot and fragrant. 'Ouch!' as she set down a cup of well-known red liquid at each place. 'Do we have to, Grandmother Grant? Well, then! here goes!' He gulped down the burning pepper tea and set the cup down with a grimace, while Sandy sniffed at his questioningly. 'Anyway, Sandy, what could be better than to come home to this, out of the storm?'

'Whew, but this tea's sure been somers where the weather's warm!' he answered, holding his mouth open after his own deep draft.

The little house stood staunch against the wind that wailed around it. The girls had left the shades up so that more light might pierce the storm, and the whirl of snow could be seen in the pale shafts of lamplight. If there were keen breezes that found their way in, they only served to deepen the feeling of comfort and shelter, though Inch-Along, hobbling round the room with an open palm to detect their source, was murmuring something about banking up the walls with earth, soon as this storm was past.

'Light, and fire, and smoking-hot good food,' beamed Haakon, having recovered from the cayenne tea, 'and your own folks.'

'Beast and human,' grinned Sandy.

Twist stretched luxuriously behind the stove, Bute thrust a black nose into Thad's hand and adored him with melancholy brown eyes, and Mignonette ——

'By the way, where is that skunk of yourn?' Sandy asked.

Janey giggled. Grandmother said nothing, but steadily sewed carpet rags. Thad rolled his eyes and pointed.

Curled up on her lap under the rags slumbered Mignonette, a sleek black-and-white ball of sheer content. Grandmother had never held with 'cosseting animals and holding them in your lap,' but the baby skunk had proved too ingratiating. Every time Grandmother sat down, Mignonette was on hand, teasing, or boldly climbing into the coveted resting-place. At first Grandmother had pulled herself upright with a grim 'Scat!' and tumbled the intruder to the floor. But Mignonette had so trustfully accepted the rebuff as accident, and so confidingly returned as soon as Grandmother was seated again, that she had won her point.

Inch-Along had settled down to his evening's task of weaving a serviceable egg-basket from willow branches; and Janey was working with a contraption of string and wire that she fitted on Susan's right wrist and fingers.

'What under the sun?' gawped Sandy.

'It's to teach the children to hold their hand the way they ought to when they write,' Janey explained seriously. 'They made us use them at Normal. See: if you go to rest your wrist on the desk you press the head of this tack and it sticks into you.'

'A pointed reminder,' Haakon suggested.

'Aren't you glad you don't have to go to school tomorrow?' asked Susan. 'Likely the snow'll be gone by Monday. They say it never lasts like it does in the States.'

'Well, then, I hazard a guess that this winter's going to be out of the usual run,' Inch-Along forecast.

He was a good prophet. During the night, the snow ceased to fall, the temperature dropped, and the sun rose red upon a frigid earth, a chill blue sky arching above the dazzling expanse of white plains. There followed frosty hours of digging paths round the White House with a shovel Inch-Along contrived from a box top and a poplar limb; and breaking a road through to the main one.

All week the temperature stayed down and the snow stayed on, but the next Saturday the sun shone benignly warm, and the whiteness melted away. When the family drove home from church, Sunday noon, most of the prairie lay bare again, and a fresh wind had begun to drive the tumbleweed before it, lodging the great airy bramble balls against the fences.

'Just take notice how the snow has all gone from these sandy roads, and they're hardly even muddy!' Susan marveled.

'Just take notice how the wind has shifted and is coming from the hills,' Inch-Along counseled. 'Ma'am, if you don't object on account of the Sabbath, my notion is we'd better bank up the shed for the critters while we can, and likewise throw up some earth to windward of the house.'

'"The better the day, the better the deed,"' Grandmother quoted, 'though we're liable to abuse the saying.'

'Aw, Inch-Along!' Thad protested incredulously, 'it ain't going to snow any more!'

'Won't we have to buy hay and grain?' worried Janey, who had complete faith in the old man's weather wisdom.

'And run up a bill?' Grandmother grudged.

In mid-afternoon, with the wind still freshening, the men were at work banking up the buildings when the curious donkey-cart jogged along, this time led by a temptingly suspended carrot. The driver pulled up and hailed them, sitting solidly and watching their work.

'You got the same hunch I got!' he bawled at Inch-Along, and Inch-Along paused to lean breathless on his spade. 'We're in for a spell of heavy weather. I never knowed it to fail, chipmunks actin' like they are, and acorns and cherries sech a heavy crop, sech a heavy crop.'

'Where you bound for, Skinny?'

'Bound fer here, jes' this minute, bound fer here. You ain't repented yer bargain, young feller?' This to Thad, who had dropped his spade and come to stroke the burro colt.

'No, sir, I ain't!' Thad assured him.

'But, Thad!' Janey worried from the doorway, 'with feed so high, if they can't graze ——'

'Costs a little less than nothing to feed a jenny, Miss, a little less than nothing,' Skinny wheezed. 'But see here, Bub!' With vast upheavals, he dragged a small buckskin bag from his hip pocket and puffingly extracted two pea-sized objects, which he held out on the palm of his hand. 'If you lack fodder, Bub, you sell these and buy it. Spuds is an ornery little devil — lazy, and twitchy round the back heels — but — well, she's my pal, she's my pal.'

He dropped the objects carefully into Thad's hand, and the boy examined the rough yellow bits curiously. He looked up, wide-eyed. 'Gold?' he gasped.

'Sure,' rumbled the old man. 'Gold nuggets. Now's there one of ye who kin ride along to town with me and bring back the outfit? My corporeal constitootion ain't such as to make walkin' a pleasure, a pleasure.'

So Thad, excused from work, bestrode Hiawatha and accompanied the old prospector to town, returning at nightfall proudly leading mother and child, to the snorting annoyance of Hiawatha, who had the usual horse's distaste for burros.

True again to Inch-Along's prophecy, the first great flakes were beginning to fall out of a leaden sky, and long before morning the earth was once more blanketed with white. That week, snow followed snow, and the wind drifted it until even the costly Colony fence was nearly covered, and ordinary ones were completely hidden.

Haakon and Janey and Thad managed to make their difficult way to school and home again each day, except when the road became almost impassable and Janey had to stay overnight at Mrs. Pertle's. Sandy and Haakon found it necessary to herd the cattle constantly, since the fences had become useless to restrain them. Their task was made easier, however, by their feed-racks of alfalfa, and by the barrel salt scattered inside the fence line.

Other cattle owners were not so careful. There was a feud between cattle-men and colonists at best. They saw the coming of the farmers as the small end of a wedge that was to break up the old open range; and they resented the high fence that enclosed the colony property. 'The Greeley hymn-singers,' they said, 'built them a fence to keep us sinners out.' Now they chuckled in their sleeves at finding the fence useless.

One old-timer, especially, let his Jersey bull wander at will over the Colony and other farms near by. He even threatened anyone who should take measures against it. 'I got a load of buckshot and a lawsuit for anybody that damages him!' Old Jed Sneeth was a terrifying figure, red of face and hooked of nose and white of hair; and tall and rugged as an old pine. The traditions of his ruthlessness in the matter of lawsuits were so many that the bull continued to range the countryside unmolested, a vicious creature, probably the only Jersey in the region.

There came a day of thawing weather and a swift return of cold that crusted over the drifts so that the whole earth seemed of burnished white metal. Next morning a herd of antelopes passed the White House, headed toward Greeley. Something had frightened them, and they raced past as lightly as thistledown before a windstorm: elfin creatures, delicately made and beautiful.

'I hope no one will hurt them,' Janey worried, as she leaped into her saddle to go to school.

'No use wasting the hope, lassie.' Inch-Along shaded his eyes against the glare of white and blue to watch them. 'You'd best turn your eyes the other way when you get to town. The beasties are headed straight for destruction.'

It was true. When the young people rode into town, they found that the flock had run into a cul-de-sac of barnyard and house, and men were already plunging toward the place with muskets. Janey flicked Hiawatha with the reins and sped past the slaughter.

'Yes, butchered the whole caboodle,' Inch-Along commented scornfully, 'and now they have meat to spoil, which seems to be the height of their ambition.'

'I wouldn't mind having some of the meat, though,' Grandmother suggested.

'We can easy get a fine tenderloin, ma'am. I wondered if we couldn't have a kind of Thanksgiving feast,' Inch-Along suggested. 'I see in the *Tribune* how the Governor of the Territory made his proclamation, and Thursday week's the day.'

'We haven't ever had Thanksgiving, Grandmother. Do let's,' Janey seconded.

'Mm. I was figuring if antelope meat and apples wouldn't make good mincemeat,' said Grandmother.

Sandy came in triumphantly next day, dragging a beautiful great bird with bronze feathers. He flung it proudly on the floor at Grandmother's feet.

'Leave it be, Bute! Here's our Thanksgiving turkey, ma'am. I met a fellow'd been off hunting and got three. He said he'd swap one fer a mince pie or punkin either, and I took him up. That all right?'

And Janey came flushed and sparkling from school. 'They're having a special Thanksgiving meeting of the Lyceum,' she said, hanging up her sacque and cap and putting away her mittens, 'and Mr. Bancroft asked me to read one of my poems. Can't we all go?'

Though the sharpest cold of the season surged upon them the day before Thanksgiving, it was not enough to chill their enthusiasm. All the foodstuffs had to be piled on the back of the stove to 'unfreeze' for use: they were hard as bullets when taken from the box Inch-Along had sunk in the ground under the floor, with a trapdoor over it. Even the bread in the can in the corner was frozen too hard to slice in the morning.

'Thad Grant,' his sister accused him after she had made the bed that morning, 'it's wonder to me you didn't take that sheep to bed with you last night. You had Mignonette and Bute, both; you can't deny it.'

'Well, garsh,' Thad defended himself, 'I gave Inch-Along my hot bricks, and I had to have sump'n. My eyelashes were froze shut this morning, anyway.'

The dinner was a great success: wild turkey browned to a crackling deliciousness, and dressing and gravy and the other regulation accompaniments; and Grandmother's special creamy corn pudding; and mince pie and pumpkin pie and apple pie.

'I sure am feeling thankful,' Sandy meditated with unusual expansiveness, leaning back and gloating over the flaky pie before him.

'Much to be thankful for,' Grandmother nodded. 'Whether it's climate, or that spring water you've been fetching me, Haakon, or the lemons, or what, the rheumatics are letting loose little by little.'

'And I feel so good again!' Susan said joyously.

'Well, I'm sure thankful — for Fidgets and Taters and Bute and Twist and Mignonette,' Thad rumbled in his heaviest young bass. 'But I'd like a few more Injuns, myself.'

'This an experience meeting?' Haakon asked. 'I can say I'm thankful the herd didn't give us the slip. I suppose I'm even thankful they're eating their fool heads off at home. But I hope to goodness there'll be some open weather by the time they've finished off our alfalfa. Hay and grain are sky high. — But it could be a lot worse,' he hurried to add, 'and it's the fortunes of war.'

'I don't know whether I'm thankful about reading my poem or not,' Janey declared.

CHAPTER XII

OLD RIP

IT WAS a festive occasion, that Thanksgiving evening, when the White House dwellers and Haakon and Sandy dressed in their Sunday-go-to-meeting clothes and drove to town. Colony Hall, where the Lyceum was held, was comfortably filled, and Janey rolled her manuscript tighter and tighter, and felt more and more fluttery.

The program opened with a debate on woman suffrage. A militant-looking woman took the feminine side of the argument, and mentioned, among other things, that it was a woman, Harriet Beecher Stowe, who had written the book that roused the country to war and freed the slaves; that women were now taking definite steps toward ridding our fair land of the blot of the liquor traffic; that women were capable of manly decision and bravery, as witness the noted traveler and writer, Isabella Bird, who had traveled through this wilderness alone, the year before, exploring the Indian country as far as Estes Park itself, with the intrepidity of a man. 'I venture to predict,' she cried, 'that the day will come when women lawyers, women physicians, and business women, will not occasion surprise and wonder!'

The negative side was represented by a gentleman whose long hair and declamatory manner combined to proclaim him the ambitious orator. His discourse was shrill with the screams of the American eagle; it bristled with the horns of dilemmas; it sobbed with neglected babes; and it wound up triumphantly: 'If women could vote, those who are now wives would live in endless political bickering with their husbands. And those who are not wives, my friends and fellow-townsmen, WOULD REFUSE TO MARRY!'

The decision of the judges gave an overwhelming victory to the masculine side.

'Makes me so mad!' Janey whispered to Susan. 'There half the judges were women, but they didn't have spunk enough to stand up for their own side.'

'Hush! Listen!'

'Although the sentiment of this company may have been seen to declare itself against extending the suffrage to its fairer members, need it be said that this decision arises from the chivalrous desire to shield these lovelier and tenderer blossoms from the rude winds of political storm and stress? In spheres where her beauty and sweetness may shine in fit setting, Greeleyites are the first to delight in honoring Woman. If the fair sex has been somewhat in the minority on these Lyceum programs, it is surely not because she lacks ability, but because she shows a natural — and may I say commendable? — timidity. It has been with some difficulty that we have prevailed upon the next speaker to entertain us with the product of her own young pen. I take pleasure in introducing Miss Jane Grant, who has fared from a far city to guide the tender minds of our youngest sons and daughters.'

Often as Janey had spoken pieces, at school and at church, this was an ordeal. The faces, little known as yet, swam before her eyes; and she was thankful that her long blue henrietta had three petticoats under it, to hide the shaking of her knees. She herself could hear the clicking of one heel against the floor.

She found Mr. Bancroft, the curly-haired principal, regarding her from the front seat with a disquieting expectancy; and Grandmother's calm face, and Haakon's proud one, and Susan's eagerly devoted, and Sandy's marveling, and Thad's feignedly contemptuous, and — off to one side — that of the 'triflin' Indiana' from Mrs. Pertle's, envious and rather resentful, while that of Long Tom, the half-wit, showed a dropped lip and a wondering gaze.

She cleared her throat, bowed, and read, to the sound of her clicking heel:

> Out on the prairie at twilight I roam,
> Under the evening welkin, whose dome
> Above me is painted with sunset hue,
> With glintings of gold and with bandings of blue,
> With cloudlets like bubbles of rosy air,
> And colors that look like a painted prayer.
>
> To my nostrils comes the breezy scent
> Of the plain, whose vast expanse, besprent
> With wildling blooms, is darkly vast;
> And a slender spire, like a ship's tall mast,
> At the earth's edge painted against the sky
> Entreats us to pass not His temple by.

By the time she had read two of the eight stanzas, Janey's eyes had cleared, and her voice had lost its earlier tremolo. She enjoyed her first experience of the fascinating sense of power that comes from holding an audience in the mesh of one's own thoughts, and walked back to her seat as if treading on air.

'Mrs. Dr. Hansom' read a paper on Thanksgiving Day; and there followed a piano solo, and finally the re-reading, by request, of Mr. Pabor's poem on Horace Greeley, written at the time of the great man's death, just two years before.

> Dead, and we to whom he stood
> As a sponsor and a friend,
> We in sorrow lowly bend,
> Like children in their orphanhood.

The final feature of the program was brief but moving. Nathan Meeker, the founder of the Union Colony, read a few of the last letters he had received from the great states-man; letters written after his bitter defeat as a presidential candidate, and when — devotedly caring for his wife in her mortal illness — he was himself sickening to death.

Mr. Meeker's eyes were moist as he stood before them — the chubby-faced, kindly-eyed man with his look of an Eastern schoolmaster and philosopher, who was in a few years to leave the town he had founded and go forth to his own dreadful death at the hands of the Utes.

'Some folks are saying that the town of Greeley will yet be a failure. Don't credit them. They are poltroons, and faint of heart and short of vision. Weather this season of financial depression, I say to you! Weather the ravages of the grasshoppers! Weather the hard, the unprecedented season! And go forth to victory! Six days before his death, with the shadows heavy upon him, this great and good man so counseled us.' He read from the precious bit of paper:

November 23, 1872

Friend Meeker — I have yours of the 7th inst. I presume you have already drawn on me for the $1,000 to buy land. If you have not, please do so at once. I have not much

money, and probably never shall have; but I believe in
Union Colony and you, and consider this a good investment
for my children.

HORACE GREELEY

As they went out of the hall, Indiana was one of the many
to shake Janey by the hand. 'I thought mebbe you'd like to
read some of my potery, too,' she said, handing her a roll
tied with blue ribbon. 'If you was to show it to Mr. Bancroft' — she added wistfully — 'it don't do a lick of good
fer me to, on account I'm only a waitress, I suppose. I've
left them a-layin' around time and again where it seemed
like if they'd been a snake they'd a-bit him. But did he ever
see 'em? No, not him.'

She backed nervously away as the gentleman in question
approached Janey, with halting words of praise. 'And
couldn't I have the pleasure of seeing you home tonight,
Miss Grant?'

Janey shook a calm head. 'There isn't a bit of need, Mr.
Bancroft, though it's nice of you to offer. Didn't you notice? — Haakon and Sandy and the whole family's right
here, and the wagon is plenty roomy.'

'I didn't think you'd be so slow to catch on, Janey! And
him *the principal!*' Susan fretted as they climbed into the
wagon.

Janey only chuckled and patted her indulgently.

'Looks 's if we might have to put our wagon bed on run-
ners, just like they do in *cold* countries,' Inch-Along observed ironically, as the horses floundered through drifts
and the passengers sunk themselves as deep as possible in
their wrappings, on the homeward ride.

'But — oh, isn't it beautiful?' Janey came out of her
muffler and her tranced silence to wave a mittened hand at

the plain, with shadows of fences painted sheer blue by the moonlight.

Haakon flapped the reins over the horses' backs. 'Giddap, Hi! 'Dap, Min! We've got to get Janey home in time to write some new poetry.'

But the budding poetry was soon blighted. When they were still a quarter of a mile away, they could hear riotous sounds from the White House.

'What the —— ?' Haakon breathed, and flicked the team with the whip. 'What on earth?'

'Maybe it's Injuns!' croaked Thad, a fearful joy in his voice. 'You g-got a pistol, Hawk?'

'You bet. Sandy, too. — Grandmother, and you, girls, you get down in the wagon bed. Hold the reins, will you?' He thrust them into Inch-Along's staunch old hands as they reached the gate, and leaped over the wheel, Sandy following, and both drawing their six-shooters. Thad followed them, and Janey slipped down stealthily, though they did not see her.

The noise issued from the wide-open door of Inch-Along's room. Crash! Splinter! Bang! Ping! and the tinkle of broken glass.

The two boys sprang to the two sides of the door, holding their bodies out of gunshot range and trying to see inside.

'By golly!' squealed Thad.

In the open doorway loomed the intruder. His heavy head hung low between massive shoulders. Small red eyes gleamed madly in the moonlight. Froth flew from his lips. A monstrous bellow shook the air.

'Sneeth's bull!'

Old Rip turned and raged back again, crash, bang, thud!

'Guess I'll have to shoot!' Haakon shouted above the uproar.

'No — wait!'

'Janey Grant, you get back in that wagon!'

Janey, who had been reaching with sure memory for something on the kitchen shelves, slipped out the back door without replying. She had a broom in one hand and a small can in the other, and she shrieked through the broken back window of Inch-Along's room: 'Stand out of the way, boys!'

Reaching in the window with the broom, she drew the attention of the big beast, so that he plunged toward her, shaking a furious head. Janey waited until she could see the glint of his eyes, and then she hurled the contents of the can full into them.

Bellowing with pain and rage, he turned and made for the door, pulling off jamb and hinges as he crowded through. There was the sound of a shot, and he lumbered into the darkness, tail high and stiff, head shaking.

'I guess you and Thad better bake you up a bed on the kitched floor todight,' Grandmother commented briefly from behind her handkerchief, as they held a lamp high and peered into the wreckage.

'Ahr-choo. Yes'b. If there's eddythig to — ahr-choo! — bake id oud of.'

'But, Jadey' — this was Susan, her eyes red with pepper-weeping — 'diddud thad bad say he'd sue eddywud who dabbidged his bull?'

'Red pebber wo'd last log,' Janey said. 'Ad you diddud do bore thad crease hib, did you, Hawk?'

'Meant to crease hib. 'Fraid I got hib id the hide leg, Jadey.'

'Well, eddyway!' Janey defied Old Jed. 'Sue us? I'd like to see hib try! Why, I'be goig to his radch first thig tomorrow ad demad dabbidges for ourselves!'

CHAPTER XIII

JANEY BEARDS THE LION

JANEY's courage may have begun to melt, even while she went sneezily about the task of rescuing trampled bedclothing and ticks to make pallets on the floor for Inch-Along and Thad. It may have oozed away before Susan's agonized murmurs.

'Janey, honest, I don't think we'd ought to let on who shot the bull. They say he cost an awful sight; and that old man's got four or five notches on his pistol.'

'You think he's likely to shoot me, Sukey?' Janey's voice was almost as dry as Grandmother's.

'No, of course not that. But he ain't afraid to do anything. And they do say he's got the law out here under his thumb, and can twist things so black looks white. Why, Janey, when those big cattle-men get on the rampage, they can drive you right out of the country, as easy as anything.'

'Pooh!' sniffed Janey, and flopped over on her stomach with her face in the pillow.

But if her determination had waned during the night, it waxed hot as Grandmother's cayenne tea, at first sight of the ruins in the thin gray light of morning. Both windows shattered, cord beds torn to pieces, clothing that had hung behind a curtain on the wall shredded to a fringe, new yellow floor paint defaced by scudding hoofs.

'It makes me so mad! I can hardly wait to face him.'

'But, Janey,' Haakon remonstrated, 'that's my place, not yours.'

'Or mine, lassie. Seems to me it's nobody's but Inch-Along's.'

Janey stamped her foot. 'It's best for me to do it. No Western man will offer to hurt a girl.'

'Can't help that, Janey.' Haakon shoved back from the table decisively. 'I don't leave that kind of work to a girl. I'll stop at his place on my way home tonight. Can't this morning: got a job that will make me pretty near late as it is.'

There was no use arguing with Haakon when his jaw set at its iron angle; but Janey had a chin that could match his jaw for firmness, and she set out at seven and trotted briskly toward the Sneeth ranch.

She kept her temper high by repeating to herself the story of their wrongs: 'And Thad's single only book,' she was murmuring, riding angrily erect, 'his "Swiss Family Robinson" that he prized so and had under his pillow, all rumpled and torn to pieces!'

She slipped lightly from the saddle, pulled Hiawatha's reins over his head so that he would stand, marched up to the door of the broad low ranch-house, and tapped sharply with the butt of her whip. She felt it an appropriate gesture.

The old man himself answered the peremptory knock, and stood towering above her, his ice-blue eyes questioning. She nodded brusquely, tilting her fur-capped head up to look him in the face.

'Good morning, sir. Are you Mr. Sneeth?'

He nodded.

'I am Jane Eleanor Grant, one of the new teachers at the Greeley school.' He looked her small self up and down in surprised amusement and waited. 'I've come to see you about your Jersey bull. Did he come home last night?'

Mr. Sneeth drew down a terrific bristle of gray brows at her and opened his mouth to speak, but she went on quickly.

'I guess he did. He was headed this way and making good time. Well, Mr. Sneeth, I came to say two things. First, it was lucky for him that my grandmother doses us with cayenne tea, or we might have had to kill him instead of getting him out with pepper. And, second, I've made a list of damages, near as I can figure them, and if you'll settle those, we — we won't say any more about it.'

Janey held out her carefully written list, footing up $9.90. Old Jed Sneeth half-extended a powerful old hand, and then drew it back.

'Did you know you liked to 'a' killed my bull, young woman?' It was the first time she had heard his voice, and it reminded her of the bull's bellow. Angry as she was, she trembled at the sound of it; but she squared her chin defiantly, and shook her head so hard that the frosted brown curls bobbed.

'No, sir, I don't believe we did. But even if we had, we were defending our own property. He just about wrecked our house — one room of it, that is.'

'Well, sir, Rip'll go lame the rest of his days, that's what!' he boomed. 'What's a little two-by-four shack to a blooded Jersey bull like Rip? What you propose to do about that, young woman?'

Janey silently held out the paper.

'IF YOU'LL SETTLE THOSE, WE — WE WON'T SAY ANY MORE
ABOUT IT'

'There are two windows,' she said, when she could find her voice, 'and paint for the floor, and wood to mend the doorway, and goods for new bedding, and work-clothes for Inch-Along and Thad. We didn't figure our time at all — sewing and carpentering and painting.'

Old Jed was still staring at her, his mouth pulled down under his bush of a white mustache, one thicket of gray brow arched high and the other quirked low over the blue eyes. He looked her up and down again, and snorted.

'You don't scar' worth a cent, Miss Snippet. Well, let me give you a piece of advice, as one rancher to another: *Don't* scar'! There's a lot of things besides bulldogs and black bears that'll back down if you stand still and face 'em. — Ma!' he shouted over his shoulder, still looking at Janey. 'Ma, will you fetch me my wallet out of my secretary? There's a little lady here's come to collect a bill.'

Ma Sneeth came amiably trotting out to them with the wallet, drawing a crocheted shawl round her plump shoulders as she met the chill air.

'Meet Mis' Sneeth,' ordered Old Jed, drawing out a ten-dollar bill. 'This is Miss — huh, what was it?'

'I'm Janey Grant.' Janey made a tremulous little bow. 'I'll bring the ten cents change tomorrow, Mr. Sneeth, and thank you very much.'

'I'm only payin' part of my bill in money, Ma. The balance — Your outfit got a good milch cow, Miss Snippet?'

Janey shook her head. 'Those Texas cows don't know the first thing about being milch bossies,' she giggled irrepressibly at memories of her attempts on them. 'We use a plain red cow now, but she doesn't give much.'

'Think she'd like one of Rip's daughters?' Jed asked Ma Sneeth. 'We don't figger to fool with any more milch cows ourself, and this one's a neat little heifer — half Jersey, of course. — Shut up!' he roared with sudden ferocity when Janey tried to stammer her thanks. 'Stop by tonight and drive her home, can you? I hope you don't think I can spare a man to take her over to you?'

He was still mumbling and booming when Janey mounted, and his brows worked up and down alarmingly on his lean red-brown face; but Ma Sneeth was smiling comfortably over his shoulder, and Janey waved a mittened hand in farewell, almost undisturbed.

That November evening, the White House menagerie was augmented by the advent of Ripetta, an 'auburn' cow, as Janey described her, whose temper bore no likeness to her terrible sire's, but who placidly gave a bucket of yellow milk morning and evening, as if she enjoyed contributing to the health and happiness of the household.

They could talk of nothing else as they sat at the table that night, Susan sipping a cup of fresh yellow milk, and all of them savoring the cream Grandmother had poured over the tapioca pudding, which she had cooked to a velvet custard, as usual, in a small pail set in the tea-kettle, after an all-night soaking of the tapioca. 'Though the cream had hardly time to rise at all. But creamier than anything the red cow could do for us, at that.'

Janey must tell them over and over, precisely how Old Jed had looked, and precisely what Old Jed had said, and precisely what she had said, and precisely how ——

Haakon chuckled. 'She looked like a belligerent bantie chirping up at an old turkey gobbler,' he interrupted. 'Oh, of course much nicer than that. Old Jed thought she was a cute infant, I could see that much.'

'You could *see* that much?' Janey questioned. 'Infant!' she protested as an afterthought.

'Sure I could see. You certainly made me mad, Janey.

When I found you'd gone hypering off, to beard the lion in his den, I came flying after you. But I was too late. Mrs. Sneeth came to the door just as I galloped up within sight, and I knew everything would be all right with her there, so I put out for school. I've met up with Old Jed before, and Mrs. Jed, too. Janey, it does seem as if you have the lucky touch.'

'Speaking of luck,' said Grandmother, 'how comes it Mignonette was so well-behaved last night?'

'Why, land sakes!' marveled Susan. 'In all that ruckus, too. I'd have thought — You know they always say ——'

Janey studied Thad's face. Thad had attention only for his tapioca.

'Tapioca reminds me of fish-eyes,' he mumbled earnestly. 'Don't it remind you of fish-eyes, Janey? And that makes me think: my trout are getting to know me: honest, they are. I've got them in a little pool down by a bend in the river and I chop a hole in the ice and ——'

Janey leveled a commanding forefinger at him.

'Oh, hush about your fish and your fish-eyes!' she said, laughing. 'Thaddeus Grant, did you have that skunk at Colony Hall last night?'

'Well, goodness, maybe it was a good thing if I did have her along!' he protested squeakily. 'I guess she didn't do any hurt if she was in my pocket, did she?'

'Luck again!' commented Sandy.

'But not everything's lucky,' Haakon said reluctantly, as they drew back from the table and the girls set about the dishwashing. He pulled two letters from his pocket, and Janey cast them an apprehensive glance: letters had been such uncertain quantities of late. He opened out the large and legal-looking one, flattening it on his knee with a deliberate palm, as if unwilling to start the reading.

'Oh, *Haakon!*' begged Janey.

'There, Janey. Well, the short of it is, it's those lawyers writing again, and they've been in correspondence with the legal firm in Norway. And they feel they must have more proof than I've given them so far. It seems — well, there's a nigger in the woodpile: somebody's been writing them that I'm an imposter, and that the real heir was killed by the Indians when my mother died.'

'Mercy-*to*-us!'

'Land sakes!' gasped Susan.

'Why, whoever could think up a wicked lie like that, Haakon? They don't take any stock in such nonsense, those lawyers?'

'Well, of course they don't say. But I doubt if they'd be telling me about it, straight out, if they thought I was such a fraud as all that.'

'Lad, how do you reckon anyone 'ud have got the address of them lawyers?' puzzled Inch-Along, his basketry neglected on his knees.

'Of course,' Haakon answered meditatively, 'there were advertisements in the newspapers for Haakon Haakonsson, with the address the information was to be sent to. But it seems like an awfully long shot that any one who saw those should know me, and how I claimed to be the heir, *and* have anything so bad against me as to try to put a spoke in my wheel.'

'Oh, Haakon!' Janey sniffled, dabbing angrily at the tear on the tip of her nose — 'if only I hadn't lost that ring!'

'Fortunes of —— '

'If you say "Fortunes of war" again, Haakon, I'll throw this tureen at you.'

'Well, but that's just what it is, Janey. I was going to say, though, that I believe our next move is to rake up a reward, as you suggested yourself,' he went on cheerfully. 'It might even pay to sell one of the short-horns and ——'

'Oh, but, Haakon ——!' Janey couldn't go on. She dropped the dishtowel on the table and buried her face in it. Haakon looked from her to Grandmother and Susan with mystification large in his face.

'She — she already did offer thirty-five dollars,' Susan explained, her face puckered with sympathy, 'and it's been six weeks, and no ring.'

Haakon whistled.

'I got fifty that's doing nobody any good,' offered Sandy. 'Make it eighty-five, Hawk, and see if that don't draw 'em.' His words were for Haakon, but his eyes, timid and beseeching, were on Susan, and he colored richly at her approving glance.

'Thanks, old man, I don't know but I'll take you up.' Haakon was pushing the letters into his pocket, but Janey sat up as they rustled, and looked at him suspiciously.

'There were two letters!' she accused.

'Oh, this other!' he waved it with elaborate indifference. 'It's just a note from a fellow in Dartmouth.'

'Fellow in Dartmouth! Hm!' gulped Janey, mopping her eyes unseeingly with the dishtowel, which Grandmother took disapprovingly from her hand and dropped into the laundry bag. 'From Ralph Farnum, that's who. You might just as well read it now, Haakon Haakonsson.'

'Oh, well,' Haakon swished it open gayly, 'fortunes of — I mean, we have to take the bitter with the sweet; or, as one of our profs always says it, "the switter with the beet." Hm. He says he supposes I must have the settlement of my estate under way by this time, and since the second ninety-day period is far advanced, he wishes to notify me that he finds himself in need of all his moneys at this time, and cannot conveniently extend the note again, when it comes due.'

'Why, he offered!' Janey was round-eyed and incredulous.

'But not in writing. It's as Grandmother Grant warned me.' Haakon's gayety slipped for a moment.

'When's this second ninety days up, lad?'

'The second of January.'

'And this is the thirtieth of November. — Oh, Haakon!'

CHAPTER XIV

SPILT MILK

THAT whole evening was given to the writing of letters. Both lamps were set on the scrubbed table-top as soon as it was cleared; with Haakon's paper in the light of one lamp, Janey's in the light of the other, and the ink-bottle between them, their two pens moved so abstractedly that the stub in its bitten black holder sometimes clashed with the tiny gold Spencerian in its ivory.

Grandmother, because they had had a fat quarter of mutton, was busy dipping candles, while Susan strained tallow into a cracked bowl, for chest colds. Inch-Along whittled and pounded mysteriously in a corner with his back toward them. Thad sat on the floor, teaching Bute to beg for bits of crisped mutton fat, while Mignonette shifted uneasily about, trying to make herself comfortable in his inadequate boy lap. Sandy sat in a corner, his hands dangling between his knees, and watched Susan wistfully, scraping his feet awkwardly on the floor or looking hastily in the other direction, whenever she glanced his way. Intense quiet held the room as the pens scratched on, for the importance of these letters was heavy on them all.

Haakon was reminding Ralph of his agreement to extend the note indefinitely. When he had finished that letter, he wrote and asked his lawyers what they would suggest in the way of acceptable proof. Janey's letter was to Mrs. Jones, offering the increased reward, and urging her to do anything she could to stimulate the search.

Janey held the letters thoughtfully in her hand when they were done — three white envelopes with their green three-cent stamps. What would they do to solve the difficult problems of these lives, or tangle them still further?

'I'm getting to just hate letters,' she thought aloud. 'They've all been unlucky, lately, except just those from Lucerne.'

Yet, if the fear of sinister replies was a shadow over the family, the hope for favorable ones was a ray of light scattering the gloom, and it was hard to believe that life could treat them shabbily when in most regards it was treating them so well.

To be sure, Haakon's crop of alfalfa was almost exhausted; the snow was too deep for grazing; he was doubtful whether, in this time of depression, he could run a bill for feed. On the other hand, the herd was doing remarkably well: the long-horns were sleek and fit, for long-horns (you could stuff them for a year without fattening them, but they could weather months of near-starvation without dying); the nine short-horn bulls were in fine shape; there would be calves in early spring, to start Haakon's grade herd on which he counted so much. And in the meantime, this unprecedented snow was excellent for his winter wheat.

If Ralph would only behave decently until he had time to prove his identity!

If he could figure out some way to prove his identity before Ralph crashed down on him!

In spite of the severe weather, the whole family was well. The intense dryness of the air made the cold endurable, even when the thermometer slid to thirty below, as it did several times that winter. Susan hadn't 'caught cold,' the whole season, and Grandmother's rheumatism was definitely better. Janey felt her energy fed by an inexhaustible spring, and school went well, though with minor difficulties, of course.

As for Thad, he was beginning to grow at last, so fast that his body seemed bent on escaping from his clothing at every exit: neck, hands, and feet looked as if they were running away. He was doing reasonably well in school. Latin was a bore, but philosophy — learning how a pump worked, and the laws of gravitation — that was good stuff. But best of all, Mr. Bancroft was, like Haakon, intensely interested in stock, and his enthusiasm over fine horseflesh set Thad dreaming.

The young principal told him of a stallion that led a band of wild horses a few miles north and east of them. Mr. Bancroft had seen him thundering along the plain, mane and tail streaming like banners in the fresh wind, while his motley band of mares galloped after him. At once Thad began to project a campaign for the capture of the splendid creature. Life was filling with ardent realities, gilded by exciting dreams.

Mr. Bancroft came often to the White House, seeming to find keen enjoyment there. Inspecting Fidgets, he confirmed Thad's idea that she was a mare of quality, fallen on evil days. Thad began to think of her as the mother of sons who might start prize lines of their own. Even the White House family had ceased scoffing at Fidgets. With good care and Thad's assiduous currying and gentle exercising, she had grown satiny of coat. Her color was beautiful, a

chestnut with golden lights. When a warm day came and
Thad washed her mane and tail in soapsuds, they sparkled
golden in the sun, and he led her around to the front door to
exhibit her, his eyes moist with admiration.

Thad fed her with meticulous care, though that expen-
sive feeding had presented a problem. Surprisingly, Old
Jed Sneeth had offered the solution.

A week after her first terrifying visit, Janey stopped
there to report on the exemplary Ripetta and inquire, cautiously, for the health of Old Rip.

Ma Sneeth was sewing carpet rags, and Janey told her of
Thad's pretended fear lest Grandmother cut up his clothes
for rags when he was asleep. Old Jed, coming in and filling
the doorway from jamb to jamb and sill to lintel, roared
with laughter at that.

'And it's no joke, either,' he shouted. 'When the woman's a rug-fiend, you got to look sharp. Don't I know?
Ain't I had to hide my pants the minute they begun to git
comf'terble?'

Ma Sneeth cast him a plumply tolerant glance and smiled
at Janey.

'An' 'tain't 's if we needed 'em.' Old Jed flourished a
great hand toward the floor, whose vine-patterned Brussels
was so protected by rag rugs as to be almost invisible. 'But
she keeps 'em on the move. I tell her every rug starts in at
the front door and moves right on back to the kitchen stoop.
This here one'll go in place of that next-to-newest, and
they'll all move down one.'

'Like children in a spelling match,' suggested Janey.

'Ain't that the ticket, Ma? And the foot of the class is
when they go to be a curtain for the chicken-coop or the
cowshed.'

'Mr. Sneeth,' Janey said demurely, 'speaking of cows
reminds me of our Ripetta.'

'Ripetta?' he boomed.

'Yes, sir; she sent me to inquire for her father. — Old Rip,' she explained, when he continued uncomprehending. 'We do hope his leg hasn't given much trouble.'

'Ripetta! Ma, ain't that the dickens? Ripetta. Well, you jest tell her her pa's swearin' and carryin' on consider-'ble, like a man-body does. But you tell her he's going to come out pretty fair this time, only she better let on to the young folks round her place to lay off their gunfire next time he comes round, if they know what's good for them.'

Old Jed had drawn down his thickety brows terrifically, but Janey smiled, though her heart beat faster at his bluster. She had an idea that Ma Sneeth was something of a barometer; and Ma hadn't paused in her placid stitchery.

'The whole family wants to tell you what a sweet cow Ripetta is,' she went on, 'and what rich milk she's giving us.'

'We keep two of her sisters out here in the barn for what we need,' Ma Sneeth observed, her rocker squeaking comfortably as she worked. 'Only we may let 'em go. Pa ain't no hand to milk, and I don't just fancy it, these awful cold days. I ain't so young as I use' to be,' she said contentedly.

'What other stock you got?' Old Jed rumbled.

Janey smiled reminiscently. 'Well, you see it's Haakon that's got the stock farm. My brother Thad — he's sixteen — he's got great plans about stock, too, soon's he's old enough. But now we've just got my pony, Hiawatha, and Susan's Gitchee Gummee, and Thad's Fidgets, and Ripetta. And Grandmother's got a dozen Barred Rocks, so she can raise chickens in the spring. That's all — well, it's practically all.' She sighed. 'I do just hope the snow'll melt off, as everybody said it would. Feed's so awfully high, and Thad's set on having Fidgets fed up like a queen. He wants to show she's worth something, even if he did get her for twenty-five dollars.'

'I s'pose he's lazy, like all the other young folks of this day and age,' Old Jed snarled, as if he were in a fury at her and Thad and the generation.

'No, sir!' Janey flared. 'Thad hasn't a lazy bone in his body.'

'He wouldn't want to take on an extra job, though, and earn enough to pay for the extra feed he's squandering, I'll gamble on that!' sneered Old Jed.

To Janey's enormous surprise, Ma Sneeth looked up from her work with a pleased laugh.

'Why, Pa, that's exactly what I was thinking. Maybe the boy *would* like to milk Star and Reddy once a day! My, but it'd be a load off my shoulders.'

Both old people looked expectantly at Janey, and her indignation and amazement melted into laughter.

'Why, Thad would be tickled to death!' she gasped. 'He's been awfully worried about that fodder.'

Thad was 'tickled to death,' and the arrangement worked out comfortably. Janey often stopped in on her way from school and visited with Old Jed and Ma Sneeth while Thad did his chores.

There was one day, though, when the visit promised to be stormy, and brother and sister had another glimpse of the Old Jed whose name had been a terror in the countryside for twenty years.

Janey could hear him roaring when she rode up to the gate, and she hurried at once to the stable, for that was the source of the tumult: his bellow, and Thad's falsetto, squeaking out of its bass completely, and Ma Sneeth's soft ripple, quavering and anxious, and the shrill blat of — what under the sun! — of a sheep!

Janey quickened her steps to a run, and stood breathless in the doorway.

There was Reddy, switching her tail and regarding them over her shoulder. And Ma Sneeth, her checked apron thrown about her head bonnetwise, tugging ineffectually at Old Jed's upraised arm. And Thad, defiantly shielding Twist from the billet of wood in Old Jed's fist. The rest of the story was told by the overturned pail at Thad's feet, and Twist's gray wool face, frothy with rich Jersey milk.

"'Tain't but jest a mite of milk, Pa!' Ma Sneeth was quavering. 'We won't never miss it; we got pans and pans ——'

'Ain't I told you 'tain't the milk?' thundered Old Jed, wrenching his arm free and banging the wall with the billet. 'Ain't I told you a million times? It's the goldarned sheep! A blame' milky-faced mutton in Jed Sneeth's barn! Ain't I swore I never would have a sheep on the place? And now this blatherskitin' young numbskull of a boy ——'

It was fortunate that Janey's sense of the ridiculous was strong. As so often, her first quick rage was overcome by laughter.

'Did Twist follow you, Thaddie?' He nodded, scowling. 'Well, you skip along home with him and I'll stay and milk, this time.' He hesitated, but her backward toss of the head was so imperative that he obeyed, and sent Twist scampering before him.

Janey washed her hands, donned Ma Sneeth's checked apron, and milked the wondering Reddy, who shifted a little uneasily and then relaxed as Janey's cheek rested quietly against her smooth side, and Janey's soft humming accompanied the ping of the milk into the pail. When she carried it in, Old Jed stood staring out of the window.

'I'm sorry he offended you, Mr. Sneeth,' she said quietly.

She had begun calling him Grampa Sneeth, and he had liked it. He snorted, his mustache working up and down violently over his quid of chewing tobacco.

'Sandy McPhee brought him that sheep when it was nothing but a little lost lamb. Sandy's a cowman, too, and he hasn't any more use for sheep than you have, but he knew how crazy Thad is for animals.'

'Hmph.'

'And they'll all follow Thad if they get a chance.'

'Hmph.'

'You should see them. We call them his menagerie,' Janey meditated. 'That's what I meant when I said our three horses and the cow were practically all our stock. But Thad has a burro for a boarder, and ——'

'Boarder?' ejaculated Ma Sneeth.

Janey explained Spuds and Taters, and told them about Bute.

'And that's all, except Mignonette.'

'Who's Mignonette? A cat?' Ma Sneeth asked interestedly.

'No, it's the prettiest little skunk you ever laid eyes on.'

This brought Old Jed round from the window. 'Skunk?' he roared. '*Skunk?* Well, what a goldarned crazy young one! Skunk!' He went off into a shout of laughter.

'But you tell your brother,' he blustered as Janey slipped on her wraps, 'if he ever lets that sheep tag him onto my place again, I'll cut off its tail just back of its ears. Mind you tell him!'

CHAPTER XV

CHRISTMAS DAY

WHEN Janey came home from Old Jed's that day, she found Thad washing the cream from Twist, who resisted, with all four legs indignantly braced. Thad had been sputtering the story to Inch-Along, and he looked up at Janey woefully.

'Lost m' job for an ol' sheep!' he snorted, giving Twist an extra slosh of water.

'Well, I don't know if I want to milk his ol' cows, any-way,' he grumbled, his face brightening as Janey reported the outcome.

'You s'pose it's just been talk, all these years — how terrible Mr. Sneeth is?' Susan wondered.

'Maybe he's getting nicer as he grows older,' guessed Janey.

'Or maybe it's just our Janey that twists him round her finger,' Susan suggested.

'No,' said Grandmother, 'he's a human being, with streaks like bacon. Mean streaks, fine streaks, soft streaks.'

'I don't s'pose he'll show us so much of his soft streaks any more,' Thad regretted; 'and all on account of an old sheep.'

Thad was mistaken. A week before Christmas, Ma Sneeth stood at the gate waiting to hail Janey when she rode to school. Ma Sneeth's shawl was clutched nervously close, and her old face was eager.

'D'you s'pose your gramma'd mind that I hain't visited her first?' she asked tremulously. 'I ain't no hand to gad about. But me and Pa got our hearts set on having you all to our place for Christmas dinner.'

'All?' asked Janey. 'But, Mrs. Sneeth, we've already asked the young principal to eat with us that day.'

Ma Sneeth's face fell like a disappointed child's. 'Couldn't he come along with you?' she quavered. 'We'd admire to have him.'

'But that makes so dreadfully many!'

'How many does it figger up? Eight? Well, the more the merrier!' She glowed with satisfaction. 'Bring the puppy, too; and even — what's its name? — Mignonette. But not the sheep!'

So the day brought right good cheer. Old Jed beamed from the head of the table, where he whetted his carving-knife ferociously and hewed off great collops of delicious goose, and succulent slices from the infant porker that flanked it, apple in mouth.

The Sneeth dining-room carried memories of more settled habitations. It was solid with dark old walnut that had come out from the East years before, banging its way across the plains by ox-cart. Above the heads of the company a hanging lamp dripped glass prisms that sent rainbows of color dancing over the room.

Inch-Along had fashioned a willow workbasket for Ma

Sneeth, and the girls had lined it with a piece of silk from his old peddler's pack, with cunning pockets for needle-book and thread and the like. And for Old Jed they had made a marvelous box of candy, Janey having learned of his fondness for sweets — molasses candy, and a new kind they had just learned to make: chocolate caramel, it was called. The two were as pleased as children over their presents. 'It's plain as a pikestaff, lassie,' Inch-Along murmured: 'those two are lonesome folks.'

'Well,' Jed asked Haakon and Mr. Bancroft, as man to man, when the feast slowed up to an oversated toying with Ma Sneeth's plum pudding and hard sauce — 'Well, how do you young men feel about Union Colony and Coloraydo Territory? You like a lot of the rest of 'em, ready to pull up stakes and hyper back East because times are hard? I suppose that don't apply to you, Bancroft: you get your selery, whether or no.'

'And I have become wedded to the region,' the young principal informed him.

'I stay, too,' Haakon was prompt in answering. 'That is, I do if I can. I'll not get out unless I'm put out.' The hardening angle of his jaw spoke plainly of January 2, and the unpayable note.

'That's the boy,' Jed approved. 'What's a year or two of sink or swim to a young fellow like you? That's the way new country's opened. But what'd you expect from a lot of Eastern sissies? White-collar clerks and schoolmarms and the like! — Present company excepted! — Come out here expectin' to find the Garden of Eden!'

They were all laughing at his uncomplimentary references, Mr. Bancroft, though his smooth young face colored hotly, joining in good-humoredly.

'The land was certain to produce potatoes as long as a

man's arm, and wheat that headed up like an ear of corn, according to the papers in my home city,' he agreed. 'And no one would have to irrigate before July; and winter was mild as May.'

'And there wasn't any insect pests. Wow!' Old Jed pounded the table with the handle of his fork. 'They come out expectin' all that; and the first month they spent all their time pickin' cactus out of their feet; and their crops had burnt to a crisp before June was over; and the canals didn't pan out according to specifications; and then come the grasshoppers; and potato scale; and next such a freeze you couldn't break ground with a pick. I could 'a' told 'em this was cattle country and not farm land. But I do like folks with the guts to stick.'

'I heard tell a man just now sold forty acres three mile from town for a velvet dress,' Inch-Along threw in.

'True as gospel, and ain't it jest like 'em? Good ground, too: I know the place.'

'That town lot I showed you on Ninth Street, Haakons-son,' Mr. Bancroft said, 'is on sale for not much more. Has a four-room adobe house, and a start of willows and cotton-woods along the ditch. There's a piece of irrigated land two miles out that goes with it, too.'

'Haakon! That little house set 'way back, that I like so well?' Janey demanded. 'I can always picture how it would look after Ma and Grandmother had put in a flower garden, with pinks and phlox down the walk to the street. And syringa bushes and lilacs.'

'Laylocks! Kingdom come!' Ma Sneeth mused wistfully.

'Your pa and ma thinking of coming out here?' Old Jed asked.

'Pa'd love to. I think Ma would, too, once she got used to the idea.'

'What kind of man's your pa?'

'Oh, Pa's wonderful!' Janey glowed with pride. 'He's the kind that starts things. Planted the first shade trees. Built the first wooden dwelling-house. Started the first school. Started the first church.' She paused, eyes roguish, mouth twitching. 'Brought the first Merino sheep into the county!'

'Bah!' roared Old Jed, brandishing his fork at her, with a juicy bit of pudding impaled on it. 'Sheep! You little snippet!'

'Lovely sheep!' Janey stared raptly past his head as if she envisioned a whole flock just beyond his great shoulders. 'Fat and white and gentle!'

'Shut up!' Then, in a different tone: 'Now, me, I don't give a snap for town. But why don't you nab onto that lot, Miss Snippet, since the fool's going to give it up for next to nothing?'

'*Me?*'

'Why not? You got guts — excuse me,' as Ma Sneeth grimaced at him from the other end of the table. 'But she *has* got guts, Ma. And why shouldn't a girl be good for something, 'well as a boy?'

Janey's face was really rapt, now. She could see the adobe house so plainly, deep in a shady lawn, with the reds and blues and yellows of flowers painting a picture in front of it, and a roomy ell behind; and all the Grants ensconced there: her slender girl-mother, and Pa, with his dreamer's eyes, and precious little Lucy, with her restless fingers in everybody's pie. All these, with Grandmother, and Thad; yes, and poor old Ingrid.

'Why not?' Old Jed persisted.

'Pa, maybe she don't want to.'

'She does so! I can see it in her face.'

The rapt look faded. 'But of course I can't,' Janey deprecated, vexed with her own foolishness.

'Why not?' barked Old Jed. 'Money? — Quit it, Ma; you can't kick this far: no use to try. Is it money?'

Janey nodded.

'What you done with all them wages? Your fancy selery?'

Haakon stirred restively, and Janey flushed. But he was an old man, after all.

'You see, we didn't have much to start on,' she explained. 'What Pa has is tied up. And we've had to use the last cent.'

'How if I was to lend it to you?'

'Oh, but I know someone else — who needs the loan a lot more!' Janey plunged in eagerly.

Haakon shook a tight-lipped refusal at her, and Old Jed's gray brows curveted angrily. She stopped.

'I ain't offering it to nobody else. And to you only in straight business. Make me a note, your wages as security. Payable in two years, if you want. Or more. Six per cent. Take it or leave it.'

'May I have till tomorrow to decide?' Janey asked excitedly.

Grandmother had interposed no objection. She was abstractedly eating pudding, her eyes narrowed at the window.

'Legal holiday anyways,' he agreed. 'But you better take the Greeley fool up quick if you're taking.'

New Year's Day dawned with Janey the amazed young owner of a town lot, a quarter-section of land, and a debt of four hundred dollars.

The last days of the year had brought also two more of the dreaded letters. They were not of a sort to scatter the clouds of anxiety that hung over the Lazy Stool Ranch. Ralph, after his long delay, dictated an ominous reply to Haakon's query: 'We have no record of an agreement to extend your ten-thousand-dollar note. Have you?'

The lawyers wrote kindly enough, under the legal formality of phrase. They asked Haakon whether he had ever heard of a valuable document in the possession of the Haakonssons, or of jewels, and — more important — a miniature of the son and heir.

Haakon had not, and, rather hopelessly, he sent letters of inquiry to the Minneapolis people who had been in business with his father, and whose names Pa Grant had given him. Twelve years — nearly thirteen now — was a long time to carry memory of another's affairs.

'Are you awfully discouraged, Haakon?' Janey asked.

'I'd not be, a bit, if it wasn't for this miserable debt. How could I be such a double-dyed idiot as to accept anything from a fellow like Ralph Farnum?'

He sat slumped at the table, where he had been writing, and Janey thought suddenly that he didn't look very grown up, in spite of his broad shoulders and his six feet of strong body. She patted his big, straight-fingered brown hand awkwardly, and he smiled at her with an evident effort.

While she tried to think of something comforting to say, horses' hoofs pelted up to the gate, and Sandy threw open the door.

'Haakon,' he gasped, 'some of the critters have got 'way off to the hills — And I just heard the panthers are thick up there.'

CHAPTER XVI
CROOKED STICK AND REDWING

THAD rode into town at once, to tell Mr. Bancroft that Haakon could not be at his desk next morning, when school convened after the Christmas holidays, but would undoubtedly be back in time for the Monday session. Anxiously then they awaited the boys' return.

And Bute's. The puppy had vanished. 'Either a coyote's got him, or he's followed Haakon,' Thad worried.

There was plenty to do, watching the remainder of the herd in addition to their regular tasks, and time passed quickly. It was on Saturday afternoon that Inch-Along suddenly laid down his paint-brush — he was painting the bird-houses that had been his Christmas gifts to the White House — and opened the door. Hiawatha had whinnied loud response to a distant nicker.

'It's them,' he called back, shading his eyes to gaze along the road that led from the north. 'Well, I do wonder — Looks 's if Haakon's ridin' double. Can't get sight of Sandy yet. Round other side of the herd, I reckon.'

Haakon was indeed riding double: a small, hunched

figure, buckskin-clad, was perched behind him, the dog
Bute in its clasp. Haakon drew up at the gate.

'Why, it's Crooked Stick!' cried Janey.

'Tell you all about it when we've looked after the herd
and cleaned up.' Janey had run to the gate and was smiling
up into the pinched face, the great eyes, of the Indian boy.
'But—Janey, suppose you mount Hiawatha and ride round
where Sandy is. He may need help. Take Susan along.'
Grinning back at her mischievously, he rode away.

Mystified, the two girls saddled hastily, and circled to the
other side of the slowly moving herd.

'Sandy's got something on in front of him,' puzzled
Susan, as they gained on the horseman. 'A bear cub, you
reckon? 'Tisn't the right time of year, seems like.'

Sandy's face was vivid with a fresh flood of red when they
overtook him. Before him on the saddle, firmly circled by
his arm, rode another buckskin-swathed being. This one
was very small and very plump, and it turned round black
eyes upon them and then wriggled about to ram its little
head into Sandy's stomach.

'The land sakes!' ejaculated Susan, the reins going slack
in her hands.

'Sandy' — Janey made her voice grave — 'don't tell me
you've gone in for kidnaping!'

But Sandy was so strangled by his Adam's apple that she
took pity on him. 'Haakon said you needed help. Hand
him to me, Sandy, if you can pry him loose.'

Sandy disengaged the clinging blue fingers, and Janey
lifted the child to her own saddle.

'It ain't him,' Sandy divulged, as he rode on. 'It's her.'

The White House quivered with an electrical excitement.
Would the boys never come, to explain this mystery?

'Explainings can wait,' Grandmother commented, stripping off the baby's grime-stiffened layers of clothing with fingers that did not flinch. 'Put these duds outdoors, Janey. Fling 'em on the roof where the coyotes won't get 'em. Maybe they can be cleaned and mended.'

The little creature, blue with cold and gray with soil, was popped howling into a tub of tempered water and lathered till the soapsuds flew like spume from her wriggling, fighting body.

'Oh, baby!' coaxed Janey, kneeling on the floor beside her, 'if only you wouldn't yell so, you wouldn't get your eyes full of soap.'

The baby's only reply was to plant a slithering foot full in her face.

'Susan, you bring me some kerosene in a basin,' Grandmother said grimly, after she had inspected the little head. 'Janey, you see what you can find to put on her. And bring me the goose-grease or the tallow: she's got a touch of cold.'

When the boys came in, the house smelled strong of soap, kerosene, and cooking, and a general sudsy dampness still prevailed. Mignonette had retired gloomily to a corner, though Grandmother was sitting in the rocker. Moreover, Grandmother was rocking, a thing she seldom did: creak, cree-eak. And sniffling in her lap was the Indian baby, swathed in a curious clean garment with slit sides, which descended past her feet. Thad looked at it askance, for it was one of his nightshirts, doubled up as to sleeves and pinned over as to neck.

It had been easier to outfit Crooked Stick. He sidled in with the boys, scrubbed and grinning shyly, and the baby held out her arms to him.

'For Pete's sake,' Thad exploded, 'when're you going to tell us?'

Haakon told, and the household dropped its work to listen.

'I won't go into the cattle end of it now' — Haakon's amused eyes were on Bute, sniffing inquiringly around this familiar-unfamiliar Crooked Stick, with his strangely soapy odors — 'except to say that there were three good cows pulled down and half-eaten, and we put an end to one of the bloodthirsty panthers. Oh, yes, and Bute — the little pest! We'd got a couple of miles from home when we found him panting along behind us. Game little pup; but of course we had to carry him across the saddle, part of the way.

'Well, we'd worked up into a little draw in the nearest foothills, when we heard something crying.' He laughed explosively. 'Never shall forget Sandy's face. His mouth dropped open, and he looked as if he'd seen a ghost. What was it you said, Sandy?—"Danged if it don't sound like a baby!" And it did, but where the sound came from was a mystery. There wasn't a thing to be seen but a great spread of snow. Not so much as a footprint. The horses shied off from it, too. "Funny," Sandy said, staring at it sort of puzzled, "I thought there ought to be a deepish draw here, with a prospector's shack in it." And just then, blame' if this little pest of a Bute didn't flounder over to where something black was sticking out of the drift. He sniffed and whined, and then he begun barking and scratching like mad.'

He stopped and smiled reminiscently.

'Haakon, do hurry!' begged Janey.

'Susan, the potatoes!'

Susan turned hastily to the frying-pan and loosened the scorching potatoes.

'Well, the short of it was that the something black was a stovepipe.'

'A stovepipe?' snorted Thad.

'A stovepipe. And under the stovepipe was a roof. And under the roof was a prospector's shack, half-smashed in. And in the good part of the shack were Crooked Stick and this little Redwing here.'

'Mercy-*to*-us, how come such a thing?'

'It's not been so easy getting all the details, seeing I didn't know any Ute, and Crooked Stick not any English or Sioux. But near as I can make it, the baby got lost when they were in their winter camp, and a lot of them turned out to hunt her. Risky business for a child out alone in the forest in dead of winter, what with grizzlies and wolves and the cold. And the Indians do love their children, same as anybody else. Apparently this one's been quite a pet, even though she's an orphan: mother just lately died.'

'How'd he make you understand all that, Haakon?' Janey puzzled.

'Sign language. Plains Indians all use it, I guess. Well, I take it Crooked Stick was the one that found her, but it was night by that time, and he made a little shelter in the snow and holed up till morning. Then he found there'd been a fresh snowfall and his tracks were all covered. The rest doesn't take so much telling, if you've been in the mountains. Easy enough to follow the wrong canyon, even for an Indian. Finally he decided he'd be safest to strike down toward the plains, and he came to this shack in the draw toward night. He seems ashamed that he didn't see it was a dangerous place: but he was dead tired, and weak from insufficient food. One nice tidbit he'd found, that had helped keep them alive, was the stomach of a bear, with a good lot of chokecherry pits in it. He cracked the pits and they ate the kernels.

'Well, they'd hardly got into the shack when there came

a tremendous roar, and a snowslide swept down over them, completely burying shack and all, and crushing in the lower end of the roof. If it hadn't been that the pipe was long, to get some draft there on the side of the hill, and well-braced, too, they'd have died of suffocation right away.'

'I thought there was always a lot of stones and earth with a snowslide,' questioned Janey.

'Not always. This must have come in a great sheet of snow. The cabin was built in the shelter of a sheer rock wall at the head of the draw: perhaps that had something to do with it. But you remember those prospectors that were caught in their cabin in much the same way — they didn't get out alive, those fellows. I must say this was a lucky stovepipe.'

He waved a hand toward the children, Crooked Stick squatting on the floor, eyes hungrily drawn toward the stove, and the baby crouched confidingly between his knees, while Bute scrubbed one face after the other with a diligent tongue.

'We'll have to crowd a little to get us all at the table,' suggested Janey, as they dished up.

'Better let these chaps have it on the floor till they get used to things.' Haakon heaped a plate with food and put it on a newspaper spread on the floor before Crooked Stick, who had emptied it, with efficient help from Redwing, before the others had asked blessing.

'What with skunks and donkeys and Indian babies,' murmured Grandmother, watching the two attack another plateful.

'Oh, their folks'll be after these fellows,' Haakon said. 'Don't tell me how they'll find out, but they will, matter of a few weeks.'

So the Indian baby stayed on at the White House, and

Crooked Stick divided his time between the two places, sleeping in Ralph's deserted bunk.

The January thaw left the prairies patchy with snow and bare ground, and then the unusual winter set in again and held them in its icy grip throughout the whole of February. Grandmother and the girls sewed busily for Redwing, who looked like an Indian changeling in the red merino and white apron they made her.

Outside of school hours, Crooked Stick was Thad's constant attendant. Old Jed bellowed at him when he came with Thad at milking time, for the cattle-man had 'no use for Injuns.' Crooked Stick stayed stoically close to his friend. Old Jed had been teaching Thad the art of the lariat, and both boys practiced it in season and out of season, lassoing everything from a straying cow to Janey and Susan.

In the meantime, Haakon had received replies to his Minneapolis letters. Yes, they had understood that Mr. Haakonsson possessed a valuable document relating to grants of land in Scandinavia; but after his death no trace of it had been found in the safe where he had kept his business papers. They had also seen jewels, supposed to be of value; these, too, had disappeared.

Grandmother mechanically emptied Mignonette from her lap and put down her knitting.

'Reminds me of some of Ingrid's gab,' she answered Haakon's questioning glance.

'But what good would it do if we *could* find them?' Haakon asked, creasing the letter between his fingers. 'How would they know I was Haakon Haakonsson, just because I had those jewels and that document in my possession?'

'And how ever could you hope to get them?' Janey had been amusing herself by rolling up the baby's black hair on curl-papers. Now she left one side rolled and the other straight and meditated on the vanished treasure.

'Twould be far worse than seeking the needle in the haystack,' pondered Inch-Along.

Ralph's letter had not been reassuring, but it had given them a breathing spell. He would hold off another ninety days, but if the money was not then forthcoming — 'Well, my name will be mud,' Haakon said wryly. 'He promises to spread it all over Dartmouth, and send it to the papers out here, that I'm a common impostor and fraud. Besides attaching my salary and all my property, of course. And that's one promise I think I could trust him to keep.'

'I'm surprised he even extended it the ninety days,' Janey sputtered.

'Well, he has an eye to the main chance, all right, and I called his attention to the fact that he couldn't realize any ten thousand dollars as things stood now, and I'd just as lieve throw up my job and starve as have him get anything out of my salary.'

Nevertheless, Haakon's tension had relaxed for the present. He had managed to borrow money — from Mr. Obadiah, who was a public-spirited citizen, even if he did enjoy his jokes — to buy fodder; and his cattle were coming through the winter in good condition.

The Indian waifs were fitting into the household with surprising quickness. 'Into the zoo,' Grandmother said grimly, even while she was tenderly nursing Redwing through an attack of colic after the baby had found her precious little sackful of dried corn and consumed it at a sitting.

Janey rode past 'her house' every day, and was planning the garden that should be planted as soon as the frost was out of the ground. Ma Sneeth gave her a dozen packets of seeds that had been sent her from the East. Janey spread

them out on the table and read the penciled names aloud:
'Cockscomb, Canterbury bell, bleeding heart, foxglove,
hollyhock, dandelion.'

'Take my advice and don't plant the dandelion,' said
Grandmother. 'Pretty and showy; but how it spreads!'

One day Janey found stray cattle in her lot. She charged
in on them and sent them lumbering out, but not before
they had devoured the budding tops of all her willows and
cottonwoods. For this was early March.

Soon after, a thaw came in earnest. With a sigh of relief
Haakon turned his cattle out on the range, where they
grazed avidly on the winter-cured grama grass and other
prairie herbage.

One mild spring evening he and Janey rode around among
the herd.

'It'll work out just the way I want it to, if only I can hold
on to them. Look at those young ones! Aren't they going to
be a lot beefier than their mothers, though?'

'What are you — doing about it now, Haakon? Ralph's
note?' Janey asked hesitantly. 'I've been trying not to
pester you with questions, but — isn't it due again the first
of April?'

'Second of April. — Well, I've mostly been finding out
what I can't do,' he said dryly. 'I've been to all the so-
called moneyed men in the Colony. They can all give me
a lot of — sympathy. And that's all.'

Janey colored angrily. 'Why, the ——'

'Whoa, there, Janey-girl! They just haven't got the cash
to lend. Not even old Obadiah. That panic of 'seventy-
three — well, it's just swept over the country like a wave.
It's taken a year for the crest to reach the Great American
Desert. But it's got here now with a vengeance. There
just isn't any money to be had. Not in Denver, either, they
tell me.'

Janey's lips folded above her square little chin and she
thumped the saddle-horn with her fist. 'Then I think it's
time you put your silly pride in your pocket, Haakon
Haakonsson!' she scolded. 'You ought to be ashamed of
yourself, not going to Grampa Sneeth in the first place.
Why you should get such a notion — just because he's
a friend of ours. It's only a straight business proposition.'

Haakon frowned, and the telltale muscle squared the
angle of his jaw. 'Well — maybe you're right,' he said at
length. 'I'll stop in tomorrow on my way to school. — But
you needn't think you're going along, Janey Grant,' he
added hastily. 'I'm not going to have him lend it to me
because a girl asks him.'

So Janey and Thad rode reluctantly on, next morning,
leaving Haakon at Old Jed's gate. Until the roll of the
plains hid the Sneeth place from sight, Janey twisted in her
saddle to watch; and all the way to town she held Hiawatha
to a jog. Haakon did not overtake them until they were
approaching the schoolhouse.

'Why, Haakon!' she exclaimed, studying his somber face
incredulously when he came alongside. 'Why, Haakon!
If Grampa Sneeth wouldn't ——'

'Whoa again, you little Spitfire!' he counseled her. 'Old
Jed was mad as a wet hen because I hadn't come sooner.
Said I'd got my own pig-headedness to blame. He just
loaned out the last of his ready cash.'

Janey blinked furiously and sniffed. 'Haakon, what ever
will you *do?*' she quavered.

'Garsh! What'll ol' Ralph do, I guess it is!' Thad
rumbled pessimistically. 'Have the lawyers execute your
prope'ty, didn't Inch-Along say?'

Haakon laughed shortly. 'Get a judgment against me,
and an execution,' he explained to Janey. 'Take my herd

and holdings, of course, to satisfy the judgment. But I'll write the old boy once more. Tonight. He's got a mean, revengeful enough streak not to stop at anything when he's roused; but he may have cooled down some in all these months. And he's lazy as the dickens — hates to make an unnecessary move. That might help some. But most of all he's greedy and grasping, and he knows this is no kind of time for a forced sale. If I can just hold him off till summer —— Every other way, I don't see how things could be going prettier.'

But they did not long continue to move so smoothly. The next Saturday evening, Long Tom, the simpleton of the district, galloped up to the White House, his horse in a lather.

''S your brand the Lazy Stool?' he stuttered.

'Yes; what about it?'

'Coupla fellas ast me to tell you. Bunch of Lazy Stools makin' off toward the hills agin. One of them big bulls with 'em. And they's a big old grizzly killin' the critters up that way. Scarfoot, they says.'

'Thanks. What next?'

Posthaste, Haakon and Sandy checked up on their cattle. True enough, a bunch of cows and one of the short-horn bulls were missing. With scant farewells to the White House, the boys set out in pursuit.

CHAPTER XVII

THE STAMPEDE

THE next afternoon, Thad came pelting into the house, his face exultant.

'Gramma! Janey! Won't Haakon be hopping, though! It was all a mistake about its being his cows. The whole bunch — the short-horn, too — are down the river a piece, as safe as anything!'

'Down the river a piece?'

'Yep! Looks just as if they'd trapped themselves there in a place where the river makes a loop and somebody's had a fence across. I can't figure out how they did it. It's right near where I made a pool for my trout. When I went down to feed them, just now, there were all those cows, grazing away as contented as you please.'

'We'd better go and tell Inch-Along,' Janey said.

The old man sat his horse and scanned the sky concernedly as Thad shouted the news to him.

'Well, the —— ——!' he muttered. 'And if I'm not mistaken, there's a dish of weather brewing, too. Now, do you suppose ——?'

'*Bad* weather?' Janey protested. 'Oh, Inch-Along! Why, I never saw such a gorgeous day.'

Inch-Along shook his head. 'A sight too gorgeous for the first of April. Hot! I've seen it like this before, in Colo-raydo. There's going to be some kind of a change, and in a hurry, too. Take note how uneasy the critters are. — Tell ye whut, Janey: I'll take out after the boys, so they won't waste a lot of time scourin' the mountins for whut ain't there. You and Crooked Stick,' he told Thad, 'you start herdin' the critters back toward the place. We don't want 'em workin' up toward the hills in earnest. I'll ride back and get me some grub, 'case I'm delayed any way.'

He was off in an hour, bundling up in an extra coat, to Janey's amusement. Before she rejoined the boys, she had ceased her scoffing. The air held a strange quality that sent the nerves tense. Even the cattle seemed to sense it: they were less tractable than usual as the young people rode slowly around them, turning them by degrees toward the home base.

'S'pose they smell Inch-Along's storm?' Janey asked Thad, watching them mill restlessly, their great horns shining in the fitful rays of the setting sun, already dimmed by clouds.

'I guess so,' he worried. 'I never did see them act this way.'

So slow was their uneven progress that darkness found them still a mile from the corral.

'I'll stop in at home and tell them how we're getting along,' Janey said, 'and then I'll bring you boys each a sandwich.'

'Aw, one isn't any good!' Thad objected. 'Bring five or ——'

If the rest of the sentence was spoken, it did not reach Janey's ears. From the starless sky, in which the clouds had thickened unnoticed, came a blinding flash, followed by a ripping, tearing crash of thunder that jerked Hiawatha to one side and left him quivering.

'Steady, boy!' Janey soothed him, her own voice shaking with the shock of the sudden detonation. 'My *land*, who ever heard of ——?'

Ominously the thunder rolled and rumbled, the lightning flickering like the waving of a curtain before a lighted window. It glinted from the wildly rolling eyes and tossing horns of the herd, bunched together in tense terror.

Then the rain descended in a drenching downpour, stopping as suddenly as it had begun, and leaving the air aching with stillness.

Not for long! Again without warning, a series of explosions split the black stillness.

In a flash the panic-stricken herd had wheeled northwest, away from the new terror.

Janey was almost unseated by Hiawatha's sidewise leap. She could see Thad for a moment, eddying through the tide of dark backs and tossing horns. Hiawatha wove this way and that, and she crouched low over the horn of her side-saddle, one hand twined in his mane. Her heart beat to suffocation as the strong wet cattle odor surged stiflingly upon her. She could see the maddened beasts rearing in air and flinging themselves across the bodies of their neighbors in their frantic haste. Once she felt her legs almost crushed by the pressure of a crowding body; and then the mass gave way and Hiawatha scrambled aside. Mighty horns grazed the horse's flank; grazed Janey's knees.

But suddenly she was out on the edge of it, and the tide was sweeping past her.

She drew a sobbing breath and vainly tried to pierce the darkness for sight of Thad, of Crooked Stick.

'Come on, Hiawatha!' she coaxed, patting his heaving neck, 'we've got to head them back.'

As well try to head back the ocean. Hiawatha galloped along the left edge of the thundering mass, but he could not overtake the van. On and on and on through the night, gaining steadily, wondering whether the boys were on one flank, trying like her, to head them back. What use? Even the three, their forces massed, could not turn the stampede until the terrified beasts had run their course.

Yet she rode on and on, scarcely conscious of her chilling wet body, scarcely conscious of the keen feel of snow in the air, until Hiawatha plunged a hoof into a prairie-dog hole and stumbled. Janey felt herself hurtling through the air, and lay dazed.

The herd had passed when at length she pulled herself to a sitting position. A few slow cows still lumbered past her, tails high in air. A few calves followed, stiff-legged and forlorn. A moist muzzle nudged her face. Hiawatha had recovered himself and dashed on, only to come back for his mistress.

Janey grasped his mane with numb fingers and pulled herself to her feet. Stiff as she was, and aching almost unbearably from the force of the fall, she was certain she had broken no bones. She felt for the saddle, and found it slipped forward and to the side. The girth had burst. There was nothing to do but start homeward afoot, and without delay. The temperature had shot downward in a freak cold wave.

As she turned, clinging to the bridle, she peered again into the darkness that had swallowed up the mass of animals. This time she made out a pale bulk. As it drew nearer, it sharpened into the form of the buckskin mare, with Thad astride her.

'Janey?' he gasped. 'Garsh, I was scaret you might be ——'

'Where's Crooked Stick?' she asked.

'Coming. Janey, what can we do now?'

'Ride over and ask Old Jed.'

'That's the ticket.' Thad's voice was husky with relief, as he swung from his mount and worked with anxious fingers in the darkness.

'Don't wait to fix that, Thad!' Janey implored. 'I can walk along beside him, just as I was starting to.'

'No.' Thad's voice was decisive, and he fumbled on, stopping to feel through his pockets for various aids to reconstruction, while the Indian boy cantered up and sat silently waiting. 'This is going to be a regular snowstorm, Janey. Inch-Along wasn't far off. But did you know thunder and lightning — and snow — could be all in one night, Janey?'

'Grandma Sneeth told about a storm like this,' Janey shivered, hugging herself and blowing a wet snowflake from her nose. 'Mr. Bancroft said it was something about sudden change of temperature and pressure areas,' she added vaguely.

Thad's fingers, eager to be quick, fumbled and twitched in the blind darkness, and his breath came noisily. But at last he had rigged up the girth so that it would hold.

'Only ride him easy!' he adjured Janey; and she held Hiawatha to an unwilling walk while the boys galloped ahead of her into the darkness.

Before she reached home, the great soft flakes of snow were plopping on her neck, down her back, faster and faster. She could barely make out the pale squares of light from the windows, through the obscuring white, and the larger oblong when the door was held open.

She called reassurance to that open door, and went on to the shed to put Hiawatha in shelter and rub him down before she herself sought the welcome warmth and light.

She had scarcely explained the catastrophe when Thad and Crooked Stick came in. Thad's face was working.

'Aw ——!' He rubbed his nose violently with the back of a mittened hand. 'I thought Old Jed had guts, like he's always saying. Say, he won't stir a step in this storm tonight! He says it wouldn't do a lick of good, and where's the use killin' three middlin' men and three good horses.'

'Likely Mr. Sneeth is right.' Grandmother was stroking Mignonette: long, heavy strokes.

'But — what's Hawk going to say?' Thad's voice shook, and he twisted Bute's ears so hard as to wring a protesting yelp from the dog.

'And where do you suppose Hawk *is?* And Inch-Along — and Sandy?' Susan quavered.

'They're all right,' Janey averred stoutly. 'They all know how to take care of themselves. I don't feel a bit worried about anything but the cattle. Not a bit.'

Nevertheless, the night was a long one, filled with troubled dreams. Monday dawned on a bleak world, with the sun making no attempt to pierce the curtains of cloud and snow. Thad's face was woe-begone as he pumped water for Ripetta and Hiawatha and Fidgets and the burros, and fed them and the chickens.

'I don't have to go to school, do I, Gramma?' he pleaded.

'I'll feel safer about Janey if you do.'

'Aw ——'

It was not very hard riding to school, along the well-known ways, where the soft snow had melted almost as fast as it fell. But all day that soft wet fall continued, and Janey's heart was heavy and her thoughts continually strayed from her children and their finger plays and I-see-a-dogs.

Did the herd still thunder northward? No, it must have slowed down long before this, with the calves among its number. Had Haakon and Sandy won shelter in the hills? Had Inch-Along's outdoor craft proved sufficient for his need?

And then her thoughts would settle down heavily on the outcome of it all for Haakon. The loss of land and stock would be hard, but Haakon, young as he was, could start over again and make a success of life, even if he could never prove his right to the estate. No, the serious element was the disgrace, the stain on his reputation. He would not wish to stay in Union Colony, and Janey realized, with surprise at the strength of her own feeling, that this was the place where they all wanted to cast their lot. She could not imagine leaving this sparkling air, this glory of mountain and plain, this something that made her feel more eager and alive than she had ever felt before — this something that made living an adventure and made adventures come to pass.

The storm was slackening when she and Thad stopped at Old Jed's place after school. Old Jed rode on home with her, leaving Thad to do his chores. The stockman was of the opinion that they could start out after the cattle bright and early next morning.

'But it ain't going to be no cinch to come up with them, Janey.'

'I thought maybe they'd be starting back home of themselves,' she said, looking up in some surprise at the gloom of his manner. 'This storm hasn't been so bad they couldn't weather it; and soon as they get over their scare ——'

'They might come home if they was let.'

Janey drew in a startled breath. 'You mean ——?'

'Well, girl, use your wits. Didn't you say yourself it sounded like a gunshot, the noise that stampeded 'em?'

'Well, but I supposed it was somebody shooting rabbits, or coyotes ——'

'That stampede wasn't no accident, Janey. Nor either was the half-wit's report about the strayed critters. *His* mistake, mebbe, but somebuddy's cute trick.'

'You mean ——?' Janey repeated helplessly.

'I mean rustlers.'

The boys and Inch-Along rode in before Old Jed started home. Though they were tired, and Inch-Along gray with exhaustion, it was evident that they had suffered no ill effects from their night and day of blizzard.

'Get the herd corraled all right?' was Haakon's first query.

'Oh — Haakon!' Janey's voice broke on the bad news. 'They're all gone.'

'All *gone?*'

'Stampeded.'

Haakon stared blankly from Inch-Along to Sandy. 'Looks like dirty work,' he grunted. 'But they needn't think they can get away with anything like that. We'll get something to eat and fresh mounts, and be after them tonight.'

'The snow's covered their tracks,' Janey reminded him.

'But the rustlers will be heading for Wyoming, eh, Sneeth?'

Old Jed nodded assent.

'We can strike north till we pick up the trail. Like enough the storm was only local.'

'I'll go in place of Inch-Along, here,' Old Jed offered. 'He's about spent, and I'm fair snortin' to go. Sure you don't want to wait till morning, though?'

Haakon shook his head.

The girls hastened the supper; the three wayfarers ate standing, and were off on the fresh mounts Thad and Crooked Stick had ready for them: Fidgets and Gitchee and Hiawatha.

'Thad, you go see Ma Sneeth, will you? And tell my men to look after things sharp!' Old Jed bellowed back to the little crowd at the gate.

'Janey, you and Susan see what you can do about school,' Haakon called.

'Garsh!' mourned Thad, 'I wish I could 'a' gone. Didn't they look like Deadwood Dick, Janey? Pistols 'n' ever'-thing.'

'Nobody can get away with five hundred head of cattle,' Janey protested. 'And all the calves branded plain, too. Can they, Inch-Along?'

'They've got twenty-four hours' start,' Inch-Along answered. 'And it's the very dickens what they can do with brands.'

'How do you mean?' asked Grandmother, her glance sharp over the steel rims.

'It don't take but a coupla strokes to change a Lazy Stool into sump'n you couldn't prove ever had been one,' he explained soberly.

CHAPTER XVIII

THE PURSUIT

THAT week dragged interminably in the White House. It was especially long for Susan, whom Mr. Bancroft had engaged as Haakon's substitute. The girl drove herself to the task with gritted teeth, fearing and disliking it. Nor did it go very well.

'Janey,' she grieved, 'I can see plain as plain I never was cut out for a schoolmarm. Only reason I went to Normal was to be along with you, I guess. And those big boys — they just pester the life out of me, asking me questions I can't answer. Even when I know 'em plain as A B C, they go scattering back into the edges of my mind and I can't find 'em till an hour later.'

She heaved a great sigh of relief when Thad, keeping a sharp eye out for the adventurers the next Saturday, threw up his cap with a yelp of delight.

'They're coming! Here's Hawk and Sandy!'

'And the cattle?' Janey dropped a flatiron on the stove with a bang and rushed to the door.

'I don't see any cattle. — Aw, they're comin' from their own place, Janey: they've likely corraled 'em.'

The two riders came splattering along the slushy road and waved a greeting. Janey searched their faces as they picketed their horses where the melting snow had uncovered the prairie grass. Haakon's was perfectly impassive, nor could she read Sandy's.

'Are you both all right?' she demanded.

'Yep. Fit as a fiddle. Fit as two fiddles.'

'And Old Jed?'

'Yep. Went on home.'

'Well, Haakon — the cattle?' Janey and Thad were both fidgeting, and Haakon smiled his slow smile at their impatience.

'Give us a bite to eat and let us stretch our legs, and we'll talk an arm off of you. But don't you feel too bad, Janey: it's the fortunes of war,' he drawled.

Janey gritted her teeth. She would not ask another question. Surely things must have come out right, or Haakon wouldn't —— Yet you could never tell about Haakon. She'd seen him as calm when everything had gone dead wrong.

'Grandmother! Susan!' she said, lifting her eyebrows in superior fashion, 'these little boys can't talk till they've been fed. Don't let's annoy them with questions. After all, what's a few hundred head of cattle? And, besides, they do just love to play the game the same way every time. They don't care for variety.'

The 'little boys' came up grinning from the wash-basin, and ate ravenously of the cold food set before them. Then Haakon made a telescope of his hands and leveled it at Redwing, in her merino and muslin.

'And who may this little person be? It's Lucy, the way

she was four years ago, only dipped in a brown dyepot instead of a blue one. Come here, Tootsie!'

'Haakon Haakonsson!' Janey shook her curls at him and stamped in the old way. 'Enough's as good as a feast.'

'So 'tis, so 'tis,' he drawled, lifting the Indian mite on his foot and trotting her: '"Nim, nim, nim, nim, this is the way the ladies go!"'

'Hawk!' snorted Thad, waiting at his feet.

'Oh, well!— "Gallop, gallop, gallop, gallop! that's the way the soldiers go!"' He gave the baby a wild ride that sent her into spasms of laughter, and deposited her in Susan's lap. 'Well, if you're all quite ready to listen properly, we'll begin at the beginning.

'We had some pretty stiff going for a while, with the snow so thick you couldn't make out your hand before your face. But the storm was local, and in an hour we'd worked through it and out into the open. We didn't pick up the trail: didn't look for such good luck as that. But Old Jed knows this country like a book, which was lucky for me, and he and Sandy agreed we'd better strike out for a little place on the road to Cheyenne. Two reasons: we'd not be losing any time, and besides that Jed had some friends at a — well, at a kind of tavern up there, and they'd let us have a change of horses. Really three reasons, there was; the town is a hangout for all sorts of queer birds, and Jed thought we might be able to learn something if we snooped around real careful.

'Well, we ran into plenty. Gambling going full tilt, and the stage just in, with this fellow Slade driving, and ugly with drink.'

'Garsh, the Slade we read about?' Thad's eyes were round with envy.

'The same. Well, with things the way they were, it

didn't seem healthy to ask many questions, but we arranged with Sneeth's friend to let us have three fresh mounts and leave our horses there until we could pick them up. We thought we'd kept a close mouth, all of us, and we didn't know anybody'd caught on to our business; but it seemed we weren't so smart after all. For up swaggers a little fellow ——'

'Queerest turned fellow,' Sandy threw in, 'so Sneeth says.'

'I didn't see him, and Sandy didn't, either; but Sneeth went into the bar, thinking there might be someone there who could give us a tip. And this little fellow steps up to him large as life, chaps and spurs and six-shooter and all, and says, "I understand you're off after rustlers. Want another fighting man along? My name's Pete the Kid, at your service." And Sneeth, he said, well, thanks, he presumed Haakonsson'd be glad to have another man, and did he have his horse handy, because we were making a quick getaway? And Sneeth said he halfway noticed that this Pete's chin dropped when he took him up so quick, but he didn't have his mind on it. But Pete peered in through the door to where Sandy and I were standing, and then he ups and out through the other door, saying he'd get his horse and meet us.'

'And he never showed up, the little cuss!' said Sandy.

'Pete the Kid!' Thad rolled the name under his tongue.

'Pete — Pete the Kid?' Janey inquired of herself.

But Haakon was going on with the story.

'Well, we rode all night and all the next day, and came into Cheyenne late in the afternoon. We stabled the horses and gave them a good rub-down. They certainly needed the rest.'

'Kind of felt the need of it ourself,' drawled Sandy.

'But we couldn't take it, yet awhile. We did sort of take turns, though: one of us stretched out in the hotel room we engaged, while the other two were making the rounds of likely places, to see if we could get wind of anything.'

'What kind of places?' Grandmother asked.

'Not such nice places, Grandmother Grant. Cheyenne's a Sabbath School compared to what it was ten years ago; but you take it at night even now ——! Music blaring out of a dozen places; and kerosene lamps glaring and smoking; and the reek of corn whiskey and beer so strong it'd knock you over; and dice clicking and cards shuffling; and — well, almost everything you can imagine. One place where we stopped, a fellow swaggered up to the bar and had some words with the bar-tender, and then quick as a flash he pulled his six-shooter and began shooting the lights out.'

The girls and Thad listened with awe, and Grandmother folded disapproving lips as she knitted.

'Well, along about midnight ——'

'When we couldn't walk straight ourself,' chuckled Sandy, 'on account of we hadn't had a night's sleep since Sattiday, and this was Tuesday,' he explained hastily at Grandmother's frozen incredulity.

'Along about midnight,' Haakon repeated reprovingly, 'we had the luck to run into a man Sandy knew — Soap-suds Sanders. Sanders is a gambler; and a sleight-of-hand performer ——'

'He c'd make you believe he'd grabbed the sun out of the sky and had it hid in his vest pocket,' Sandy exclaimed. 'So to speak,' he added, with a hasty glance toward Grandmother.

'Well, this Sanders, he really did know something — overheard some fellows that were past watching their words. He pointed them out to us, and we sat down at the next table and ordered ham and eggs and listened to them whooping her up. Pretty soon two of 'em got into an argument.

'One of them kept insisting that safe and sure was his motter, and everything done decent and in order. They had time to make things shipshape — change the brands, he evidently meant — before the Greeley tenderfeet could come up with 'em, and then the aforesaid tenderfeet could go to a warmer country, for what else could they do about it?'

The room was breathlessly silent, except that Thad twisted Bute's ears too tight again, and the puppy yelped his protest.

'And the other fellow — he wasn't carrying his liquor any too well — he said they needn't go to all that trouble. They'd push on to Laramie and sell the whole bunch to a fella who didn't give a rap about brands — you understand there was a lot of language in their talk: swearwords peppered in at every breath — and who'd tend to them himself if he wanted them tended to. Then the first one said what if the Greeley saints caught up with 'em before they got to Laramie? And the second one says they weren't likely to; probably were still up in the hills hunting their short-horn bull and the old grizzly killer. And if they did, he said, what the dickens would it matter? Didn't they have seven men and plenty of hardware? But the first fellow says, yes, and all the other four so far gone they couldn't hit a barn door.

'Then the second one says, grave as a parson, well, they'd go out and let the other four have a good night's sleep, and they'd ride herd themselves that night, because weren't the three of them a match for any dozen Greeley hymn-singers? So they pushed back their chairs and got up, solemn as you please, stepping all over their own feet, and they threw down a couple of silver dollars in front of the bar-keep and staggered out.'

Haakon took a deep draft of the milk Janey had set at his elbow.

'Well, you can bet we watched the direction they rode. Easy enough, for they went shooting and yipping out of town. And then we made a dash for the barn where we'd left the horses, and had 'em saddled and were off before you could say Jack Robinson.

'It was the brightest moonlight I ever saw, and we galloped ahead full speed for a ways, and then, luckily, we could follow along in the shadows of the cottonwoods on the river. And by jinks if we didn't almost run over the four cow punchers that the others had relieved. They'd tumbled off their mounts as soon as their friends came out from town, and there they were asleep on the ground. Well, then, I tell you we had to do some fast work.'

'It was Haakon worked fast,' Sandy exclaimed, his bashfulness overcome by the memory. 'Whillikins! First off, he had us lead their four horses back a ways and tie them, down in a hollow we'd passed, where the shadows were thick. Then he rode off, real cautious, to get the lay of the land, and dang if he didn't find those three idjits at the bottle again. Anyway, he seen one of 'em, plain against a light patch of sky, and he was jest tippin' back his fool head to take a long swig. And the others was croonin' to keep the critters quiet, and hiccuppin' at every other word. And there were the critters, a few of 'em layin' down chewin' their cuds peaceful, but the most of 'em uneasy, millin' around kind of wild-eyed and res'less with the calves huddled in the middle. You know, ma'am, once a herd gets nervy like that, it's awful hard to git 'em ca'med down.

'So Hawk comes back an' tells us whut's whut, and we decide it's as likely a chancet as we kin look fer. So ——'

'So Sandy does his little stunt,' Haakon took it up again. 'We three work round to the north and east of the herd, and all of a sudden Sandy lets out the wildest yapping, like a dozen coyotes. And right on top of that he comes at 'em with a panther scream. And Sneeth and I, we blaze away into the air with our six-shooters.

'Gosh! That scary herd, all edgewise anyway, why, it fairly jumped out of its skin. It was stampeding south before you could wink an eye.'

'And the rustlers?' croaked Thad, his eyes wild.

'I'd of give a pretty to really see them!' Sandy chortled. 'But we didn't have time to stop.'

'I'll bet the four that were asleep went staggering around for an hour trying to find their horses,' said Haakon. 'The other three were so taken off guard that they didn't get into action at all till the stampede was well under way. Then there was some pretty lively shooting.'

'Shooting? At you?' Janey gasped.

Haakon chuckled and reached under the bench where he had dropped his hat. 'They didn't have a show, really, with the liquor inside them, and the cattle surging round them, and us all scrooched down on our horses. This was the nearest they came.' He held out the hat, neatly drilled through at the top of the crown.

'Well, I forgot to say we'd tipped off the town marshal at Cheyenne,' Haakon went on, while the hat passed from hand to hand. 'He was waiting for us with a bunch of deputies. So we headed the herd toward the edge of town, and the law did its bit as neat as you please. Nobody killed; but one of the rustlers had his horse shot out from under him, poor beast; and they were all three taken.'

'And then what?' demanded Thad.

'Well, of course there was no stopping the herd yet. So Sneeth and Sandy went on to keep them headed home, and I stopped long enough for formalities. Folks came streaming out of the saloons, and it looked for a while as if they were going to let Judge Lynch deal with those rustlers — string 'em up to the nearest pole. But they got 'em safely in jail, the sheriff and his deputies did, and then sneaked out to bring in the other four, I guess. Soon's they'd taken my deposition, I came on after Sandy and Sneeth.' He yawned mightily.

'And the cattle are really safe in your own corral?'

'All except' — Haakon's mouth twisted in another prodigious contortion — 'a few. Some calves lost, poor little fellows. The short-horns are all there, anyway.' And he sat staring at them owlishly, rounding his eyes with an effort.

'Mercy-*to*-us!' Grandmother rose and emptied Mignonette from her lap. 'You go home to bed. Thad and Crooked Stick'll look after the stock in the morning. I don't know but you better sleep than go to church!'

'I'll bet we'd sleep if we did go to church, so maybe we might as well do as you say.'

'But what do you make of that Pete the Kid and his acting so queer?' Janey pondered a half-hour later, as they sat down to their own supper. 'Pete the Kid. Pete.'

CHAPTER XIX

'MORE BEESKIT!'

THAD and Crooked Stick, going over to look after the stock, that Sunday morning, had shoved the shack door open and looked in.

'Place was cold as a barn,' said Thad, 'and we went in, real careful, and made up the fire in the stove. Sandy threw a shoe at me,' he chuckled. 'Maybe he thought I was a rustler. But Hawk, he just pulled one eye open far enough to see, and stared at me like I was a stranger. After a while he said, "Um! Thad!" and let the eye go shut again.'

'They'll be sharp set by dinner-time,' said Grandmother. 'Put a few more potatoes in the stew, Susan. And brew a cup of wild sage tea. It can't hurt 'em.'

'Sandy,' Haakon inquired, when dinner had been served and eaten, 'is there anything like being dead for sleep and sleeping, and empty from top to toes and filling up with food like this? I answer, No! Unless it is seeing your herd stampeding north, and stampeding it south again. Only it's April, and my note's overdue, so it's a little like making merry on the lid of a volcano, after all. Oh, well, it's the fortunes — ouch!'

Janey, moving painfully about to clear the table, had paused long enough to prick him with her collar-pin.

'Well, for that, Janey Grant,' he said severely, 'I've a good mind not to tell you who it was we passed, as we were hypering home with the herd. Not so far out of Greeley, either, but it wasn't convenient to stop just then. I was surprised, for it's early for them to be making their trek; but you couldn't fool me about Weenonah, not a mile away you couldn't.'

'Honestly? Weenonah?' Janey asked eagerly.

'Weenonah and Two-Toes and their band.'

They were all looking thoughtfully at Crooked Stick. He wore an outgrown suit of Thad's, and his hair had been thoroughly combed for church, so that its comic feather stood more noticeably erect than ever.

'Cowlicks aren't so very uncommon,' Janey said slowly. 'And I suppose lots of Indians have those big black eyes, like his and Weenonah's. I don't think it means a thing, myself ——'

'Well, *I* do.' For once, Susan spoke in flat contradiction of Janey's opinion. 'I've got a feeling in my bones.'

'I'd like for Weenonah to see the boy, myself.' Grandmother measured him consideringly.

'What worries me,' said Haakon, 'is that there are buffalo coming up from the south. Small herd, of course; but nowadays the Indians are on the lookout for the smallest. I'm afraid Colorow will be down from the hills and take the boy away before Weenonah has a chance to see him.'

'You don't figger the Sioux would cotton to him?' Sandy was incredulous. 'Poor little twisted fellow like that?'

'Smart's a whip, though,' said Grandmother.

'And nice in his ways.'

'I — well, I'm just fond of Crooked Stick,' Janey summed it up. 'And he's so folksy.'

The Indian boy, able to catch only a few intelligible words besides his name, was nevertheless aware of being the center of attention. After he had hidden his shyness by playing with Redwing for a time, he turned an anxious face on Haakon, and his hands flickered in swift signs.

'He wants to know if anything has been learned about his people,' Haakon explained, and his own hands flickered in answer.

'I told him we were wondering whether Colorow would be coming soon; and that we felt him a friend and a brother. — Best not bring in Weenonah at all.'

The dark face had closed up at repetition of Colorow's name, and not only Haakon, but the others also, comprehended the flash of his arms across his flat chest, the tap of the forefinger upon it, and the slow shake of his head.

'Either he doesn't love Colorow, or Colorow doesn't love him,' Janey said.

'Likely it works both ways,' said Grandmother; and she handed him the piece of pie that was left in the tin.

With their minds focused on the Indians, none of them were surprised by the news the afternoon brought them. A lumber wagon stopped at the gate, and the ponderous body of Skinny, the prospector, let itself down over the wheel. The wagon drove off, and he squeezed in at the narrow gate.

'Well, Bub,' he asked Thad, who came to the door, 'Spuds gettin' along all right? Gettin' along all right?'

Thad nodded, and held the door wider, to let him in.

'No, thank ye. Help me hitch up my little jenny if you want, and I'll be getting along. I'll be getting along. Got that young skunk yet, Bub?'

'Just a minute, Mr. — Mr. Skinny.' Thad scooped Mignonette out of Grandmother's lap, where she lay contentedly under the open Bible, and ran into the room he shared with Inch-Along, to scoop something out of his Indian pouch with his other hand.

Skinny's huge bulk shook with laughter at sight of Mignonette, her black-and-white coat sleekly handsome.

'Bub, you're the beatenest! — Whut's this? Whut's this?' And he peered down inquiringly at the wad of paper Thad had pressed upon him.

'I didn't have to use the nuggets. I got a job,' Thad explained, thrusting Mignonette inside his buttoned-up coat and going around to the shed, where the cart was stored. 'They're grazin' somewheres around.'

Skinny made a trumpet of his hands and wheezed out a 'Spuds! Hyah, Spuds!' of surprising volume. Presently, over a little rise of ground, the burro came trotting, the small one running at her heels.

Skinny watched their approach fondly, and Janey, who had followed them, felt something pathetic in the expression on the old face; something still more pathetic when the burro nudged him with her nose, and then, in her joy of welcome, braced her legs and loosed an ear-splitting song: 'Eee-haw! Eee-haw! E-haw, e-haw, e-haw!' The prospector's eyes were ludicrously soft, and when he caught Janey's look upon him, he cleared his throat noisily and laughed his gusty laugh.

'Joke on an old feller, ain't it, Miss? This little jenny's all the folks I got — all the folks I got.'

He fed Spuds a sugar lump and a bunch of alfalfa that he

produced from voluminous pockets, and smote her mightily with the flat of his hand.

'An Injun boy!' he ejaculated, when Crooked Stick emerged from nowhere and helped Thad hitch the burro to the queer old cart. 'Where've I saw that Injun boy before? Don't pertend to know the run of 'em, one from t'other. But this here one, with his great big eyes and his humpy little back — well, if he ain't the spit of Colorow's brat, Colorow's brat. Dern Colorow's hide, I met a prospector that seen him hyperin' out this way this very day. Buff'lo in the vicin'ty. Well, I hope he gits his buff'lo and puts out fer some'rs else, some'rs else.'

He climbed ponderously into the cart, waved a pudgy hand at Thad and the White House, and set out for Greeley, while Taters was forcibly restrained in the shed, with a cooky for consolation.

Janey played 'This is the church and this is the steeple,' with Redwing's little brown hands, tiny and delicately formed and now grown astonishingly clean at the nails. Susan brushed her shining black hair and tied her muslin apron bows perkily on her shoulders. And everyone had an extra kind word and smile for Crooked Stick, whose mournful eyes continually turned toward the window that gave toward the town.

But Sunday passed, and Colorow had not appeared.

'Maybe Skinny got it wrong — about Colorow,' Haakon said at breakfast. 'You know, if the old reprobate hasn't showed up when I get home from school, I've got a mind to ride along up the road a piece and see if I can't hurry Weenonah. Likely they've camped somewhere.'

When he and Janey reached home that night — Thad stopping reluctantly at Old Jed's — they were greeted as usual by Crooked Stick and Redwing.

'Then I'm off,' Haakon declared, flicking the reins at Minnehaha and galloping away.

He was scarcely out of sight to the north when a group of horses appeared from the west. Astride one of them was a rider too obese to mistake, especially when Colorow's stovepipe hat could be distinguished, and his gay shirt, vermilion on this occasion.

Inch-Along hobbled in at Janey's call. 'Look at the little lad!' he scolded. 'It don't seem right to hand him over when he feels like that. But I s'pose you can't keep a pa from taking his son.'

Crooked Stick stood silent against the wall, his face closed as it so often was, and the look of hopeless passivity that a trapped animal might show, eloquent in every line of his tense body. Redwing stared wonderingly from one to another, and took Susan's face between her hands in a rare caress, and frowned questioningly into the girl's tear-filled eyes.

'I — I wisht Sandy was here!' Susan quavered. 'S'pose he won't be coming for an hour and a half at the best. Oh, Janey, maybe they'll go past.'

They did not go past. They had evidently been informed as to the whereabouts of the children, for they drew up at the gate, and Colorow sat his horse for a minute, staring fatly at the little white shack, before he slid to the ground, shoved the door open unceremoniously, and waddled in.

His contemptuous glance made a circuit of the room, dismissed the withered old Inch-Along, curled a lip at the statue-still Crooked Stick, and measured the girls and Grandmother. Grandmother's gaze met his coldly, levelly, over her spectacles, and Janey felt a thrill of comfort when he gave back a step. His eyes shifted away uneasily, and he snarled a guttural command at Crooked Stick. The Indian

boy started forward, and Redwing, curled unnoticed in
Grandmother's lap, whimpered. He looked at her questioningly, drew down a scornful mouth at her clean finery, and
crooked an arrogant finger. The baby caught her breath in
a frightened sob.

At the sound, Janey felt her temporary paralysis give
way. She darted to the shelf and held out to Colorow the
well-filled sugar-bowl.

'For you!' she offered eagerly, while Grandmother and
Susan and Inch-Along watched wonderingly, and the two
bucks who had accompanied the chief pressed into the room.

Janey poured the precious sugar into a sack Colorow
formed of his vermilion shirt tail, and nodded at the others
behind him.

'More!' she promised them (over her shoulder, frantically,
'Make up the fire, somebody. Quick!'), and opened the
sugar crock, dishing it out recklessly into a green shirt tail
and a yellow one.

Susan had flown to do Janey's uncomprehended bidding.
Colorow barked another order at Crooked Stick, but again
Janey made him pause.

'Biscuit?' she asked, dragging her face into lines of
enthusiastic hospitality. 'Big biscuits? Me make! Sit
down.' And she motioned to herself, to the stove, to themselves, to the floor, nodding vigorously.

Colorow knew the word well, and his face relaxed with
oily satisfaction. 'Beeskit!' he grunted, acquiescent. 'Heap
quick!' He and the young bucks settled themselves on the
floor where they stood.

Janey made that batch of biscuit in record time, her
hands shaking and her mouth paper-dry. Sifting the flour
and soda and salt together with a vigor that sent the white
spray out onto Colorow's dirty plug hat; measuring the lard

and cutting it through in a vicious hurry; slopping the sour milk in recklessly; mixing with an arm so tense that it ached; rolling and cutting and testing the oven and sliding in one tin — two — of the smooth white rounds. 'Whatever will they be like?' she wondered with a little gasp.

The Indians had watched approvingly, nothing moving but their eyes, except now and then when the younger ones laughed at her flying hands, or at the shower of white on Colorow's hat. They sat patiently watching the oven door, while Janey set out a dish of butter and a jug of molasses, and plates, on the scrubbed table. Everyone was silent, and Janey, stealing a glance at the silver watch, which she had tucked out of their sight behind the flour barrel, found that a half-hour had passed. She climbed over the Indians to the door, to look anxiously along the road to the north. There was no one in sight. The Indians stirred restively, and Colorow, growling, put out a grimy hand and tugged at her skirt, nodding imperatively toward the stove.

Breathlessly Janey stooped, her full skirts flouncing out around her, and opened the oven door. What if she hadn't put everything in? What would Colorow do if the biscuits were flat and bad-tasting? If they were yellow and strong with saleratus? She'd heard so many stories of his cruel whims.

She slid the top tin out, and Colorow's unctuous chuckle judged it for her as soon as her own eyes and nose. Such puffy browned circles!

'Not bad, Janey!' Grandmother commented coolly.

Janey slid them onto the plates and took out the other tin. The Indians squatted awkwardly on the benches and went to work.

Never have biscuits disappeared more rapidly. Janey

stifled an impulse to laugh at Susan's expression: she was gazing with such wide amazed eyes at their unwelcome guests. A biscuit at a mouthful was Colorow's portion, and these were not of a dainty tea-size: they were cut with a tumbler top. His method was to dip the biscuit in the butter and then into the wide-mouthed molasses jug, and bear it, lusciously dripping, to a mouth stretched wide to receive it, while beads of molasses trickled unheeded down the vermilion shirt. As he saw the plates emptying, he reached out a sticky paw and dragged them both in front of him, growling a warning at the younger men through a crammed mouth.

Still the window gave no welcome tidings. Still the fat silver watch had ticked out only another ten minutes. Janey folded her hands in an attempt at calm, and pulled at her fingers till the joints cracked. Then she flew at the flour-barrel again; at the basket-sieve.

'Please light the lamp, Susan. I'm going to bake another batch.'

'Mercy-*to*-us!'

By the time Colorow had sooped up the last dripping mouthful and drawn his cuff across his sleekly shining face, Janey could nod and motion toward the oven, where two more tinfuls were puffing roundly. This time she did not wait, but started another batch as soon as the second was baking.

'I've had to use vinegar with the sweet milk for these,' she murmured tensely. 'All the sour milk is gone, and I've scraped the bottom of the flour barrel. If Haakon doesn't get back soon, they'll just take Crooked Stick and Redwing and go. — Where's Susan?'

'She's lit out after Sandy. Afraid he might be waiting for Haakon.' The only way Grandmother betrayed the least excitement was by the slow creak-creak of her usually motionless and silent rocking-chair.

Colorow and the others finished the second batch without slackening their pace. Janey refilled the plates, and emptied the molasses keg into the jug, quivering with impatience at its slow stream. Still they ate, while she strained her ears for sounds outside. Utter silence!

The two younger men pushed back from the table. Colorow sighed vastly and folded his hands over his great stomach; turned heavily and growled again at Crooked Stick.

'More beeskit!' urged Janey, almost hysterically jocund. Colorow hesitated, unwrapped the blanket from about his waist, poured into it the remaining plateful and knotted it loosely, paused in tossing it over his shoulder, and scowled toward the door. Steps sounded on the walk, hinges creaked, and in thrust Haakon's fair head.

'Did you — did you get Weenonah?' cried Janey.

He motioned backward with his head.

'Coming. But it doesn't look so good for Crooked Stick. — Janey, they'd already found their lost son.'

CHAPTER XX

THE FEATHER OF HAIR

WEENONAH had already found her lost son.

The words burst Janey's bubble-dreams for poor Crooked Stick. Susan, coming in the back door with Sandy, stood poised, her face blank with disappointment. Grandmother's rocker went cree-eak.

The Sioux pressed into the house, Weenonah with hands outstretched to Janey in eager welcome. Dear Weenonah! If only the little Indian boy might have been hers! Kind, that face; self-controlled and sweet-natured and generous.

Thad, pelting in at the door a moment later, found the house so full that the walls seemed to bulge. The two young Utes hunched themselves on the bench, too sated to stir, Colorow majestically sleepy beside them. Grandmother rocked, stiffly erect, Redwing in her lap clutching at her with both hands. Crooked Stick stood pressed against the wall behind her, as far as possible from the Utes. Susan was fussing around the stove, with Sandy drooping his great height protectively near her, his eyes elaborately on nobody at all. Inch-Along whittled steadily, for once letting the

shavings fall where they would. Janey crouched beside
Weenonah on the floor, the Indian woman's hand gently
patting hers, but the Indian woman's eyes pondering on
Crooked Stick. Two-Toes had taken his place on the bench,
opposite Colorow, and beside him sat a handsome Indian
boy of some sixteen years, his black eyes roving boldly over
room and occupants.

Thad slipped inside breathlessly, Bute pressing after
him, and Twist's woolly head nudging the door open again
as it swung shut.

'Shoo!' Grandmother clapped her hands smartly.
'There's too many varmints in here already.'

'The air's thick enough to cut with a knife,' observed
Inch-Along, 'but it's an ill wind that blows nobody good.'
He motioned wisely toward Colorow, whose head nodded
till it fell on his chest, jerked up while he blinked dull eyes,
nodded again. 'He won't be in a hurry to go.'

'Janey,' Susan spoke softly, 'want me to make some of
that new chocolate candy? Seems like we haven't got anything to offer *them*.' She nodded toward Weenonah and
the other Sioux.

'Do, Sukey!' Janey approved. 'And, Haakon, tell us
about the — the son.'

'Well, of course, they've always been hunting for him,
and there are few that don't know it. And it seems it wasn't
but a few days ago that some Utes — yeah, Utes, but
Douglass's band, not Colorow's — brought this fellow and
said they'd had him since he was a yearling. He looks like
a Sioux, all right; and he's the right age; he's got that high
nose like Two-Toes', besides — though that's common
enough among his tribe.'

'You mean — him?' Janey looked with distaste at the
strange youth.

'Yes. Fine-built fellow, isn't he?'

Janey nodded reluctantly. 'How did they happen to come so early this year?'

Haakon addressed Weenonah, and she replied in fluent Sioux.

'She says,' Haakon interpreted, 'it was on account of the old medicine-man, her grandfather. You know, that awfully old one that frightened Lucy so, years ago. What was it she called him?'

'Why, the Monkey Man!' Janey recalled.

'The very same. Harka is his Sioux name. It was on his account,' Haakon repeated. 'You know he's as old as the hills. This winter, Weenonah says, he almost slipped from them, time and time again, at those periods when life ebbs low in the earth and all its children. But in the moments when the flame flared up in his old body, he set his heart on coming to one of their springs of healing, here in the Old Red Land — Hue Hue Tlappallan. He thinks if they will set up his tipi beside it, so that he can bathe morning and evening and drink hourly of its life-giving waters, his days may be renewed. So Weenonah and Two-Toes promised to start as soon as spring should set in; and from the day the first robin sang, he has given them no peace.'

'But where is he?'

'He will come in tomorrow, with the rest of their band. They halted long in camp, for his sake.'

Colorow dozed, his fat face shining with perspiration. Weenonah was intent on Haakon and Janey by turns, as if she could hear through her eyes, and she smiled and nodded and stroked Janey's responsive hand. But Two-Toes sat moody, his gaze on the table. And the new son continued to inspect room and people, until suddenly his regard fixed itself on the wall beside him, and he smiled and frowned and tilted his head. Janey laughed aloud, seeing that he had discovered a fragment of mirror tacked against a two-by-four.

Again Weenonah spoke, hesitantly, anxiously, with a sidewise jerk of the head at the strange lad. Haakon listened with downcast eyes.

'She says, Is he not a fine upstanding lad, that one?'

Two-Toes added his word.

'He says, He rides and shoots with the bravest and best.'

Thad broke in indignantly, as if his friend were belittled by this praise of the other. 'Well, I guess Crooked Stick's as brave as anybody. You know what he did when we found a few buffaloes off here on the prairie a ways? Well, we made it up that the first one that lassoed a young bull, why, the other one'd have to ride him. And we did. I got him first, and Crooked Stick rode him — garsh, he stuck like a bur! Maybe you think that don't take grit when you're little as him.'

Haakon snorted with appreciative laughter, and interpreted quickly to the Sioux. Weenonah regarded Crooked Stick with a glance that was almost tender, but Two-Toes, after a searching gaze, shook his head stubbornly, and motioned toward the other boy.

'He says, That one has been called among the Utes, the Magpie; he does not know why. But he will call him Chaska, the first-born son. He is a fit chief's son.'

The Magpie, though it was evident he knew little Sioux, had ceased to preen and grimace in the mirror, and caught proudly at the few familiar words and the intonation of praise.

'But he has no cowlick!' Janey protested.

Haakon spoke to Weenonah and Two-Toes, unconsciously stroking down his own fair plume. Two-Toes answered loudly, gruffly.

'He says, He does not remember the feather of hair Weenonah talks so much of.'

Two-Toes glanced at Crooked Stick and turned his eyes away, almost angrily, but Weenonah's gaze rested wistfully on that comic disorder of black locks, on the wide and patient eyes beneath, on the frail shoulders. She spoke, her voice rising into pathos at the end.

'She says, The Magpie's head is smooth as a beaver's pelt. She says, Her heart does not open and flow out to him as she thought it would.'

The Magpie had risen. He was strutting as best he could in the close-packed room. He was taking the center of the stage. Susan looked up from cutting a great platter of brown candy, and pulled down her lips at Janey as he grunted and posed.

He drew the bow. He lashed an imaginary horse. He flexed his strong right arm. He measured his proud height. Colorow had wakened enough to stare up at him from bleared eyes, and the lad was transparent in his wish to impress this chief of his adoptive people. He broke out in a flood of talk, interspersed with the sign language of the plains.

The effect of his words was striking. Weenonah drooped beneath them, and Two-Toes sat straighter, lifting his chin and fixing this new son with a keen eye.

'Haakon, what was he saying?' Janey begged softly, in the stillness that followed.

Haakon spoke, stiff-lipped, his scornful eyes not leaving the Magpie. 'He says, What will the Chief Two-Toes, my father, pay for such a son as I? How many swift ponies will he give me for leaving these my friends the Utes?'

For a moment the tableau held. Then Two-Toes spoke, quietly, with decisive dignity not to be appealed.

'He says — Gosh, but this is good! — He says, Chief Two-Toes would pay all his ponies, the fleetest and the strongest, for his son. But it is no son of his, no son of Weenonah's, who will come to the arms of parents lost from babyhood with cold thoughts of payment in his heart!'

While the Magpie's plumage drooped, and he stared, uncertain, Two-Toes spoke again, incisively. Haakon struck his hands together.

'He says, Chief Two-Toes will gladly pay the Magpie two of the finest of his ponies and a buckskin suit, well embroidered with quills and beads — these will he pay him — to go back to his friends the Utes and have no more traffic with Two-Toes and Weenonah!'

Silence, followed by a babble of sound. The Magpie spoke with jerking head and a semblance of scornful satisfaction. Colorow spoke. Weenonah cried out uncontrollably, in a crooning voice, and Haakon answered her. Both were looking at Crooked Stick, and Two-Toes turned his eyes full on the boy at last. He spoke, and the boy answered.

All the others sat and stood about the stuffy little room like the audience at a drama. Now and again Haakon interpreted, mechanically.

'He says — Colorow — He will trade the Sioux his worthless offscouring of a Crooked Stick for this strapping Magpie.'

'Two-Toes says, He wants no dog of a Ute for his son.'

Colorow felt for his gun, his thick lip curled in a snarl, but thought better of it, and spoke, head jerking toward the cowering child, hands flying in the sign language.

'He says — Gosh! — He says, Crooked Stick is no Ute. That the Utes have no offspring so ill-favored. He is a Sioux, picked up by the wayside where his parents had flung him away.'

Weenonah's eyes widened, glowed. Two-Toes pondered, chin in hand, studying the boy, whose timorous gaze met his. He spoke, and Weenonah pulled her blanket across her face and rocked to and fro as Colorow snarled his answer.

'He says, You mean it, you will trade? And Colorow says, How much you give to boot, for your fine bargain?'

Again Two-Toes spoke, impassively.

'He says, I give two ponies, as I said, and count the bargain a good one — for me.'

Janey cried out softly, 'Redwing, Haakon! Ask if he won't let Redwing go, too!'

Haakon complied, with sign language and a word or two of Ute, but Colorow shook his head, though he looked contemptuously at the cowering baby.

'Tell him she's only a bother, and cries much at night.'

Colorow pondered the information. Then his pudgy fore-finger shot out toward Janey. Haakon laughed reassuringly as she shrank away.

'He doesn't mean you, Janey; he means your necklace. But you don't have to let it go.'

Looking at Redwing's shining black head and tiny clutching hands, Janey could scarcely pull the twisted gold chain from her neck quickly enough. The Ute took off his hat and dragged the bauble over his head, thrusting out a thick lower lip as he admired the display on his vermilion breast. Then, with a negligent wave, he gave over the baby.

Grandmother studied him coldly. 'He mean we're to keep her?'

'Grandmother, she won't really be much trouble,' Janey urged anxiously.

'Mis' Grant, I'd — I'd like to bring her up myself,' begged Susan.

'I don't doubt Weenonah'd take her, for that matter,' said Haakon.

'He mean we're to keep her? For good?' Grandmother's scornful voice brushed aside the irrelevant remarks.

'Yes, he does, Grandmother Grant.'

'Mercy-*to*-us, I'd 'a' liked to see him try to get her away!' Grandmother smoothed the shining black hair severely. 'The oily old heathen,' she added.

There was little more of the ceremony. With mock courtesy twisting his gross body like a sneer, Colorow waddled across the room, took the hand of Crooked Stick in a grasp that tightened till the boy paled with pain, waddled back with him, and placed his hand in that of Two-Toes. Two-Toes led him to Weenonah and presented him gravely, with the one word, 'Chaska!' which was to say, 'Our first-born son.' Then he took the hand of the Magpie with a courtesy as grave, and laid it in the palm of the Ute chief.

The three Utes and the new son of the chief had started to file out when Colorow turned, remembering.

'Candee!' he demanded.

Susan, giggling weakly, pried up a part of the still soft brown candy, emptied it into a bit of newspaper, and handed it to the chief. He and his followers padded out the gate to their horses.

'Leave that door open,' Grandmother ordered. 'A window, too, Susan.'

They all gulped in the fresh air and looked at each other happily.

Crooked Stick — Chaska — sat quietly beside Weenonah on the floor. His thin little face was expressionless, but his body had relaxed from its tensity.

'Do you suppose — really —?' Janey worried. 'What's a cowlick to base relationship on?'

'And what does it matter?' Grandmother asked wisely.

'That's a true word, Mis' Grant.' Inch-Along had whittled his stick to nothing and offered no word before. 'A fine lad, if I'm any judge; and fine folks; and needing each other — happiness all round. What's the odds if they ain't blood kin?'

As they all munched the remaining caramel appreciatively, Haakon turned to Grandmother.

'I'll take them over to my place, Grandmother Grant.'

'They've eaten? Well, we'll have breakfast at the usual time.'

'Have your special pancakes, Grandmother Grant?'

'Thad'll have to ride over to Sneeth's and borrow flour and molasses.'

It was time to start for school next morning when the rest of Weenonah's band drew up to the White House. How well Janey remembered the other times she had seen them, in Wisconsin and in Minnesota: dapper young braves and stalwart old Indians, riding arrow-straight; shapeless squaws each with a child before her on the horse's back and a baby's head bobbing at her shoulders; horses drawing the characteristic travoises, like buggy thills dragging on the ground and with miscellaneous bundles strapped midway — tipi covers, camp equipment, young puppies, babies; and before and behind and underfoot, the skulking, fighting, yelping Indian dogs.

One travois supported a litter with a basketwork canopy. In it reclined the Monkey Man — Harka.

Four years earlier, when the band stopped at the Grants' Wisconsin farmhouse, Janey thought no living being could look older than the Monkey Man. Now she saw her mistake. Shrunken like a dried apple, the skin pleated to his fleshless bones in deep dry furrows, the eyes peering dim and small from cavernous sockets, the body withered to the semblance of a mummy, today he seemed nothing human.

He peered at Janey, mumbled something that Weenonah and Haakon interpreted as a request that she come closer; peered again, tremulously intent. Then his lips drew back from his toothless gums in an eerie smile.

Janey smiled back, shivering. 'Would he — would he like some sugar?' she asked Haakon.

'Sure thing. But didn't you use it all?'

'I hid part,' she confessed, and running back to the house, she brought him some in a little cloth bag. He dipped in his fingers and sucked with the avid pleasure of a child. Then he pointed a skeleton hand toward the mountains and spoke to Weenonah in a high, cracked whisper.

'He says, They must hasten to the spring of healing,' Haakon interpreted.

Inch-Along had been thoughtful at breakfast. Now he spoke, turning to Grandmother, who stood in the doorway with Redwing clinging to her skirt.

'Ma'am, would it put you out any if I was to join up with these chaps? Just for the present? I know this spring he talks of, even if it is so awfully secret. And I surely do hanker after a spell of the water, myself. Getting along in years, Inch-Along is.'

'Wouldn't sulphur and molasses do just as good?' asked Grandmother reluctantly. 'Well, of course ——'

The upshot of it was that Inch-Along rode away with the Sioux, and the White House, thrown wide again to rid it of the reek of Colorow and his men, seemed empty indeed.

CHAPTER XXI

THE MONKEY MAN

It was the most beautiful of April evenings. The prairie
was wakening: a faint tinge of green could be seen through
the brown. That morning Janey had heard the liquid gurgle
and trill of a meadow-lark, the first song-bird she had heard
on their claim. 'Meadow-larks follow the fence-posts,' said
Grandmother.

An exquisite fragrance of wild flowers lay about them,
and Janey and Susan, seeking its source, found starry white
blossoms nestled close to the ground in rosettes of slender
leaves. One of 'Janey's children' had brought her wild
anemones that day, gallant flowers, their lavender cups
thick-furred with silvery down, like baby garments. And
Janey had found spring beauties and purple filaree on her
own town lot that noon.

'My own town lot! — Redwing, don't twist Mignonette's
ears: it's Bute that likes his ears twisted. — Isn't it strange
how things work out?

'Now, me: I supposed of course I'd live all my days in
Wisconsin: Fall Rapids seemed big enough for anybody.

And then everything changed and our road led to Lucerne. And now it's led to Colorado Territory, where we certainly never dreamed of coming.

'And there's Haakon's road — and yours, Sukey. And this little mite's, and Crooked Stick's — I mean Chaska's. — Oh, Sukey, will you mind Redwing awhile? I'm coming down with a poem.'

Susan insisted on her reading it aloud at the breakfast-table next morning.

'It's awfully rough,' protested Janey, smoothing back her curls with both hands and then pulling the notebook out from under her on the bench. 'Really, I don't believe I ought to read it to anyone till after I've polished it up. There's one rhyme especially that ——'

'Aw, let's have the pome, Janey,' Thad blurted with brotherly resignation. 'I don't see why you always have to say that first — about its being rough.'

'Well, you and Redwing and Bute and Mignonette might as well run out and play,' his sister retorted bitingly. 'I naturally couldn't expect any of you to care for poetry.

'I think I'll call this "Winding Roads," maybe.' She cleared her throat self-consciously and read:

> So many roads beneath the shining stars,
> Beneath the silver rain, the golden sun;
> Uphill and downhill wearily they wend,
> With questing feet upon them, every one.
> By wood and stream, by sea and boundless plain,
> So many, many winding roads to roam.
> Who knows? Mayhap they'll all untwist again,
> Those tangled trails, and lead us safely home.

'You know,' she explained hastily, pressing the page down with nervous fingers, 'as I was telling Susan, it's the way we've gone here and there, when we didn't expect to, that made me think of this. Especially Chaska. How if we hadn't been here, if our trail hadn't led just the way it did, he'd have had to go on and on, instead of coming safely home. And really, all of us, Haakon, I guess, and Sandy, and Redwing here ——'

'And Bute and Mignonette and Taters,' Thad said seriously. 'It isn't so bad; not for a pome, Janey. And there isn't so much of that "where'er" and "yon" stuff in it. Only one place — what was it?' He craned over her shoulder and reached down a stubby finger to trace the penciled lines. '"Mayhap." That's it. You don't ever hear folks saying "mayhap" and "where'er." Why do you put them in pomes?'

'If you didn't,' Janey dismissed the question firmly, 'how would you know it was poetry? Besides, if I'd used "maybe," the meter wouldn't have come right.'

'It's perfectly wonderful, Janey!' Susan cried indignantly.

'I — like it,' Sandy said. 'About the trails leading — home.'

Haakon didn't say anything, but he smiled at Janey as if he were proud of her writing; and his face was gentle. Doubtless he was thinking of the twists and turns and darkness of his own road, and that its happy end was quite, quite hidden.

For his problem was no nearer solution. In the midst of all the excitement of rustlers and Indians and sons lost and found, Haakon had received another missive from Ralph. It was distinctly not a nice letter. It warned him that the ninety-day period was past, and enclosed copies of the letters he had ready to send to the college paper, the *Rock County Herald*, the *Fall Rapids Comet*, and the *Greeley Tribune*: letters that exposed to the full the false pretenses, the broken promises, the defalcations, the general unreliability, of one Haakon Haakonsson. He also gave Haakon final notice that he had put the matter in the hands of 'my attorneys,' and after generously allowing him thirty days' grace, he would let the law take its course, leaving Haakon a broken and discredited young man.

It seemed a contrary twist of the road that brought an answer to one of Grandmother's letters two days after Weenonah and her band had gone their way.

Dear Mother [it ran], I've been slow about replying to your question. But you know how Ingrid is. First off, we made the mistake of asking her a direct question: Pa was so anxious to know, he plumped it out at her, and the poor old thing fell to trembling and whimpering so we couldn't get a word out of her till we'd let the matter rest for a few days.

But I finally did get news. Real news, too; but how it will be of any use after all these years I don't see.

You know Ingrid wears one of these black rubber rings the boys make by burning the middle out of a coat button. I led off from that to rings in general, and then I said how pretty it would be to have a ring with a red set like the buttons on Lucy's merino. You know she loves to brag about her family, and how much more they had than we have. Well, just as I hoped, she began to stammer out in a great hurry that *her* lady had rings with sets, and even sets that they didn't bother to put in rings — just for looking at and dropping between her long white fingers. She said there were some like red currants, but bigger, and some green like gooseberries, and yellow ones.

After she'd talked awhile, meandering on while I basted up a dress, I asked her, sort of careless, where they kept such valuable things — laughing a little as if I thought she was making it up about their being so costly. And she flared up and said the master kept them in a big iron box with keys he always carried; and when he didn't have them in the box, her lady wore them around her neck under her dress, they were that precious — 'in a little bag, like, made of soft leather.' She went on, pretty indignant with me for doubting, and said her lady wore the bag on a golden chain, and she knew because she always fastened the chain herself. Why, she said, she fastened it that last day! And then she fell to weeping and shivering again, poor creature, so that I was almost ashamed to have put her in the way of such a remembrance of dread and fear. Yet I thought it was worth what it cost, perhaps, to have definite news for Haakon. Only who would know, after thirteen years, what happened to the bag the poor lady wore round her neck on the fatal day?

'Yes, who would?' Janey echoed, when the letter had been read aloud in the breathless silence.

Haakon sat chin in hand, brows bent. 'Who would?' he asked slowly. 'Likely no one. Yet if there's one who knows always what goes on among her people, it is Weenonah. We must ask Weenonah.'

'Why in tunket couldn't this have come two days sooner?' fumed Susan.

'I've had to be away from school so many times, I grudge to ask leave again,' Haakon pondered. 'Yet, with Ralph getting so nasty, I need any news there is, and right quick, too.'

'Too bad Inch-Along isn't here.'

'But, Haakon, Thad can look after things a couple of days — it won't hurt so bad for him to miss a little — and with you home nights ——' Susan's voice was eager. 'Sandy's the one to go! Sandy'd go, wouldn't you, Sandy?'

Janey was startled by the expression of perfect confidence that Susan turned upon the young cattle-man. As for Sandy, he opened his mouth and closed it, while the brick red welled up to his roan red thatch; and he gave back to Susan a gaze of gratitude mingled with something deeper and tenderer.

'Yes'm, thank you, Susan, I'd be awful obliged,' he

gulped. 'I know where they were headin' for, and I'll go right off, not to waste any time.'

Before they could discuss the matter further, Sandy was mounted and away, leaving the rest of the family staring at each other blankly.

'Golly, what made him so sudden?' rumbled Thad.

'He's a bold knight doing a fair damsel gallant service,' Janey said solemnly.

'Janey, honest ——' Susan melted in scarlet confusion.

'I hope he knows what's the message he's taking,' Grandmother said dubiously. 'When young men get that ailment ——'

Sandy was gone two days. Friday evening he returned, accompanied by Chief Two-Toes, Weenonah, and Chaska.

'Weenonah says she would come back many days' ride for you, Janey — or for me, either,' said Haakon. 'But why in thunder did she have to come back? With Inch-Along knowing the sign language pretty well, and a lot of Sioux, and Weenonah some English, I thought ——'

Sandy cast a beseeching glance at Susan. 'I — I'm afraid I spilt the beans, Hawk. I — wasn't that what I was supposed to do? Bring her back?'

Haakon laughed at his humiliation. 'Well, now we've got her — can we give them a good feed, Grandmother Grant? — we may as well see what we can learn.'

While the girls hastened around preparing a hearty meal from a larder sadly depleted by the recent inroads on the white flour and lard and sugar, Haakon and Weenonah talked, Haakon listening with bent-browed intentness, and throwing an occasional interpretation to the tensely interested family.

At first Weenonah sat impassive, staring down at her

hands as if she scarcely heard his questioning. At length she
spoke, slowly.

'She says, She does remember such a bag, tanned softer
than the softest buckskin. She says, She even saw a Sioux
wrench the chain from my mother's neck and hide away the
bag. She is searching in the back of her brain for the face
and name of that Indian.'

Again Weenonah sat impassive, silently regarding her
folded hands. Suddenly she lifted her head and spoke, her
face puckered with concern.

'She says it was Wolverine!' Haakon smote fist into
palm resoundingly, hopelessly.

'Why is that bad news?' asked Janey.

'Because Wolverine was one of the thirty-eight Sioux
hanged on the gibbet at Mankato.'

But Two-Toes was leaning forward, finger raised. He
spoke, jerkily, and Haakon's face brightened.

'He says — well, of all things! — he knows of a pouch
that Wolverine possessed. After the hanging, it seems,
Wolverine's son came and offered it to him for one pony, because his mother was poor.'

'Is he sure it was the same bag?' Janey asked eagerly;
and Haakon put the question in Sioux.

'He does not know, for he would have no traffic with the
belongings of the murdered whites, and he did not even look
inside. But it was not the work of Indian hands, that
pouch; of that he is sure.'

Two-Toes still leaned forward, his face broad with the
pleasure of one who has more to impart. Haakon turned
a willing ear, and his face widened in turn, his smile incredulous.

'He says Wolverine's son finally sold it to — listen! — to
this Harka. You know, Janey, the Monkey Man. — But

what Harka did with it he does not know, as he was displeased with Harka for buying it, and no word has passed between them on the subject from that day to this.'

There followed excited questionings. Would Harka still have it, secreted about his person? Two-Toes was sure he had not. Had he sold it, long ago? Perhaps no one but Harka knew. Would he tell them?

At that query, Weenonah shook her head.

'She says, Harka has grown stubborn as he has grown old, and secretive. When questions are asked, he turns his face away, and lets his mind go floating far and far. — I'll ask her whether she hasn't influence with him, herself.'

Again Weenonah shook her head, her expression at once rueful and indulgent. Suddenly, however, she thrust out her chin toward Janey and suggested something to Haakon.

'She says, Perhaps if Janey would go and talk to him. It seems he has taken a great fancy to Janey.'

'Probably because I gave him sugar,' Janey said with a surface modesty, thinking it much more likely that it was her bright brown curls, so unlike Indian hair, or her pretty dresses, with the ruffles and pleatings and the frills of lace at the throat. 'Oh, I'd love to go.'

'She says, There is no hour to spare, because at any minute —— And for once we're lucky in the time of week,' Haakon added. 'Friday night. We start out bright and early tomorrow, after a good night's rest for man and beast, and make it up to the spring tomorrow night. Why, we ought to get back, anyway, in time for school Monday morning, Janey, though we may be pretty sleepy.'

It was a wonderful ride, out and out across the rolling plains almost guiltless of road or fence. Janey looked over her shoulder at the great red ball of the rising sun, peeping over the far earth-edge; looked before her at the unbelievable rose and blue and gold that lighted the snowy peaks to dreamlike beauty, while the foothills and the lower range still slept in untouched shadow. Prairie dogs stood up and chattered at them, and slim gophers streaked across their course. Watching sharply, she could see the flicker of horned toads darting to the shelter of the bristling yucca plants. As the sun rose higher, a flock of antelopes eddied away to one side; jack-rabbits bounded out of sight; Haakon flicked his whip toward a sinister diamond-spangled coil in the sunlight. 'The Indians always tell their children to keep their hands out of the clumps of sagebrush when they're gathering kindling,' he said, 'and it's good counsel, Janey.'

It was a relief to come at length into the shadow of the foothills, though the going was slower, and the horses must pick their way more cautiously. The day had been warm, as sunny April days so often are in Colorado, and the cool of the ravines was grateful. They stopped to eat some of the lunch they had brought, and let the horses browse on the sparse mountain herbage and drink at the brawling stream. But they did not tarry long. What if Harka's tired old spirit were this very moment flitting from the withered husk of his body? That thought made Janey grit her teeth against the aching weariness of a body unused to the jolt and twist of mountain riding. That thought rode with them and drove them along the trail.

With the coming of night, they emerged from a rocky defile into a cupping of the canyon where a few tipis clustered close, and the smoke of fires ascended. Haakon leaped buoyantly from the saddle and stopped to help Janey, who was so stiff and tired that she could scarcely keep her feet.

'Go slow! We go slow!' urged Weenonah, as her daughter

Mitsu came to greet them, and children rolled out of the tipis to survey them wonderingly. 'First, we eat.'

So, schooling themselves to cover their impatience with the quiet calm of their host and hostess, Haakon and Janey sat down in the dusk of the tipi and ate by the light of flaring pine knots.

Janey marveled at Haakon: he slipped back so easily into the ways of his life among them. If it had not been for the glint of his fair hair in the smoky light, the flash of his gray-blue eyes, Janey would have thought him a Sioux among the Sioux, sitting there nonchalantly in the posture Janey found so cramping, eating with decorum — and his fingers — the food that was set before him. Why, he even seemed to take time and thought to relish it, even while he must be on edge with impatience, as she was, to be at the old man's side and learn whether he had good news or bad — or none at all. Well, Janey had brought along a poke of sugar. That might help.

Calmed by the quiet around her, she, too, began to savor the strange viands, watching curiously as Mitsu rolled between her slender brown palms the dough of flour and water and salt, flattening it to a cake and pulling a hole in the middle, and then dropping it into hot fat and boiling it there until it was puffy and crisp and — yes, actually! — delicious. A stew of venison bubbled richly on the fire, and Weenonah, laughing at Janey's uncertainty, ladled some out onto her large round of fried bread. There was choke-cherry gravy, too, such as Haakon had described to her; Janey, tasting it politely, could only pretend to enjoy it.

They ate; and outside was the sound of crying babies and the yelping of dogs, and the sighing of the wind high in the spruces. Inside was the fragrance of wood smoke, and the sight of dark faces around her. Janey wondered if this were really she, or if she were only dreaming of being a part of strange places and strange lives, as she so often did dream.

Weenonah rose, wiping her lips carefully with her fingers, and spoke to Haakon.

'She says, Now we will go to Harka, who has eaten his own meal of delicate broth and marrow in his tipi beside the healing spring.'

Single file, they climbed along a narrow trail lighted by white moonlight and shadowed by trees and cliffs, and came into the lone tipi, grouping themselves silently around the pallet raised from the ground on wicker rests: Weenonah and Two-Toes, Haakon and Janey. Harka lay with eyes closed, so still that they watched a perceptible time before they could be sure that his buckskin shirt lifted and fell with breath.

'Old One!' said Two-Toes, and he opened his eyes, slowly, unwillingly. 'Old One ——' Two-Toes sat on his heels and talked to him, quietly, his voice rising at the ends of his sentences.

The old man only frowned and moved his head feebly from side to side. Two-Toes spoke again, and still there was no inflection of impatience in his tone, but a quiet courtesy.

Again the old man moved his head in petulant negation. Two-Toes rose and motioned Weenonah to take his place, and the same performance was repeated, Weenonah quietly urgent, Harka unresponsive. At length he muttered briefly, and Haakon interpreted under his breath:

'I am too tired and old. It is past. The medicine was evil.'

Weenonah asked another insistent question, and he shook his head.

'She asked, Did he sell the pouch to another? And he said, No.'

Weenonah spoke a word or two over and over, and the old man's eyes opened at length, and moved dimly over their faces till they rested on Janey's.

'What the deuce?' Haakon murmured. 'Weenonah said that his medicine maiden was here, and it was she who wished to know. His medicine maiden?'

Weenonah motioned Janey forward, and she leaned over the old man, smiling and taking from her pocket the poke of sugar she had brought. He thrust in a feeble finger and sucked it and smiled, but his eyes did not leave her face.

At length he nodded as if satisfied, and began to talk, slowly, and in so broken a whisper that Weenonah bent low, and Haakon, too, leaned close and listened with a fierce absorption until the words had died away and the old man turned definitely from him, with a last lingering look at Janey, and closed his dim eyes.

Haakon drew a deep breath and addressed Weenonah with the brusqueness of anxiety. Again she questioned the old man, but he showed no sign of hearing her. She spread her hands wide. 'Not any more,' she said, and led them from the tipi.

Outside, they hastened to satisfy Janey's palpitating curiosity.

'He did buy the pouch,' Haakon told her. 'He thought it was a "white" medicine bag: a little smooth drawing-up-tight pouch like that, with precious objects inside. He said there were colored stones that flashed in the light, and a white thinness with strange markings upon it.

'But when he was banished from Minnesota — you know they were, after the massacre — and wandered to and fro far from his home, he began to think that this was not good medicine: it was bad; perhaps without it Wolverine would not have gone to the gallows and had the breath stifled within him so that his unhappy spirit can never enter the Happy Hunting Ground.

'So Harka tried to sell it. First to his own people. Then to white men who were coming down from the hills with the yellow stuff they hold so dear: because he didn't care what happened to the foolish white men. But none would buy. And in the meantime nothing was right with him, Harka, who had been a medicine-man strong and wise.

'So, in despair, he buried it then and there, where the Red Lovers of Hue Hue Tlappallan could look down upon the bright stones forever and forever.'

'The Red Lovers?' Janey demanded, aghast.

Haakon nodded wryly.

'And then what?'

'That's all. The Red Lovers. He said the medicine maiden would understand.'

Weenonah, who had been watching them anxiously, spoke.

'We ask him again, when morning,' she said. 'Now too ——' She fluttered her hand as a tired old heart might flutter.

CHAPTER XXII

THE MEDICINE MAIDEN

WHEN morning came, and they went to the tipi by the side of the healing spring, they found Inch-Along standing mute beside the opened flap.

'With a smile on his face,' he said. 'The old chap's gone on, with a smile on his face.'

'You can't mean — Harka is gone!' Janey gasped. 'Oh, Inch-Along!'

Soberly the three 'palefaces' stole away, leaving Wee-nonah and Two-Toes to do what must be done. When they had found a quiet place, Janey and Haakon told the old man the story.

'And now, just within a word of it, maybe, it's all lost,' Janey said, biting her lips and blinking back the tears.

Inch-Along had listened with the closest attention, tugging at his thin gray beard and whistling soundlessly. 'What was that he said, lad? About the Red Lovers?'

'Just that.' Haakon's tone was lifeless. '"Buried it in the Old Red Land, where the Red Lovers could look down on the bright stones forever and forever."'

Inch-Along's soundless tune took voice and he whistled thinly to himself, his eyes opaque with thought. Suddenly he smote his thigh resoundingly.

'By gollies,' he said solemnly, 'if I don't believe I've got it!'

Doubt struggled with hope in their faces as they waited.

'You see, I've been much amongst these Injuns, as often I've told you before. They sometimes call this region the Red Land, but especially the deestrict down where the brick-red sandstone rocks begin, and even the ground is red because it's made up of that sandstone. Begins a few miles south of Denver City, and crops up again in a place called Perry's Park, mebbe thirty miles south. But the best-known locality is near Coloraydo Springs. You know: Garden of the Gods is its new-fangled name.'

He looked at them to see that they were following, and they nodded him on, Janey's face scarlet with excitement, Haakon's jaw flexing and hardening.

'You've been there, Haakon? Then you know the outlandish shapes there are, most of them in bright red rock, as if one of their old heathen gods — and him stark crazy — had sculped them out. White folks are beginning to tack names to 'em now, but some of 'em have old names back beyond the time of the white man in this country. And there's one — I don't know what the whites have seen fit to call it, but the Injuns have a great story how a daughter of the gods dared love a mortal man, and this was their funeral pyre, hers and the man's she loved. Seems they had to be killed, but the gods changed 'em into rock, so that they could kneel and kiss each other — or anyways look into each other's eyes — forever.'

'Red rock?' whispered Janey. 'The Red Lovers?'

'Well, of course I don't know no more than what I've

told you; but I'd gamble on it that those was the Red Lovers.'

Obviously, then, the thing for Haakon to do was to go to the Garden of the Gods as soon as possible and see whether Inch-Along's gamble was right. He and Janey waited only long enough to have the old man describe the position of the formation — which was marked by an arch of stone forming a circular aperture — and to bid good-bye to the chief and his family, and then they turned their horses' heads toward Greeley, hastening in order to make the trip before night-fall.

Weenonah, talking rapidly to Haakon in her own tongue, gave them each a parfleche of pemmican — dried meat mixed with fat and berries and preserved in a box of tanned hide — and a few cakes of fried bread, so that they need not stop even for eating, but might nibble as they rode, dismounting only now and then to drink long and deep of the icy clear waters of the stream, still edged with winter's ice.

'Weenonah says that Harka went away happy, she knows,' Haakon said abruptly, when they could ride abreast and talk, 'because he had seen his medicine maiden and she had smiled on him and given him gifts.'

'Whatever did he mean — medicine maiden?' Janey demanded. 'Haakon, have you any idea?'

'Well, that's what I asked Weenonah. You know when they have their medicine dream, or trance, Janey, they hold communion with some object that is ever after sacred and magical to them — linked up with all their fortunes. And it seems you typified Harka's "Medicine."' He chuckled.

'But do you know what it was?'

'Well, suppose we leave it that Harka's trance brought him a lovely maiden with hair like honey in the sunlight

and like the ripe acorn in the shadow; and with eyes like
a forest spring; and a mouth ——' He paused, his eyes
dancing.

'Why, Haakon Haakonsson!' It didn't sound like
Haakon at all, though she couldn't help liking it. 'But
you're laughing at me. That wasn't his medicine — a
maiden?'

'Don't you think you'd better leave well enough alone?'

'Now I just simply have to know. Haakon, I'd die of
curiosity.'

'Well, then, I'll plump it out: Harka's medicine had to do
with the wild turkey.'

Janey stared.

'A kingly bird, the wild turkey. Did you ever see its nest?
And the eggs — all sprinkled with — well, with freckles?'

Janey's stare took on shocked comprehension.

'*Freckles?* Oh, Haakon, honest, was that it?'

'Well, now, Janey, let's put it like this. Here old Harka
meets a lovely maiden, bearing sweet largess in her hands;
and her hair is — well, like I said; and her eyes, too, and her
mouth ——'

'You didn't describe that,' Janey suggested demurely.

'No, and I'm not going to,' Haakon said hastily. 'And
she had such a — well, such a nice little face, all golden tan
and dusted with freckles like the stars in the sky — or like
the delicate splashes on the precious eggs of the magic wild
turkey. Well! You see, all you need to tell anyone, Janey,
is that he took you for the medicine maiden of his vision.
I won't let on.'

'But of course *I* will!' Janey laughed. 'It's much too
good to keep. — Poor old man.'

'I'd give a farm if I could go right on to the Garden of the
Gods tomorrow,' Haakon said.

Janey was glad and sorry to get away from the medicine maiden story. She had liked to have Haakon speak as he did, and yet for the first time she felt as if he were almost a stranger, instead of the foster-brother she had known and loved.

'Goodness, can't you go tomorrow?' she exclaimed.

'Would it be exactly square? I feel mean enough about the number of times I've skinned out already, and Bancroft so decent about it. Of course, I've tried to make up for it by doing extra work outside hours.'

'But just once more, Haakon?'

'No; if the pouch is there, it's pretty likely to stay a few more days. And if it isn't — Gosh!'

'Then, when will you go, Haakon?'

'Start next Saturday, I guess. It must be close to a hundred and fifty miles, and I don't know but it'll pay me to go by train. Get there Saturday and start back Sunday, if I should by any chance have good luck; or Monday if I had to keep hunting.'

'Oh, Haakon, if you only find it!'

'Yes, but, Janey, I can't see quite how it cinches the thing, even if I do. Just as I said before, I might have the Haakonsson jewels, or even that document they talk about, whatever it is, and the ring, too, Janey-girl; and yet how would that prove I'd come by them rightfully?'

'At least the document and the ring would have some writing to show what they were; and it does seem as if Ingrid's testimony, and Weenonah's and Two-Toes' ——'

'How far would their testimony go?' he scoffed gently. 'A poor old woman whose brain's as weak and uncertain as Ingrid's — and Indians?'

'And Pa and Ma!' with spirit.

'Well, I'll acknowledge their word would be good any-

where. But there are such holes in the story. Such gaps.
So many chances for some other little tow-headed boy
to come in. Well, it's the fortunes — of Haakon Haakonsson, Janey!'

CHAPTER XXIII

PAIUTE PETE

THE following Saturday, Janey and Susan and Thad rode down to the station with Haakon, to wish him luck on his fantastic expedition.

'There's another of those what you call imitation bad-men, Haakon,' Janey said, reining in the prancing Hia-watha. 'Look, Susan!' She pointed with her whip, but the theatrical buckskins were moving away, and they had disappeared before Haakon could tie Minnehaha and look around.

It was not until the train had snorted away, with Haakon waving his hat from the platform, that Janey looked around again for the picturesque figure. It had sauntered into sight once more, and the three young people stared with frank interest at its Wild West regalia.

On it came, halting dramatically when abreast of the group, returning their stare, and sweeping off its concealing hat.

'Peetohlemy!' cried Janey.

'Miss — Grant! Miss Sloane! And ——?'

'This is my brother Thaddeus, Peetohlemy.'

'And you are living in this vicinity?' Ptolemy asked with vast apparent surprise.

'Yes. Do come out and have supper with us, Peetohlemy,' Janey invited hospitably, her conscience prickling at thought of the pain she had cost him. 'You could ride Minnehaha. We're leading her back.'

Peetohlemy had his own nag, he told them condescendingly. Presently they were riding homeward together, Ptolemy keeping close to Janey's side. She glanced at him curiously, silenced by a stiff constraint. It was not only that she had wounded him so deeply, but that she had wondered — persistently wondered ——

He was the same Ptolemy, in spite of the curls that straggled on the collar of his beaded buckskins; in spite of the six-shooter in his belt. Janey eyed that revolver with awed curiosity.

'Peetohlemy,' she asked suddenly, 'you *aren't* Pete the Kid, are you?'

If a rider can strut on horseback, Ptolemy strutted.

'So you've heard of Pete, have you? That's me. Pete the Kid, or Paiute Pete; take your choice!'

'Why Paiute Pete?'

'Well, any skulking Paiute that's run afoul of Pete, he's been one Paiute less,' Ptolemy bragged largely.

'Why, Peetohlemy Jones, do you really mean you've ——? I did hear them say you had — *notches* — on your six-shooter. Why, Peetohlemy, whatever would your mother say?'

Ptolemy looked back to see that nobody was near enough to overhear.

'It's true as Scripture that those notches mean killings, Janey — at least the old Injun fighter I bought it off of took his solemn oath to it. You know if you want to make any showing at all out here you got to shoot somebody. So I just let it go that way.'

He swaggered resentfully at her laugh.

'All the same, they better not try to come any of their shenan gans on Pete the Kid,' he blustered. 'I don't mind adding a notch of my own, any time,' he added darkly. 'I suppose your Eastern friends are such softies they never pull a six-shooter.'

'Softies nothing!' Janey disclaimed good-humoredly.

'Still stick up for the big Swede, do you?' he bristled. 'After his name's blackened for an impostor? Or hasn't he told you the mess he's in? Maybe you'll wish you'd chosen your friends a little bit more carefully. Prince, you thought he was, didn't you? Hm, fine prince he is!'

'I never thought he was a prince!' Janey snapped. 'You just hush up about Haakon, Peetohlemy.'

'I'll tell you one thing,' he taunted her, 'when he's poor as poverty, Peetohlemy Jones'll be rolling in wealth, maybe. You just wait!'

Janey giggled. 'What are you going to do, Peetohlemy? Find a gold mine?'

'Something bigger than that, my good girl! Pete the Kid is about to embark for the jewel fields of the Southwest. What are perils? What are hardships? What is pain and — and danger, when the heart is gallant? No, sir, Pete the Kid will stake his all on a single throw.'

'You mean those stories they've been telling about the diamonds they found down in the corner of Colorado Territory? Near the Indian villages?'

'Where the ground glitters with such skintillating brilliance,' he declaimed, 'that the human eye is dazzled and the reason staggers.'

'We saw some of the diamonds and garnets,' Janey said doubtfully, 'but Haakon thinks it's a hoax — jewels loose on the ground that way.'

'Haakon!' He spat the word from his mouth. 'And how could it be a hoax? You acknowledge that you saw some of the gems? Why, Janey, a Pima Injun came in with a diamond bigger than my thumb — worth a king's ramsun, it was. And it's not reasonable to suppose that if there's stones as big as that, there aren't more of 'em, and bigger, too.' His eyes shone. 'Janey, I'm willing to forgive and forget, I am. I want to be manganimous. Say the word, and I'll bring you back diamonds and rubies as big as hens' eggs!' he promised recklessly. 'What's a measly old ring with green stones compared to that? And a big rawboned Swede to boot?'

Janey flashed him an indignant glance — a suspicious one.

'Peetohlemy,' she cried, 'honestly, sometimes I think you know more than you ought to about Haakon's affairs — and about that ring, too! You didn't think it would be a joke to hide it somewhere and get even with me? Because I must say I'd call that a pretty poor kind of joke ——'

Ptolemy's face had flamed with angry color.

'All right for you!' he shouted, clapping one hand to the beaded pouch that flapped at his belt, 'I gave you your chance, didn't I? A lot of use being manganimous to you!'

Setting spurs to his horse, he shot off on a crossroad to the south. A little distance away he drew rein and called back defiantly:

'It's good-bye this time, Jane Grant. Pete the Kid never offers his friendship three times to the same ungrateful and blinded person.'

Once more he spurred his horse to a gallop and was gone in a cloud of dust.

'Good land!' Susan stuttered, as she and Thad came up with Janey. 'What was all that, Janey? Isn't he coming to supper?'

'I wish I knew what all that was, Susan. But he certainly isn't coming to supper.' Janey laughed shortly. 'I don't suppose there's a thing to it, though I wish Haakon was here. Peetohlemy's just so set on being a character out of a dime novel that he's not any realer than they are. Thad Grant, if I ever find another of those Deadwood Dick stories under your pillow, I'll write Pa about it; honest, I will. I'd hate to have them go to your head like that.'

'I s'pose you want I should read the Rollo books,' Thad grumbled.

Grandmother had supper ready to dish up when they came in, and as soon as they were seated, they told her and Sandy what had happened.

Sandy took it more seriously than the rest.

'I had a sneakin' notion I saw that fella hangin' round town yesterday,' he said. 'Prob'ly waited till he seen Hawk clear out. Just like he faded when he heard Hawk's name up to Midway that time. I've a good mind to ride after him and see ——'

'See what, Sandy?'

'Well, it wouldn't do no harm — I'll eat first, though, on account of he's headed for Evans, sure as shootin', and he'll put up there tonight, like enough. What you say his nag's like?'

'Sorrel with a white foot and a star,' Thad said. 'Fancy Mexican saddle.'

'Let us go along, Sandy!' begged Janey.

'No, ma'am, it wouldn't be fitting. They's tougher towns

than Evans, but you don't need to risk your neck in any.'

'Aw, Sandy, me?' Thad persisted.

'And not leave any man to look after things? No, sir.'

'I'm going, all the same,' Janey whispered to Susan behind the dishtowel. 'Sandy's pinto's slow as molasses in January, and I can catch up, even if I do get a late start.'

'I'll go if you do,' Susan said, paling at the thought.

Evans was only a few miles south of Greeley, and, urging their horses to a brisk canter, the girls soon were in sight of the first scattered houses, and of Sandy's pinto, its grotesque white patches showing plainly through the dusk. They held their distance, watching anxiously lest he catch sight of them, but he did not look back.

Once in the town, he proceeded directly to a corner building where several saddle-horses were fastened, tied his own with them, and went in. When the girls reached the place, they saw that the sorrel with the white foot and the star was with the rest. Slowly they turned the corner. A partly open window gave on the street. Janey slipped from Hiawatha's back and peered in. The whole large room was clearly visible.

'Janey, let's don't!' Susan's voice hissed feebly in her ear. 'Isn't this awful dangerous?'

'Hush!' Janey hissed back. 'If they should see us at all they'd know we were girls; and, anyway, we could mount and be gone in no time. Trot home if you want to, Susan. I'm going to stay.'

Ptolemy was lounging against the wall, watching the activities of the room with a manner slightly bored and patronizing, when Sandy sauntered in through a side door with a man the girls had never seen. He was a typical gambler, sleek-haired, with a flashing pin in his tie, a flashing ring on his finger. He and Sandy talked quietly for a few moments, and then their voices rose in such animated discussion that the words came clearly through the window.

'—— willing to bet a fiver on it!' Sandy's drawl, that was, but without an atom of the shy uncertainty the girls associated with him.

'Well, say, young feller, it don't take me a split second to show you up on that deal!' The other voice was aggressive.

'What you fellows differin' about?' the bar-tender asked with mild interest, and the attention of the room focused on the answer.

'He says'— the diamond-studded one jerked a thumb at Sandy — 'he says I can't pull my old trick on anybody but a hayseed, and I bet him Soapsuds Sanders is as quick with his fingers as he ever was.'

He pulled from his pocket something that looked like a bar of soap, and from his wallet a roll of bills.

'Look close!' he challenged the room. 'You will observe this bill, ladies and gentlemen. Twenty dollars. Twen-ty dol-lars. Observe that I remove the paper wrapper from this bar of soap — a pure white soap, fit for the fairest and most sensitive complexion of infant, lady, or gent. Observe that I *wrap* this twenty-dollar bill *around* this soap and *replace* the wrapper.

'Now — I make this unprecedented offer: Who will give me five dollars — FIVE dollars — for this bar of soap?'

He waved it above his head as he spoke. The girls had watched his hands with breathless absorption as they flickered around soap and paper.

'Whyee!' whispered Janey. 'How can he? I *saw* ——'

Ptolemy took a step forward, his mouth opening, closing, opening again to say, 'Me! I will. Don't you come any of your tricks, though. Just keep your hand up till I take the soap out of it. I ain't going to have you slippin' it up your sleeve, I ain't.'

'Does the gentleman question my honesty?' Soapsuds
Sanders scowled fiercely. 'Then I shall request that he place
his five-dollar bill in my other hand before he removes his
purchase.'

Ptolemy pulled at the string of his pouch and drew out
a small roll, Sanders's eyes scowlingly upon him. He pressed
the five into Sanders's left hand, seized the soap from his
right, and crowed with triumph as he unwrapped it. 'That's
once you didn't get a chance to switch on a fellow! Learn
you ——' His voice trailed into silence and he stared
blankly at the bill neatly folded round his soap.

'Some mistake, ain't there, stranger?' asked Sandy.
'Looks like a one to me.'

Sanders laughed genially and held out the five-dollar bill.
'All in fun,' he said. 'I'll swap you. Wouldn't do you out of
four dollars for anything. Take your money and run back
to nursie.'

'You can't do that again!' Ptolemy shrilled furiously.

'Oh, yes, I can, buddie. The hand is quicker than the eye.
My hand, your eye. Why, my dear lad, I can pick your
pockets and you'd never know it.'

'Bet you a tenner,' snarled Ptolemy.

'The question is, have you the tenner?' Sanders's voice
was silky. 'Or have our bad-mans fleeced the little lamb
long since?'

Ptolemy pulled out his roll again and waved a ten-dollar
bill in his tormentor's face. Sanders sneered at it, flicked it
with a contemptuous forefinger.

'Try that on another hayseed. It's counterfeit.'

'It is not!' Ptolemy raged.

'Oh, ask the bar-keep,' Sanders said negligently. 'Ask
anybody.'

Furiously, Ptolemy turned to the bar-tender, who

straightened his face with an effort and bent a close scrutiny on the bill.

'Sorry to differ, Mr. Sanders. This here looks good to me.'

'In that case I beg your pardon, Mr. — Mr. —— But pardon me again! Is this something you have lost?'

Soapsuds Sanders held out on his palm the object that his flying fingers had just abstracted from Ptolemy's pouch. It was a massy gold ring from which the girls at the window could detect a tiny twinkle of green and white light.

Ptolemy's mouth fell open again and his face paled. He laughed uneasily.

'You win,' he said. 'Here's your tenner, and I'll thank you for my ring.'

'Jest one minute.' There was a dangerous quality in Sandy's drawl. 'I've got a curiosity to know how you come by that trinket, stranger. I've got a friend that lost a ring answering that general description.'

Sanders's hand closed over the jewel as he waited for Ptolemy's explanation.

'Well, I guess I can prove ownership,' he sputtered. 'Just ask any of these gentlemen to look this ring over. See anything peculiar in its construction, gentlemen?'

The ring passed from hand to hand. One after another took it to the flaring oil lamps and turned it this way and that, while Ptolemy watched with a sneering smile and a defiant out-thrust of chin. The girls forgot caution and pressed toward the middle of the window, but no one glanced that way. Hiawatha nickered, but the company was too engrossed to notice the nearness of the sound.

'See anything peculiar?' Ptolemy challenged.

They shook their heads.

'Well, look here!'

He took the ring, while the others crowded round to watch, and the girls tried vainly to see what was going on within that close-pressed circle.

'By jinks, that's a cute contrivance!' someone ejaculated.

'Anybody but the owner be likely to know that little secret?' Ptolemy triumphed.

'Jest the same, it looks mighty like a ring that was lost by this friend of mine,' Sandy spoke stubbornly. 'And, besides, that looks a heap like ——'

'Prove it!' said Ptolemy.

It was more than Janey could stand.

'Why, Peetohlemy Jones!' she cried indignantly from her window. 'I never would have really believed it — not in all my life!'

That voice was as startling as an explosion. A dozen heads gaped toward the window, and Sandy strode across the room purposefully.

Ptolemy turned white. Then he laughed boisterously and flipped the ring in their direction. It struck the wall just below the sill and dropped to the floor. Janey, reaching into the room, breathlessly retrieved it.

'The lady wins!' Ptolemy declaimed; 'and Paiute Pete rides out of her life forever!'

He swaggered to the door without a backward glance, and a moment later they heard the beat of his horse's hoofs, muffled by the dusty road.

CHAPTER XXIV

THE RED LOVERS

WHILE Janey and Susan were watching at the window in Evans, Haakon was impatiently awaiting the morning in the little town of Colorado Springs, some hundred and twenty-five miles away.

It was a moonlight spring night, and the treeless village was dominated by the snowy splendor of Pike's Peak, which seemed to tower at the end of every street. Haakon had no eyes for it: the evening and night stretched before him, maddeningly long. He found a clean-looking little hotel, where he engaged a room, and then wandered out to see what was to be seen.

Like Greeley, this was a temperance town, and its streets were quiet. At one corner store, however, men jostled one another for entrance, and Haakon paused and peered in curiously.

A man at his side chuckled.

'They call that the Katy King Spiritual Wheel,' he told Haakon. 'After the famous medium, I guess. See? You put your money in a can on the rim of that wheel, and it rolls around into the back room, and then another can brings out your beer or whiskey. Very mysterious! Nobody sells it. Nobody buys it. But the law'll soon run 'em out, and then the drinking folks'll have to go to Colorado City, like they always have.'

A carriage bowled past them, and Haakon's mentor plucked his sleeve and nodded toward its occupant.

'Ever see a lady authoress?' he asked. 'That's one: Helen Hunt: she lives here in the Springs. Gone on the Indians, she is.'

That would be something to tell Janey. He recalled the girl's enthusiasm over Helen Hunt's novel, 'Mercy Philbrick'; recalled also the writer's crusader-indignation at the cruelty of our Indian policy. He had heard that she was contemplating a novel which should deal more graphically with the red man's wrongs, as Mrs. Stowe had dealt with the black's. Well, he thought, as he detached himself from his chance acquaintance and went to bed, he had seen Katy King's Spiritual Wheel, and Helen Hunt, the 'lady authoress,' and Pike's Peak by moonlight: now he must consume the remaining hours till daylight would let him start for the Garden of the Gods. He felt like a small boy on Christmas Eve — a small boy who didn't know whether his stocking was to reveal a pair of skates or a hickory stick.

Morning came at last, after a long night of fitful dreaming on the lumpy hotel bed. Haakon dressed hastily, found the hotel dining-room stale and deserted, and hunted a lunch-room where a lamp burned murkily and a sleepy proprietor served him muddy coffee in a thick chipped cup, and flap-jacks that were burned on the outside and moist in the center. It made small difference to Haakon: he gulped down the food and drink without tasting it, and was out again and headed westward in the morning twilight.

Colorado City was sluggishly stirring when he passed through its huddle of wooden houses and out toward the bold red crags now visible against the background of the Rocky range. From Manitou, he knew, good roads ran out to the Garden of the Gods, for it was already thronged, in summer, by the tourists who came to the big hotels to drink at the medicinal springs near them. He could not wait to go around by roads, however. His high boots were stoutly made of cowhide, and need not avoid the rocks and spiny cacti of the foothill country.

The sun was climbing the sky now, and calling forth the small denizens of prairie and hill. Striped chipmunks darted away ahead of him, tiny tails straight as exclamation points. Lizards and horned toads slipped through the sand. Handsome black-and-white magpies flew up and away, lumbering awkwardly through the air with their over-long tails. The sharp spears of the yucca pricked his knees.

His breath labored a little, for he had unconsciously increased his swinging stride to a lope. His eyes were fixed on a circle of blue sky seen through a rocky red ring on the summit of one of the Garden's great masses. Sometimes it was lost to sight as he dropped into a hollow; sometimes it was screened from him by a clump of firs or cedars; after a half-hour's brisk approach it seemed no nearer than when he had first seen it: such was the illusive clearness of the thin air.

His face was prickling with moisture when at length he gained the valley, jagged with red and gray outcroppings of sandstone. He had lost the circular aperture some time since, and now he stood, wiping his face and looking about him.

You had to pass red rocks that were like giant slices set on their edges cornerwise, Inch-Along said. And there they were! The picture puzzle was beginning to work out!

Beyond them, as the old man remembered it, loomed jagged groups of red crags that 'favored so many shattered church steeples, to my thinking.'

Here indeed were the shattered spires! Haakon shouted aloud at sight of them, and plunged forward across the hilly ground.

There should be a long rampart of gray, so Inch-Along had said. Well, here was the gray, though not very long. One couldn't expect Inch-Along to drag a complete map from his memory after a dozen years.

And here — he uttered another hoarse shout of triumph — here he could see the round hole again, with blue sky showing through. The Red Lovers! Between the Lovers' meeting lips and the pyre beneath them the opening was almost perfectly circular, the old man said.

The vast slab of rock, though lofty, was not so high as Haakon had expected from the description, but it was vertical on this face. Impatiently he dashed around it, stumbling heedlessly through the tangled grasses of last year, leaping rocks and low bushes.

Its other face was scarcely less precipitous, but it had been so furrowed and ridged by water that it offered possible footholds. And within its rocky, skyey curve — what might await him?

Starting a little back from the base, Haakon ran up the grassy shoulder and on up the first few feet of stone, seizing a projection at which he had aimed. On, up and up, slipping backward, scrambling sidewise, scraping knees and hands viciously against the granular surfaces, zigzagging from foothold to foothold on the bleak red expanse.

Yet it was only his six-feet-two of bone and muscle, only his strong length of arm, that let him complete the ascent at last. For he found himself on a short ledge in the rock, not far from the summit, with an unbroken face above him, presenting not even a handhold except for one sturdy knob just above his head. Haakon grasped that knob, drew himself up — not for nothing had he chinned himself a hundred times in succession — caught one toe in a shallow depression, and scrambled onto the narrow summit, where he lay panting.

He was on top!

On hands and knees he clambered along the ridge until he reached the rust-red arch that was his goal. There, quite as he expected, fragments of the sandstone lay heaped at the base of the circular aperture.

Haakon scooped the smaller ones into his hand and tossed them down the abyss; pried out a larger one; reached for another. It slipped from his fingers and dropped out of sight. While he stared, troubled, the remaining rubble sucked downward and the hollow was empty.

It was not a mere hollow: it was a shaft, extending blankly down, down, down ——

Haakon knelt and pressed his face to the opening. He could see no end to it. He dropped in a handful of pebbles and thought he could hear a muffled clatter far below. It was evident that the rock was cleft, probably from summit to base.

He knelt there, limply considering the situation. The crack was much too deep and narrow to admit of any search. Had it appeared after Harka's visit? Was the object of his search buried forever at its bottom?

He slid recklessly down the hundred feet and ran around the base, looking for possible openings. Unbroken rock confronted him at both faces and one edge, the other screened by a growth of scrub-oak. Haakon thrust an impatient foot into the leaves there, and heard a warning rattle, but too late: the diamond-spangled length leaped from its coil and struck.

Just as it struck, Haakon crushed the body with a stone, and pulled it away from his leg by the lashing tail.

'Gosh! Thanks for the good, thick cowhide!' he ejaculated fervently. The fangs had not pierced the heavy leather of his boot top.

More cautious now, he cut himself a stout stick and prodded the débris, killing another rattler and satisfying himself that there were no more.

At the same time, he had satisfied himself that there was no opening at the base. If the pouch had fallen down the cleft, it was walled up irretrievably against the ages.

Another hope flickered in his mind. There might be other arches of rock, other round openings.

He climbed a knoll that commanded a fair view of the 'Garden,' and studied the skyline. Here — and there — and yonder — were indeed patches of sky showing blue through rock borders. He clambered down again, and walked from side to side, to see whether there was any angle from which one of these took circular shape.

Here — and there — the openings remained angular or disappeared, when he made patient circuit of them. Yonder — yes, at last he found points from which that one little window stood round as a ring.

Carefully he looked about him. There were the sheets of sandstone perched perilously cornerwise, and there the shattered steeples; but where the gray rampart?

Haakon stumbled through bushes and rocks to the other side. There stretched the great gray wall, only less lofty than the red one topped by its rocky arch — its rocky arch that was formed by the heads of the Red Lovers.

This time Haakon felt a profound conviction: these were the Red Lovers. Their very garments swept outward and downward upon the rock; their mouths and brows met in an eternal salute.

Yet how had Harka ever ascended that splendid height? He had been an old man, even a dozen years ago. The mass towered above Haakon's head a hundred and fifty, two hundred feet, without a shrub or a twisted cedar clinging there to give support; much of the way with no footholds or handholds to be seen.

Haakon stood alone between the giant red wall and the giant gray one, like a mouse in the bottom of a dry well.

And then his busy eyes caught a shadow low on the face of the rock: so faint that he would not have noticed it but for another two feet above it, another two feet above that.

'Steps! Almost worn away by wind and rain. But if someone else did it, I can, too.'

There ensued a long and patient digging at the soft stone with the large knife he always carried, deepening the first impression till his toe could cling there; deepening the next; the next.

'It's like the boy in the reader,' he said aloud, 'cutting his way up the cliff to safety.'

Six or eight steps, and his arms ached and his face dripped from the heat of the sun full on that red expanse. His hat was pushed from his head as he hugged the sandstone, and he had no hands to catch it as it fell. He gritted his teeth and kept on.

Ten steps, and the ache had grown intolerable.

'Gosh!' he gasped, 'there are limits.'

He stared upward at the interminable distance, swinging

his head to throw the tormenting hair out of his eyes. Not far above him swung something slender and dark, like a lariat. It was a length of rawhide rope.

His heart leaped. Another step, and he could pull himself up by the rawhide to a shallow ledge, and from thence his eye traced a possible path, tacking to and fro across the face.

On the other hand, did the presence of the rope mean other visitors to the summit? And did other visitors mean the loss of the treasure?

The first thing to do was to gain the top. With new energy he hacked at the shallow foothold, climbed up, seized the rawhide with a gingerly hand, tested it by little and little, and drew himself up.

The rest of the way was tedious, but comparatively sure, and another half-hour's climbing brought him, faint and dizzy from sun and exertion, to the crest.

This arch was much larger than the first he had investigated, and Haakon crawled bodily into its cradle, smiling feebly at the thought that he was under the gaze of the Lovers at last.

Another rubble-filled hollow at his feet. As his fingers ladled out the first handful of sand, they made the disheartening discovery that the sand was wet.

He looked up. A groove led directly down the face of one of the Lovers from what must have been a depression on their heads. Rainwater had doubtless gathered there and trickled down into the sand. And he had counted so greatly on the stony burial place to keep pouch and paper dry and intact.

His sore fingers went on scratching and scrabbling in the rubble, flinging aside pebbles and larger fragments. It was only a few moments before they closed on a different sub-

stance. Drawing a deep breath, Haakon pulled out a dark
and mouldering fragment of thin leather, stiffened and
decayed. He dug again, frantically, and brought out a
scrap of what had once been paper.

Slowly he drew his handkerchief from his pocket, spread
it beside the hole, and laid the bits upon it. Then he
reached into the hollow once more. This time there flashed
from the pebbles the rich red of a cut ruby. More fragments of paper and chamois skin. A garnet. A sapphire.
A diamond. A topaz. He passed wounded finger-tips
through the hollow again: a tiny rough length — the gold
chain. And that was all.

There was no miniature.

Haakon sat there in the shadow of the stony arch, staring
at the contents of the handkerchief. Jewels. Yes, they
would help his new beginnings, if they were what they
seemed. But they could not establish his identity.

An eagle screamed stridently from the gray wall, but
there was no other sound. He shivered sharply as the
shadow chilled his sweat-drenched body.

'Well,' he said, 'it's the fortunes of war.'

Carefully he knotted the handkerchief over the de-
spoiled treasure, thrust it deep in an inner pocket, and
made his perilous descent.

CHAPTER XXV

TRAIL'S END AND TRAIL'S BEGINNING

JANEY was awaiting him next afternoon at the station, her eyes searching his face eagerly as he waved his hat from the steps of the train.

'Great of you to meet me, Janey!'

'Haakon, did you find it?'

'I did, and I didn't. No, I'm not trying to pester you this time. I found all there was to find, I guess. But it's not conclusive. It's not evidence, Janey.'

'Oh, Haakon!'

She was thoughtfully silent while they cantered out of the town and onto the prairie; yet, if she was deeply disappointed, she concealed her feeling well, Haakon thought. When they reached a fork in the road, he turned his pony's head away from home.

'Mind if we stop here by the river, Janey, while I show you what I did find?'

'Mind? I think I've been pretty patient to wait this long.'

They sat down on the bank, where the cottonwoods were unfurling their shiny little leaves, and the pussy-willows glowed golden. Hiawatha and Minnehaha browsed quietly beside them.

Haakon pulled the handkerchief from his inner pocket and laid it in Janey's lap. She untied it, her fingers trembling.

'O-oh, Haakon!'

There lay the stones, a sapphire, deep blue of an amazing purity; a ruby, blood-red; a topaz, clear sunshine; a garnet; a great square-cut diamond. There lay the old chain, and the scraps of useless paper. There lay the mouldering leather. That was all.

'No miniature,' Haakon said heavily. 'No writing, even. But never mind, Janey-girl. I'll have a notary witness all this, and I'll get depositions from your father and mother, and then send the whole caboodle to the lawyers and see.'

'But the stones are wonderful, Haakon!' Janey cried again, turning them rapturously in her palm, so that they caught the sun and flashed forth a rainbow of color. 'Like Aladdin's lamp or something. Do you suppose they're real?'

'Pretty sure of it, Janey-girl.'

'Well, they ought to be worth more than a hundred dollars. Oughtn't they, Haakon?'

He nodded, grave under his amusement. 'Considerably more.'

'Then they'd anyway help — get started again?'

'Yes, they'll help get started.'

Janey was still playing with the gems, turning the diamond so that it flashed blinding darts of color from its faceted edges. She smiled at him, but his face was somber, and she laid the baubles back in the handkerchief and knotted it again, and then fumbled at the collar of her blue henrietta dress.

A cord hitched upward from the ruching under her square little chin. The Haakonsson ring jerked out, and she dropped it into his astonished hand.

'At least,' she said, 'here's their initials on the inside. That may add a grain of weight to your claim.'

'But, Janey, where under the sun ——?'

She explained the return of the ring, while Haakon turned it caressingly in his hand.

'Who'd have thought the odd genius would play us a trick like that! — Well, Janey, it may not amount to so much as evidence, but I'd like to see it put to a good use, at any rate. Won't you let me put it on your finger until we have to send it to the lawyers? *Will* you, Janey?'

Obediently Janey held out her hand.

'Funny little Janey! I didn't mean your right hand. But maybe I oughtn't to say anything about your wearing it on the other, now. I may have to begin all over again, without a sou markee — except for the jewels — and with a debt besides, if those lawyers stick too close to technicalities.'

'Oh — but I wouldn't mind that!'

Janey caught her breath sharply, and her eyes were wide as she held out her left hand and let him slip the queer old ring on the unaccustomed finger. She looked at it with her head on one side, and Haakon looked at her. She met his glance and smiled shyly, while Haakon's smile seemed to shine away all the dark gravity that had settled over his face during these past months.

'Janey,' he said, 'I know how those old knights felt when their ladies gave them a token. What couldn't a fellow stand! What couldn't he do!'

'I was thinking,' Janey said thoughtfully, 'that I'd like

to teach — oh, maybe till I'm twenty. And then — oh, Haakon, wouldn't it be fun if — Well, wouldn't it be glorious to — Oh, you know I do think a trip across the ocean to where your forefathers lived in Norway ——' Again she broke off, shyly.

'But, Janey-girl, you know there's a lot of chance that they'll throw out any evidence I have, even now. There's a big chance I may never be able to prove I'm Haakonsson.'

'I don't think so, Haakon. Though it wouldn't matter to me if you hadn't a sou markee, whatever that is. But — Haakon, do you mind if we ride home first and show Grandmother and Sukey and Thad? They'll be fairly counting the minutes.'

She cantered ahead of him all the way, looking back now and then with shining, excited eyes and flushed cheeks. Reaching the White House before him, she had tethered Hiawatha and was opening the door before he could overtake her.

'Thad!' she was calling, her voice bubbling with eagerness. 'Oh, Thad, come on in! We've got such lots to show you!'

Thad dashed in from his chores, Bute close at his heels, and Grandmother ran her knitting needle into the heel of the big gray sock and laid it down on the black-and-white ball of fur in her lap, while Susan sat down opposite Janey and Haakon, her eager eyes fixed inquiringly upon them.

Haakon pulled the handkerchief from his pocket, laid it on the table, and unknotted it. The gems spread out in an iridescent mass on the white linen.

'Garsh!' croaked Thad, his eyes starting.

'Land sakes!' breathed Susan, stretching out an involuntary hand.

'Mercy-*to*-us!' said Grandmother.

'But no miniature!' mourned Janey. 'No document. No proof at all, Haakon says.'

Haakon knitted his brows and looked at her wonderingly.

'Janey, I can't make you out today. You act as if it were funny. Girl, have you got something up your sleeve?'

'No, Haakon,' she said demurely, 'but you must remember I have something on my finger.'

Radiantly she held out her left hand to the others, the Haakonsson ring on its third finger.

Susan's eyes misted, and Grandmother looked soberly from her to Haakon.

'Did you want I should say I was surprised?' she asked. 'Well — as far as I can see, both of you could have gone further and done worse.' Grandmother's voice was very gentle.

'I don't know whether I should have let her, Grandmother Grant,' Haakon apologized. 'I'll have to start all over again, likely, and with a debt, too, since there's nothing to prove who I am.'

'Aw, Hawk!' Thad interrupted them with a hurt, incredulous snort. 'You and Janey — Hawk, you always said we'd bach it together on our cattle ranch some day! I never saw anything like the way a girl can spoil things!'

His face had grown red and his eyes stormy, and he pulled away from Janey and started toward the door.

'Oh, now, Thad!' she coaxed. 'I have something so funny to tell you. No one but Susan knows — and Sandy.'

Thad stopped at the door and stood with his back to them, listening reluctantly.

'I hardly know how to tell it,' Janey went on. 'It's about Peetohlemy. He didn't do us such a disservice as he thought, and I mean to write and tell him so.'

'Now it's you that are doing the teasing, Janey-girl!'

Haakon puckered his brow at her in the funny way he had, and his plume of blond hair waved as he shook his head, and his tightened lips deepened the scar just to the left of his chin's center, like a one-sided cleft. Janey, watching him, laughed suddenly.

'Well, you see Peetohlemy's queer, and all that, and those millions of dime novels he's read have come near turning his head. But with all that, you can't deny he's awfully ingenious, Haakon. Why, the things he thinks up and contrives —— Haakon,' she broke off anxiously, 'do you think he'll ever settle down and amount to anything?'

'He might. I imagine there are plenty of solid citizens who've been worse than Pete.' Haakon was evidently not so concerned for the Kid's reformation as was Janey. 'But for goodness' sake, you little tease, why don't you come to the point?'

'Garsh, yes, Janey!' grumbled Thad.

'We-ell,' Janey drawled, touching the ring with a loving finger, 'during the year Peetohlemy had the Haakonsson ring, he learned something we'd never guessed. Of course we'd noticed the initials and the motto and the crest, but there we stopped.

'Peetohlemy didn't stop there. He must have puzzled about the thickness of the gold under the emeralds. And he must have noticed how this little diamond at the side sticks out as if it were mounted higher than jewels usually are. And so he fiddled with the little diamond, until he discovered ——'

Janey 'fiddled with the little diamond,' and inserted her thumb-nail in the crack that appeared at the base of the mounting. She pried gently, and it swung back.

'Je-hosh-a-phat!' said Haakon.

Set into the ring, and covered by the emerald-studded

and crested top as by the lid of a tiny box, was a miniature, painted with exquisite delicacy on an ivory disk a half-inch in diameter.

It was the face of a boy of three or four years. With an uncanny faithfulness to detail, the artist had depicted the tiny plume of silver-gold hair at the crown of the baby head; the funny pucker of the brow; the scar that simulated a cleft, to the left of the chin's center.

Haakon laughed, sheer joyous relief bubbling upward to his lips.

'Oh, Janey-girl! Janey-girl!' he cried. 'That trip to Norway — won't it be great?'

THE END

DATE DUE